CURSED

BOOKS BY J. C. MCKENZIE

Embrace the Flame

CURSED

J. C. McKenzie

COPYRIGHT INFORMATION

Cursed

Contact Information: jcmckenzie@jcmckenzie.ca

Cover Art: Olga Sauchenia

Publishing History:

First JCM Publications Edition, 2024

First Black Rose Edition, 2016 (*Shift Work*, Wild Rose Press)

ISBN: 978-1-990143-59-5 (print)

ISBN: 978-1-990143-60-1 (ebook)

To Hannah.
If you hadn't devoured fantasy books when we were
younger, and if I hadn't followed you like a shadow
wanting to do everything you did, I wouldn't have
discovered the world of urban fantasy.

This series contains explicit language, open-door spicy scenes, ghosts, violence, gore, torture, PTSD from past SA, threat of SA, murder, assassinations, sociopaths and narcissists. This series also contains death, grief, and loss.

Please read with care.

I

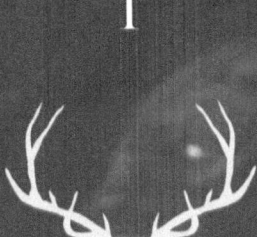

The skin of my inner thigh pebbled into hundreds of goosebumps as Tristan's fingers slid up my leg to hook into my satin panties. His hot breath fanned the burning inferno in my core. At last! We'd waited for so long. Finally, I would feel him deep inside me.

I gripped the silk sheets, twisting them in my clenched fingers. A piercing sapphire gaze, framed with porcelain skin and midnight hair, met mine before travelling down the length of my body.

Something in my mind twisted. As if setting off an alarm, only to get smothered before it could make any sound.

"Can I join in, Andy?" a deep husky voice, chilled whiskey over warm cream, shattered the silence. Wick stood naked by the door. His tall muscular body glistened with a sheen, his body hard and ready.

Tristan waved him over.

Something niggled in my brain, like a worm working its way through an apple, but I shushed it and arched my back against the soft sheets. Wick appeared at my side, and his devilish mouth clamped on my skin. Something pulled at my neurons. This wasn't me, was it? Two guys... silk sheets? Why had Wick appeared? I'd chosen Tristan, hadn't I?

"If I'd known your kinky little mind had a hankering for ménage, Little Carus, I would've suggested joining in a while ago." Another voice fractured the air. An unwanted voice. A voice of intrusion.

Sid the Seducer. Demon.

I bolted upright in bed, my cotton sheets clinging to the thin layer of moisture covering my body. Sweaty, like Wick's had been... I shook off the remnants of the dream and the fading sound of Sid's laughter. The sickly sweet smell of perspiration soaked through the linen and wafted up in waves to my face; tiny bitch-slaps telling me to get a hold of myself.

Threesomes would never be my thing. Never tried it, and never would. Despite having a choice of men, I would *never* become a supernatural who delved into the land of promiscuity. Just not my thing. That damn Demon knew it, too.

Tristan mumbled in his sleep and threw an arm over my lap. Even in slumber, he tried to comfort me. We'd been doing more and more sleep-overs recently. Although the relationship progressed slowly because of me, we both craved the closeness. His citrus and sunshine scent, laced with honeysuckle, broke through the nause-ating smell of my fear, and I breathed deep.

Fucking Demons.

Did Sid plan to torment my nights indefinitely? This was the third dream-nightmare in a row. Obviously, my blood gave him access to my mind, but what else did he gain from the connection? Aside from feeding off the sexual energy, what else could he do?

My cell phone trilled in the darkness. I glanced over at the device, the latest i-something on the market that Lucien the Master Vampire had given me. I'd decided to keep it as a token of my service when I kicked Lucien's bond to the proverbial curb. My phone trilled again, and I picked it up to look at the screen.

Allan.

My scalp prickled, and my hand clenched the phone. What the hell did he want?

As Lucien's second-in-command, his call meant nothing good. No longer tied to the Master Vampire, I cared what happened in that court as much as I cared about the true contents of a hot dog. I hit ignore, placed the phone back on the nightstand and curled up into Tristan's heat.

My phone vibrated with a message. And then started trilling again.

"Mmmphh," Tristan mumbled into my hair. His nose dipped down and rubbed against the sensitive skin on my neck. "Are you getting that?"

"No," I said.

The silence had little chance to descend and carry me

off to a hopefully Sid-free dream-land before my phone started making incessant noises again.

I snatched my phone off the nightstand, punched the accept button and yelled into the phone. "WHAT?"

Tristan startled and sat up beside me, hands flying to his face to rub his eyes.

"Lucien's dead," Allan said and hung up.

THE TORRENTIAL DOWNPOUR PUMMELLED THE bay windows and signalled the end of summer. I sat up in bed and rested my back against the headboard. Less than five minutes had passed since Allan's phone call, but my mind still reeled.

"Lucien's dead?" Tristan pulled himself up to sit beside me, then ran his hand through his disheveled black hair. "That's all he said?"

"Yup. I assume he means the Master Vampire is truly gone." The neurons in my brain kept firing signals, but my body refused to react. Numb shock.

Tristan leaned in and kissed my temple. "Didn't give you a chance to point out Lucien was already technically dead, did he?"

"No."

"You're quite cute when you sulk."

"This is serious, Tristan. Why'd Allan contact me? If Lucien is gone, that makes Allan the new Master. What does he want with me?" My heart thudded in my chest. What would this mean for me? When blood bonded to Lucien, I'd been employed as an ambassador by the SRD to work as a liaison between the government and the Vampire horde. Remaining tied to a sadistic supe hadn't been an option, and after I slipped the chains binding me to Lucien, I'd spent the last month avoiding the Vampires and looking for alternative job solutions. Naturally, I'd also been planning the ultimate revenge assassination for Lucien. With him taken care of... Maybe I could continue working as a liaison without a blood bond. Would it be that bad?

"Maybe Allan called out of courtesy," Tristan suggested.

I gave him a dark look, made easier by the early morning hour and lack of caffeine. Unfortunately, my powers of bitch-face were totally wasted on Tristan because he watched his fingers slide up and down my forearm instead of watching my expression.

"Maybe Lucien never told anyone you kicked his bond." Tristan moved his hand from my arm and gently placed his fingers on my lips. His action stopped whatever denial I planned to fling out. "Think about it. Why would the Master Vampire let anyone know? It would make him look weak."

"Lucien hated looking weak," I mumbled.

"Exactly."

"But if I was still bound to Lucien, his death would mean mine."

The falcon in my head screeched.

5

"Allan's not an idiot. Maybe he suspected and you answering the phone confirmed it."

I grumbled. On one hand, had I not answered the phone, the Vampire court would've assumed I died, like all those blood bonded to a Master Vampire. The horde certainly wouldn't waste resources searching for me. In fact, the Vampires would finally leave me alone and stop thinking of ways to use me.

On the other hand, I needed a job, and with Lucien dead, my main reason for avoiding the Vampires had been removed, quite literally. The horde now represented a potential employer. As much as I hated Vampires, I didn't need to like them to take their money, but I would need a good explanation for my beating heart. No one blood bonded to Lucien would survive his death, including Clint, and... A shiver lanced up my spine and struck the back of my skull. Wick. "Oh, god."

"Shhhh." Tristan ran a hand up my arm. "Wick and his pack aren't blood bonded. Just like my Vampire Master's death didn't kill me, Lucien's will have no ill effect on Wick's life, nor anyone in his pack."

Lucien had possessed certain skills as an older Vampire. His age and strength made it possible for him to bind two humans servants—me and Clint—and call wolves, any wolves, to do his bidding. This meant Lucien had controlled Wick and his Werewolf pack, just like Tristan's previous master, who called leopards, had controlled Tristan and his prowl. This special skill also meant Lucien had no need to blood bond Wick to make him do what Lucien wanted.

A long breath escaped my lungs, and I tried to ignore Tristan's intense scrutiny of my face. Tried. It didn't work. Sometimes his perceptiveness freaked me out. He read me too well. I hadn't spoken Wick's name out loud.

"It does have one effect," Tristan said.

My heart pounded in my chest again. "What's that?"

Tristan smoothed my hair down and tucked a strand behind my ear. "He's free."

"Oh," I said. The pronoun didn't need a name. Wick's tie to Lucien had ultimately led me to break things off with him. Too many times, Lucien had used the Alpha Werewolf against me, and I couldn't take the pain anymore. Did his freedom change things? I looked into the deep blue of Tristan's eyes, sparkling even in the dim light, and smiled. No. I'd made my choice a month ago. I leaned forward and planted a kiss on his full lips.

THE RAIN ABATED A LITTLE DURING THE DAY while Tristan and I ran errands. The little things we did together, like make oatmeal, drink coffee and buy groceries on a lazy Sunday, brought us closer and melted my heart. He held my hand as we walked down the aisles and read labels as if we cared about caloric intake. As a Wereleopard and Shifter respectively, Tristan and I didn't need to worry about what we ate like norms did. The transformation process took so much energy, we could binge on junk food every day and still look trim and in shape. The fashion world would love us except we often wore T-shirts and sweatpants for easy shifting.

Tristan had been uncharacteristically quiet all day. Sweet, but not his normal talkative self. Not possessing the same perceptiveness as he did, I had no idea what had sent him into deep-thinking mode. Maybe he worried about my job prospects as much as I did. I'd been essentially unemployed since dispelling Lucien's mark from my body.

At the end of the day, Tristan and I went to the bedroom to change. Tristan for bed, me for Vampire Court. Since Allan knew I still stalked the mortal realm, I may as well find out if I could continue working as the ambassador between the Vampire court and the SRD without a blood bond.

Tristan turned to me, gloriously naked. "Does this change anything between us?"

"What do you mean?" I pulled a mint green shirt over my head. I tugged a pair of ripped skinny jeans from my bottom drawer and mentally selected the flats I'd match with the outfit. I could fly to Lucien's, or Allan's place, but I didn't want to beg for a job naked or in a house robe. "I've been involved with the Vampire court since we met."

"Do I need to say his name? The one that still hangs heavy between us?"

With my jeans still in my hands, I bit my lip. Well, something did *literally* hang heavy between us. My gaze drifted down Tristan's toned body. I licked my lips.

Tristan cleared his throat. "I'm up here."

I shook my head and forced my gaze to make eye contact. "I made my decision."

"Good." Tristan's shoulders relaxed and he stepped in close. He ran his hands up my arms to cup my face. Keeping his gaze on my face, he paused as if soaking in as much detail as possible, as if memorizing every freckle. "Good."

He pressed his lips to mine, hard, before deepening the kiss. The air sucked out of my lungs, leaving me breathless and lightheaded. He always had this effect on me—as if oxygen was inconsequential, as if I could live without air as long as we were together.

He pulled away too soon, and traced a finger along my bottom lip. "Good," he repeated.

Still gasping for breath, I clutched the pants in my hand. "I'm going to the Vampire court to ask for work. Why'd you get me all hot and bothered?"

Tristan smiled. "Trust me. Smelling like you do right now will only help your chances of employment."

I growled, but Tristan just laughed and swaggered into the bathroom. With the tangible need to follow and give him a goodbye kiss of my own, I tugged my jeans on and turned toward the living room instead. Tonight, I needed a clear head to get a job—one that didn't require any blood swapping.

2

The cool air caressed my face, carrying with it the deep fragrances of blood, death, and decay. Lucien's grand hall seemed less grand and *emptier* as I walked down the red carpet to stand in front of the former Master Vampire's austere, throne-like chair. Allan sat in it, barely. He perched on the edge with a rigid posture and looked ready to leap off at the slightest provocation.

As a Carus, I possessed more than one animal familiar, known as a fera, to shift into. With one of these forms so dark and filled with malice she scared even me, Allan's restlessness made sense. Not that I could necessarily take him down surrounded by the horde, but I'd do some damage if I felt compelled.

Allan. The largest Japanese man I'd ever met, easily stood over six and a half feet. He packed about three hundred pounds of muscle, and a brain bordering on genius. Smart and strong, he could read my mind like I devoured books. My skin prickled at the reminder, and I forced myself to reminisce about the forest behind my parents' old house.

Allan's lip twitched, but he said nothing as I completed the final steps to reach him. We studied each other for a silent minute, or five. My skin itched to shift to a mountain lion, and my palms began to sweat.

No sign of Clint. Was the death of his master the one and only thing that could kill him? Despite defying all reason, I doubted it. He'd been pretty indestructible until now, surviving a torn out throat and getting shishk-abobbed with a sword multiple times. The hairs on the back of my neck prickled my skin as they rose. Had Clint run off somewhere to plot my demise?

"You look remarkably alive for one tied to a Master Vampire." Allan broke the silence.

"As do you, for one who's actually a member of the living dead tax bracket," I replied.

"Second-in-commands are not blood tied for the sole purpose of a more streamlined succession. We're blood sworn."

Blood sworn to prevent them from backstabbing their masters. He didn't need to explain. As the name implied, Vampires in a horde swore an oath in blood to their Master. This oath worked much like the relation-ship between an Alpha and his pack, pride or prowl. It prevented underlings from going against the word of their Master or from betraying them. There were ways around blood oaths, though, just like ways existed around an Alpha's order, or telling the truth.

"Did you do it, then?" I asked.

Allan's eyes narrowed. "Did you?"

"No, not that I didn't want to." I opened my mind so he could read the truth from me. The mountain lion cohabitating in my head hissed at the move. She didn't like company from the outside. Allan would see every-thing—including my revenge plotting and the anger simmering beneath my skin because someone stole my revenge.

He pulled his cuffs down. "You couldn't kill Lucien when your life was tied to him, and it's no secret you despised his control over you and his methods of... persuasion. Many suspect your hand in his true death."

Methods of persuasion, my ass. The blood flowing in my veins grew hot as memories of Lucien's methods flooded my mind. The Master had promised to gut Wick repeatedly and make me watch unless I did as he ordered. Fetching coffee for the egomaniac would've been tolera-ble, but his tasks either caused great shame and debase-ment, or put me and loved ones in danger. Allan was right. I had plenty of reasons to kill Lucien. I'd spent the last month thinking of ways to pull it off and get away with it.

"Well, it wasn't me."

"So I see. Thank you for opening your mind. You can shut it now. I have no interest in seeing what you've been up to with your pussy...cat."

Jackass. He meant Tristan, but Vamps couldn't resist the not-so-original play on words. "You're hilarious," I said.

Allan shrugged.

We studied each other for another long minute. "Why did you call me?" I asked.

"Courtesy."

"How'd you know I survived Lucien's death?"

"After making his inner circle blood swear to secrecy, he told us about your little blood bond escaping trick." He levelled me with a dark look. "You're fortunate someone took his life. He had plans for retribution, kitten."

My heart played hopscotch in my chest, but I ignored it. Allan didn't tell me anything I didn't already suspect. Lucien couldn't take the blow to his ego without reacting, and it was only a matter of time before he sought revenge.

"Do you plan to pick up where he left off?" I asked.

"Where you're concerned? No." He shrugged. "There are more important things to attend to."

"How'd it happen?" I glanced around the room, looking for...what, exactly? Not sure. Maybe a pile of ash with a sign stuck in it reading, "Lucien's Remains." The vacant chamber held nothing but the stench of Vampire and cleaning products. The room had been freshly sterilized and only the recent milling of surviving Vampires had ruined the clean smell. No ash, no blood spatter, no signs of a struggle. Maybe the true death didn't happen in this room.

"That's none of your concern," Allan said.

"As the ambassador between the Vampire Court and

the SRD, a supernatural death is exactly that—my concern." I held my breath.

Allan chuckled. "You were the ambassador between *Lucien's* Vampire Court and the SRD. You were also *absent* for the last month. Now that Lucien is gone, it is my court, and I have no wish for the meddlesome SRD to be needlessly involved in my affairs. Especially not with a representative who most of the surviving Vampires believe assassinated Lucien. At the behest of the SRD, no less."

I choked on my breath. "But can't you use the liaison thing to your advantage?"

"Do you honestly want me to use you, kitten?"

I froze.

Allan smirked. "I thought not. I am doing you a favour by releasing you of your service."

"Do I get a severance package?"

Allan laughed. He could've just said no.

3

T here's nothing I despised more than the thought of walking into the SRD's downtown headquarters to face Agent Tucker. Except facing Agent Tucker *and* asking for reinstatement as an agent. My hand clasped the cold metal handle, and I yanked the glass entrance door open. The stale and fresh scents of norms and supes flooded my nose. When I woke up late this morning after my visit with Allan, I realized I needed to do something more proactive about my work situation. Unfortunately, that meant the SRD and one particular agent.

Agent Tucker Fucker. ATF. *How do I loathe him? Let me count the ways...*

Elizabeth Barrett Browning probably groaned in her resting place as I adapted and butchered her work as a mental mantra to gather self-restraint. Hopefully, she'd forgive me. Only hatred this intense led me to revise and spout poetry.

I padded across the massive foyer of the SRD's down-town headquarters and nodded at my Witch neighbours who stood at the security desk. We'd gotten off on the wrong...note...but now, I counted Ben as one of my best friends. I loved this guy.

"Hey." Dirty blond hair hung in his eyes when he glanced at his clipboard. He and Matt guarded the SRD from unwanted visitors. Their naughty list would include me very soon. "Didn't expect to see you until tonight."

"Yeah." Matt looked up from the computer, green eyes twinkling. "We're still on, right?"

"Of course."

"Then why are you..." Matt trailed off. "Oh."

"Here to beg for a job?" Ben asked.

I might've vented about my lack of job prospects with the Witches on more than a few occasions. They held as much optimism for this option as I did.

"I don't think it will come to that," I said. Inside, my mountain lion yowled at the thought of such a submissive act. My falcon screeched.

Peck! she said, over and over again, while replaying memories of Tucker's bugged out eyes from when I strangled him.

"I do. No way ATF will let you off that easy," Ben said, using our acronym for Agent Tucker Fucker. Another reason he was one of my best friends. We'd thought about using FAT for Fucking Agent Tucker, but came to the agreement we couldn't say it in public. Plus,

I just disagreed with using fat as an insult, even if it was an acronym for something else.

"No. I don't either," I replied. "But it won't come to that because I'm not going to let it go that far. If he says no, he says no."

"And then what?" Matt asked. "I can tell you right now, you won't make it as a freelance singer."

I scowled at him. "No. But maybe I can do something else freelance."

Ben's lip curled up, and Matt started laughing. To them, "freelance" referred to prostitution or stripping, but among assassins, it meant something entirely different.

"That's not what I meant," I said.

"Sure." Still chuckling, Ben handed me the clipboard to sign in.

ATF. I RECITED MY POEM AGAIN AND BOLSTERED some courage to walk out of the elevator. Angelica, one of Tristan's Wereleopards, greeted me with the condescending smile she reserved just for me. She loved Tristan, as a leader and probably as something more. They had no history like that, nor would they ever if my hissing mountain lion and I had anything to say about it.

The icy glare trying to freeze me on the spot spoke

otherwise. Along with immaculate up-dos, Angie liked power, and Tristan had it.

Mine, my mountain lion hissed, sending me images of Tristan's naked body.

The incinerator in my core kicked up a notch, and Angie's ice-queen antics held no effect on me. The SRD office wasn't the place for dominance games. My best behaviour meant keeping my mouth shut instead of bitch-smacking Angie like she deserved.

What Angie really needed was a new man to set her sights on. Maybe Allan needed another lady friend to scare the crap out of. Not exactly Angie's type, but the match-up worked for me.

"I know a single Vampire if you're interested," I said in way of greeting. Sure, Allan didn't technically count as a friend, but she didn't need to know that.

Angie waved me off with manicured hands.

"Super powerful. Super freaky deeky."

Her dainty little face pinched up as she scowled at me. "I assume you're here to speak with Agent Tucker? He's been expecting you since we got news of Lucien. I'll let him know you're here."

What the hell? How did Tucker know I lived? I paused and took a deep breath. ATF stole my thunder. I'd planned to give him a rude shock. "How'd he find out I survived Lucien's death?"

Angie shrugged. "Wasn't from me."

Huh. Maybe ATF had more contacts in the supe community than I suspected. Or maybe he had me watched. My skin prickled, and my mountain lion yowled for release.

Angie pushed a button on her desk, and Tucker's nauseating voice trickled through the speakers. "Yes?"

"Andrea McNeilly to see you, sir." Angie's voice dropped several octaves to morph into one of a throaty phone sex operator.

Hmm. Last time I'd stomped into the office, Angie had been on her best behaviour with ATF, almost nervous. What changed?

Maybe Angie no longer prowled for a power player. Maybe she went norm and saddled Tucker. God, I hoped so. That would make my day. ATF wouldn't stand a chance against Angie.

"Send her in," Tucker responded.

Angie somehow puckered and curled her lips in a look that screamed mean girl, and nodded toward the door.

"Thanks," I said. My lie stunk and it made me smile.

One step into Tucker's office and I had to take a deep breath to fortify myself from the bombardment of images assaulting my eyes. Tucker decorated his office using pictures of himself with important people, or at least, people he thought held some clout, including his father, the director of the SRD. None of those big names could stop me if I decided to let my feras have their way with Tucker.

Obscure books lined his bookshelves and today Tucker had *The Catcher and the Rye*, by J. D. Salinger, facing out for all to see what a complex individual he really was.

The room reeked of Tucker's expensive cologne and his bland, boring as paper norm scent. I ground my teeth and approached him. He sat behind his desk, leaning back in his chair with his hands folded across his lap. My thin file with the coffee mug ring stain sat ominously on the smooth desk surface between us. The folder used to be stuffed full of documents, none of which I'd been privy to, but Booth had cleaned the file before taking off.

"Ms. McNeilly." Tucker waved his hand at one of the faux-leather seats across his desk. "What an unexpected surprise."

Foul-smelling, like a manky chicken truck, his lie moved through the room obliterating all other scents. This, in addition to my folder on his desk, contradicted his words. I plastered on a fake smile and set my shoulders back. "Agent Tucker," I said and sat down.

"What can I do for you?"

"Well, given that you addressed me as Ms. McNeilly instead of ambassador, I assume you're already aware of the power shift in the local Vampire court."

"Of course." His bright hazel eyes bore into mine, his only remarkable feature. Everything else about the man came across as bland, average, nondescript. That wasn't me being mean either. Honest truth. The man would've made a great undercover agent. Blending in with any crowd, he could've slipped in and out of crime scenes. Too bad he was soft and *Daddy* handed everything to him instead of making him work for it.

With the urge to throw insults at him somewhat suppressed, I decided to cut to the point and make this as professional as possible. "The new Master Vampire made it expressly known he doesn't wish to continue the liaison relationship with the SRD."

"You could have informed us of his decision via the phone." Tucker stretched his arms out before leaning forward and resting them on his desk. "Why are you really here?"

"I want to be reinstated as an agent." I held my breath and cringed on the inside. My blood pumped slowly with a gritty sensation, as if asking Tucker for something left grime in my veins.

Agent Tucker chuckled and flopped back into his chair. He smiled at the ceiling. "Priceless."

"I'm glad you think so." The desire to leap across his desk and finish what I started months ago pulled at me hard. We'd seen each other more than I'd like since our first fateful meeting, but the urge to hurt him hadn't dissipated. I clutched the armrests of my chair and dug my toes into the soles of my shoes.

"Answer me this, Andrea."

I nodded, not trusting my speech at this moment. Sure, I was capable of saying something, but whatever came out of my mouth would be accompanied by a string of curses that would make a salty old sea dog blush.

"How'd you survive?" he demanded.

I pursed my lips and forced my breathing to remain controlled. How'd he know I survived before I showed up at his office? That's what I wanted to demand in return. I bit my tongue instead, and forced the tension from my muscles before responding. "What do you mean?"

"How'd you survive Lucien's death?" he asked again. "You were blood bonded to him and should've died."

Burnt cinnamon rolled off his body. So, Agent Tucker was a bit pissed I lived. Had he heard the news about Lucien's death and danced around in his office because he thought I'd died as well? Did news of my survival crash him back to reality? *Sorry to disappoint.*

"Oh, Agent Tucker. I didn't know you cared." I forced my body to stay relaxed, and shushed the animals snarling in my head.

Tucker recoiled, and his hands balled into little fists. "How?"

I shrugged. "Lucien must've released me from the bond before his untimely demise."

Tucker pursed his lips and drummed his fingers on the desk as he studied me. His narrow gaze an amateur attempt at the stink eye, as if he willed me to divulge all my secrets with the power of his pissy face.

Not happening. Not ever.

They might know I survived Lucien's death, but my survival had plausible, if not inaccurate, explanations. If they ever found out about my beast, I'd end up on the run or in their lab. A tremor ran through my body.

Tucker's gaze faltered, and he broke the silence. "So Allan has no wish to sully his own veins by re-establishing a blood bond."

No point in correcting him. I had no wish to go through another blood bond either.

He grabbed the file with my information and flipped through it. His gaze focused forward, but he didn't pause long enough to read anything. His irises didn't contract; instead, his pupils dilated like someone staring off into space. As he shuffled the documents, the paper crinkled and rustled in time with my twitching eye.

Bite, my mountain lion snarled.

Peck, said my falcon.

I wanted to reach across the desk, haul Tucker over the smooth surface by his smarmy rich-boy shirt, and stomp on his face.

Best behaviour, I reminded myself. *Be good.*

ATF finally sighed and closed the file, placing it gently back on the desk. Apparently, he didn't plan to share any of the file's contents with me. He laced his fingers together and peered at me. "You're of no use to the Vampire court."

I frowned. "I'm not asking to be of use to the Vampire court."

"No. You're asking to be of use to the SRD. Given your previous criminal activities, which should've been pursued instead of waved off..."

I started to object, but ATF spoke over me.

"And given that you no longer hold a connection with the Vampire court, I'm afraid you have no value to us here at the SRD. No use to the Vampires means no use to us." He paused and slid his gaze to mine, daring me to contradict.

Or did he want me to beg? Neither would happen. I'd lowered myself to ask for a job from this man for nothing. My skin crawled. My fingers itched to claw his face. My blood heated.

"Well," I said as I stood up quickly. "Thank you for your time."

Agent Tucker's eyes widened, and he hesitated before also standing.

I held my hand out and waited. My falcon sent me pictures of pecking out his eyes, and my mountain lion begged me to shift and rend him from head to toe. Neither would happen. At least, not right now. As much as I despised Tucker, killing him today would only add to my problems.

Tucker stared at my open palm as if it could transmit rabies. If only.

I waited. And waited.

Finally, he clasped my hand in a weak, sweaty grip. I slipped my hand forward in his limp handshake, clenched hard and pulled him over the desk, close enough to whisper in his ear.

"You just threw away the one thing protecting you," I hissed. "Thank you."

I released his hand and smiled as he staggered back.

Oh Feradea, that felt *good*.

4

Unfortunately, immediate gratification rarely paid the bills. In fact, I'd argue right now, it kind of screwed me over in the long run.

I was officially unemployed.

My fingernails dug into the steering wheel as I turned off Lougheed Highway and headed toward Port Moody. I shouldn't have attempted retail therapy after meeting with ATF. Now my car chugged along with the rush hour traffic, and it always bottle-necked around the corner. Tristan said he planned to work from home today, so I'd hoped to surprise him at his place without any of his prowl present.

Now, I had to worry about possible spectators along with my lack of employment.

My savings would cover me for another six months; years, if I moved out of the Lower Mainland.

Move away from Tristan? My heart flopped before convulsing in my chest.

Live with leopard man, my mountain lion purred. She and Tristan had been dropping not-so-subtle-hints about cohabitation. Like he didn't spend most of his days and nights at my place already.

I might not be ready to officially live with Tristan, but I sure as heck wasn't moving away, either.

Still, I didn't want to sit in my home and twiddle my thumbs. I'd lose my mind. And no one needed a nut-job Carus rampaging around. If knowledge of my skills spread, the SRD would find a new use for me. They'd send a retrieval unit out and throw my cat ass in a specimen cage.

My skin crawled. Nope. No desire to end up in the SRD lab as another specimen. ATF would probably come by and poke me through the bars.

I pulled up to a large house in the Port Moody neighbourhood. The last time I'd been here, I'd been scouting Angie. Watching her dance around in her undies and waiting for her to lead me to the rival Master Vampire, Ethan.

Unlike a Werewolf pack, where most individuals lived in their own homes and came to the Alpha's place for meetings and get-togethers, the entire Wereleopard prowl lived under one roof. They'd *all* moved back in. Good thing the house was huge.

The idea of multiple spectators to the budding romance between me and Tristan made my skin crawl. My past experience with a Were-group-gone-bad didn't help, and Tristan always came to my place, or we went out. I'd yet to visit his home since choosing him over

Wick, and I knew my inaction pained Tristan. Despite assuring him I wasn't rejecting his prowl or this part of his life, I'd seen the creases in the corner of his eyes, and smelled the sour air, bruised with his hurt.

I had only met two of the prowl—Angie, who I had to refrain from punching in the throat from my general dislike on a regular basis, and a submissive male who'd seen me strapped naked to a gurney. I didn't fault him for not helping. His choices had been taken from him. His timely appearance had spared me from more suffering, removed the sick torturer from the room, and ultimately led to my escape.

Maybe he'd be home as well and I could thank him.

Or maybe I could just turn around and do this meet and greet another time.

My mountain lion yowled, her irritation running down the inside of my skull like claws.

Coward! My falcon squawked.

They were right. What was up with me today?

I mentally pulled up my big girl socks and clambered out of the car. The heat radiated off the stone walkway and caressed my legs before I climbed up the three steps to the entrance. The large red double doors stared back at me, daring me to knock or run away. I stood frozen with self-doubt. Tristan said he'd work from home today. He also said I could stop by *any* time. Why did I feel like I intruded before I even stepped over the threshold?

With a long inhale, I rapped my knuckles against the painted wood. Citrus and sunshine spiraled through the door seals and encircled me. Fresh and warm, despite the cold nip in the air. Not Tristan's scent, the one laced with honeysuckles, but one belonging to a prowl member. My mountain lion purred from deep within, wanting to shift and roll around in the smell.

The person behind the door hesitated before opening it. The hinges creaked a little before revealing a large male Wereleopard with deeply tanned skin and a body that rippled with muscle. Despite his strong appearance, he held himself in a slightly diminutive posture. A sub. And not any sub, the same one I'd met in the torture room of a sadistic Werehyena.

"You." His large brown eyes widened.

"You," I said.

We stood in silence. I enjoyed the smells emitting from the house; pumpkin spice, vanilla and cinnamon mixed in with Wereleopard. Someone had baked. My mouth watered.

"Uh, can I help you?" the sub asked. He ran his hand through thick brown hair.

"Oh, sorry. I'm Andy." I put my hand forward. The Wereleopard stared at it and then frowned. Had he not heard of me? Surely, Tristan would've mentioned my name. Even if he hadn't, his prowl would sense his...well, his feelings for me.

Unless a prowl's bond with their Alpha didn't work like a pack's. I operated under that assumption, and now, staring at an uncomfortable, if not bewildered sub, I kicked myself for my ignorance.

"I'm dating Tristan..." My voice trailed off, and I took a deep breath. What the heck? I distinctly remember pulling up my big girl socks. Where did they go? I straightened my shoulders and met the sub's eyes. "Is he here?"

"Oh!" he exclaimed. "That Andy! I'm so sorry. I didn't make the connection. I just...well. You remind me of a time and place I hoped to forget." He bowed his head and started mumbling at his feet. His fear and turmoil swirled around me. Of course he'd recognize my scent, but he had more tact to comment directly on the incident.

My shoulders dropped a little, and I instinctively reached out. "I'm sorry you had to see me on Mark's operating table, but I can't thank you enough for your interruption."

The sub's head snapped up.

"I escaped because of you and Angie. Thank you."

His eyebrows turned up in the middle, and his lips trembled.

"Nelson!" A familiar voice yelled out. "Who is it?"

At the sound of Angie's voice, ice flowed through my veins to wipe out the warmth from my moment with the sub. The mountain lion inside clawed to get out, wanting to attack Angie and claim her territory. Dang it. She beat me here.

Nelson jumped back. "I'm so sorry!" he said to me. "Please come in."

I flashed him a quick smile and stepped inside the house with heavenly smells and two Wereleopards, one sweet, one bitchy.

When I rounded the corner of the foyer, the house

opened up into a large living room. Angie lay on one of the couches with her feet up. She wore spandex pants that showcased her toned, albeit short, legs and curvy waist. The fuchsia work-out top squeezed her magically enhanced boobs to the point they looked like they'd pop out if she completed a burpee.

"Angie." I nodded and squashed the urge to take the final steps necessary to punch her.

My mountain lion hissed in my head, and my fingernails stung to elongate.

"Andrea." She flicked two fingers up in some sort of salute, but all I got from the gesture was attitude and derision.

I took a deep breath. Angie tried to bait me. Why else would she remain sprawled on Tristan's couch as if I posed no danger, as if she owned this home, not Tristan?

How angry would Tristan be if I beat her up? I could do it, too, but she hadn't crossed the line…yet.

I could always hope.

"Why are you trying to piss me off?" I cocked a hip.

Nelson swayed from foot to foot behind me, and a gust of his nervous energy hit my back. If things came to blows, he'd be stuck between a dominant prowl-mate and his Alpha's mate. I didn't envy his choices. Technically, he should choose my side, if I'd formally been welcomed, finalized the mate bond, and joined the prowl, but he'd just officially met me and although I'd accepted Tristan's claim, we hadn't slept together yet, nor had we completed the bond. My stomach lurched. Nelson's lack of attachment to me was entirely my fault.

Angie smirked and wiggled into the couch. "We could always sort our differences out."

"I think you spend way too much on your magical enhancements to risk a confrontation with me."

"I don't plan on losing." She yawned.

"That's your first mistake."

Her attention snagged on my face and a finely plucked brow arched. My mountain lion hissed to swipe the smug expression off her face. "You might have an advantage with your gangly limbs in human form," she said. "But a mountain lion is no match for a Wereleopard."

She stood and stretched, making a point to look away as she bared the soft tissue of her stomach. She didn't act in a submissive way, but in a you're-beneath-my-concern way.

I snorted. "Who said I'd pit my feline against yours?"

Angie laughed; a trill sound that raked my nerves like fingernails on chalkboard. "Your wolf?" She scoffed. "Like it would have a better chance. I gave your intelligence too much credit, it seems."

"You gave your own too much." Maybe I should shut up and let her continue to underestimate me. Maybe I should stick to my best behaviour? My fists clenched. My knuckles popped, and my canines elongated to puncture my bottom lip.

No. First time in Tristan's house, confronted with another dominant female, challenged, even if a bit passive aggressively? No. I had to throw down or get thrown down. No other option. I'd turn this into a bitch fight if needed to assert my dominance and my position above Angie in her own prowl. She'd peck at me like carrion until she reached bone, otherwise.

Angie blinked.

"Do you honestly think I'm limited to only three forms?" I took another step forward so only a foot separated us.

Angie's eyes widened. "You have more? If the SRD found—"

"The SRD will never find out. Not from you. You've already sworn to your Alpha not to reveal my nature, either directly or indirectly." And thank Feradea for that. Angie chewed her lip in a thoughtful way, entirely too calculating. It made my skin itch.

Angie lifted her chin. "What would you use then?"

My smile widened.

"Well?"

Her nervousness wound around me, and I inhaled the sweet smell deeply. I leaned in. "I want it to be a surprise."

She rolled her eyes, but couldn't hide the relaxing of her shoulders or slowly released breath.

Go in, my cougar hissed. *Go in for the kill. Shush, you!*

"Tristan's not here," Angie said. "He got called to work." She folded her arms across her chest, and looked out the large window with the view of Burrard Inlet.

"So I see. I'll text him." I plastered on a fake smile. Maybe I'll insist he kick Angie out to live in her old place. "Thanks for your hospitality." I didn't mean it.

"Anytime," she said, not meaning it, either.

Andrea McNeilly
Code name: Serendipity
Employee number: 16113

Dear Ms. McNeilly,

Subject: Termination
CC: Personal file

We regret to inform you that your employment with the Supernatural Regulatory Division has been terminated effective immediately.

Termination was based on a combination of two factors: 1) The untimely true death of Lucien Delgatto, the Master Vampire with whom you shared a blood bond; and 2) The refusal of the current Master Vampire, Allan Akihiko, to renew the horde's ties with the SRD.

Considering these two factors, your position as liaison between the Vampires of the Lower Mainland and the SRD has been made redundant. As no contract was signed for the ambassador position, we must fall back on your previous agreement with the SRD, which stipulates no severance package or notice of termination is required by the employer (Section 10.1 d).

A record of employment has been issued, and you may apply for Employment Insurance through the government at your earliest convenience.

Thank you for your service. We wish you much success in your future endeavours.

Sincerely,

Randall Tucker

Randall Tucker,
Executive Director, British Columbia Branch
Supernatural Regulatory Division

604-555-5555
401 West Georgia Street, Vancouver, BC,
V6B 5A1

rtucker@srd.gov.ca
SRD.GOV.CA

5

T crumpled up the letter signed by Agent Tucker's father. Tucker probably wet his pink panties drafting this piece of crap. He didn't have the gonads to sign it, though. Got daddy-dearest to scribe his fancy-dancy signature on the termination notice instead. What a lovely reminder of his family's importance and power.

Like that would stop me from gutting him.

I shot the wad of paper at my office's recycling bin, my form perfect, like a professional basketball player.

The crumpled paper bounced off the rim, and the wall, finally settling on the floor beside the waste bin.

ATF.

Somehow this was his fault as well.

When I slowly applied the brakes, my early model canary-yellow Poo-lude lurched to a stop in front of the Vancouver Police Department downtown head-quarters. I'd spent a pretty penny from my savings getting this hunk-of-junk repainted to cover the bright red cock and balls some wannabe thug had emblazoned on the side with spray paint. Ben had laughed and asked why I went with the same colour. For some reason, I'd grown attached to the effervescent shade of radioactive urine.

I pulled the handbrake, grabbed my keys and hopped out of the car. Officer Stan Stevens had left a cryptic message for me to stop by during his shift. He wanted to discuss something. Or at least I assumed he did when he said, "Get your scrawny ass down here."

With curiosity worthy of my feline nature, and having a wide open schedule due to my current unem-ployment, I found myself walking into the precinct with a bounce in my step.

The desk clerk admitted me to the secured area after I signed in. I wove through the cookie-cutter cubicles and work stations while lingering emotional scents washed over me. Grief, heartache, anger, guilt, and a slew of other unpleasant smells assaulted my nose, but more pleasant scents made it bearable—relief, happiness, deter-mination and gratitude. Cops often got a bad rap and there were certainly bad cops out there. People forgot too easily all the great things the good cops did within the community.

When I approached Stan's desk, he looked up and beamed at me. Middle-aged and sarcastic, he held nothing back when it came to his opinion. His uneven teeth pointed in various directions as if they were sunflowers trying to find the light at a disco party. In the last month, we'd met a few times for beer to bitch about...well, whatever we wanted to bitch about. I called them B&B sessions and found them almost as therapeutic as belting 80s songs karaoke-style with my Witch neighbours.

Stan leaned back and clasped his hands in front of his firm belly. "Andy, I'm glad you made it."

"Well, your vague message left me in a state of wonder." I pulled a chair back and sat across his desk from him. "What's up?"

"Well, there's been some drug activity."

"It's Vancouver, not the Vatican."

Stan snorted. "This is different. There's a new drug on the scene, and it's deadly."

"I think I heard of it on the news. What are they calling it? Special K?"

"That's Ketamine. The new stuff is called King's Krank, or KK. And, yeah, we've been trying to keep a tight lid on it, but somehow those damn reporters got a hold of the story."

"So how does this involve me?" I had a feeling—an itch at the nape of my neck threatened to race down my spine. My finger beds ached as my nails pushed against the tender flesh to shift to claws.

"We need your help."

"Could you elaborate?" I plucked a small five by seven inch frame off his desk and flipped it around. A wedding picture of Stan with thicker hair beside a pretty brunette with dark eyes. His wife, Loretta.

"I've discussed you at length with my serg—"

I glanced up from the photo. "Tony Lafleur?"

Stan nodded. "We'd like to bring you on to the force, as a direct transfer from the SRD or as a consultant. The way we figure it, we can do faster police work if we have a supe to collect evidence for supe-norm and norm-norm crimes. With this new drug, we could really use your nose to investigate."

"I think that's the longest I've ever heard you speak."

"Fuck you." He snatched the frame from my hands and gently repositioned it on his desk. He smiled. At the photo, not me. "What do you think?"

"I think you want to use me as a drug dog."

"That's why you're perfect for this job." He leaned back and clasped his hands behind his head. "You're a complete bitch most of the time."

"Har de har har. Like I haven't heard that before."

Stan smirked.

"I don't…" I studied my twisted hands on my lap. "I don't have my wolf form anymore."

Stan straightened. "You can no longer shift?"

"Yeah, about that." I took a deep breath. "This has to stay between us and your sergeant, okay?"

"Yeah, okay, whatever." Stan waved his hand in the air as if it was no big deal.

"Seriously, Stan. No leaks."

He leaned forward. "Shit, this has got to be good."

"Good enough to land me in the SRD lab if you can't keep your yap shut."

Stan paused and pursed his lips. "I get it, Andy. You can trust me."

"Like I could trust you to brief your fellow officers not to shoot me?"

Stan groaned and flopped back in his chair. "That wasn't my fault. Dubin...er...the officer was a rookie and totally rattled. Those massacres were intense. He would've shot down a mosquito if one dared to fly near him."

When the Demon, Bola, had found a loophole allowing him unrestricted use of a human form, he'd used his mortal realm free time to cause mass slaughter and mayhem. The VPD used me in wolf form to sniff out the massacre sites and when I'd shown up to one, an officer freaked out and shot me in the ass. My blood bond to Lucien at the time meant quick healing and only about thirty minutes of intense pain, but it still pissed me off. And Stan knew it.

Stan leaned forward in his seat again and clasped his hands together. "On my life, Andy, your secret is safe with me."

The fragrance of his truthful statement flooded my senses and warmed my heart. I laced my fingers together. I whispered, "I have more than one form."

"Huh?"

I glanced over my shoulder and leaned in. "I can take the shape of more than one animal."

Stan's eyebrows drew together and his mouth gaped open, giving me prime seating to study his snaggled teeth. "How's that even possible? I took Supernaturals 101 as a prerequisite for the force. Shifters bond to one animal fera."

I shrugged. I'd once believed my multiple forms made me special, but a meeting with Feradea, the goddess of beasts and hunters, taught me I was just a genetic throwback to her original demigod offspring. Of course, Stan didn't need to know any of that. Bad enough more and more people knew my shifting secret.

"Wow," he said after a moment of silence. "You're like a freak of nature."

Relief flowed through my veins, and my shoulders drooped. "Thanks."

He shook his head and looked down at his hands. "The SRD lab would like to get a hold of you, wouldn't they?"

My muscles tensed.

Stan looked up, and his intense gaze met mine. "Wow, Andy, you really trust me."

"Don't make me regret it."

He nodded. The space around his desk grew quiet while we studied each other. Stan shifted in his seat. "You don't want to hug this out or something, do you?"

I snorted.

He relaxed. After a silent moment, his expression

quickly grew serious. "So you can't shift into a wolf anymore?"

Technically, I could. All it took was reintegrating the wolf into my body to shift, in a semi-fluid transition, but the pain of having the wolf's mind in my own...the wolf's heart beating along with mine...the wolf's wants...the wolf's needs... I couldn't take it, the pain of letting Wick go too fresh and too raw.

"No," I answered. "I can't."

Stan peered at me. "Are you sick?"

"No. I just..." I sighed. How to explain this to a non-supe? "I got rid of the wolf because I chose not to be with Wick, the Alpha Werewolf."

Stan's lips compressed. "You supes are so..."

"Complex?"

"I was going to say fucked up, but sure, let's run with that." Stan tapped his fingers along his desk. "What other forms do you have? Can any of them sniff things out like your wolf?"

"My sense of smell is still heightened in human form and sufficient for most crime scenes, but yes, I have other forms with more than adequate noses." Technically, the bear would be the best option, but I just couldn't picture lumbering around the crime scene in the form of a two-hundred-and-fifty pound black bear.

"Could you elaborate?"

"On what?"

"On which forms."

Mountain lion, falcon, wolf, fox, bear...and the beast. The latter, known in the supernatural community and historical documents as the Ualida, would be a bit overkill for most situations. Pun intended.

Stan's death stare urged me to speak.

"I plan to use the mountain lion unless the situation calls for something else." Although better than a human, mountain lions actually had a poor sense of smell, but the falcon had none to speak of whatsoever. My fox had a great nose, but like the falcon, the body of a fox was small and vulnerable. No way would I leave myself exposed like that at a crime scene. Well, not unless necessary.

"A mountain lion?" Stan sputtered.

"Yup."

Stan peered at me. "You really could kick my ass, couldn't you?"

"Well, probably, but one of your coworkers might take another pot shot at my butt, and that shit hurt."

"Seriously, Andy. Will you let that go?"

"No."

"I wouldn't, either." Stan sighed. "Will you do it?"

Of course I would. I needed a paying job. If the VPD had finally loosened up enough to bring on a supe, I wanted to be a part of it, even if it had taken them eighty years since the Purge. "What's the pay?"

His gaze cut away. Crap! Not much then.

"You'll have to negotiate your salary or fee with Lafleur." Stan said. "And I'm not sure how they run things over at the SRD, but you'd probably have to get approval from them, and maybe even a release."

Well, that just proved not everyone in the city knew my business. True, moments ago I told Stan my biggest secret, and I'd tell him about the SRD, too, but I wanted to keep my termination under wraps until after I negotiated my salary with Lafleur.

"I'll have to leave my job," I said. "That will factor into the figure I name."

Stan shrugged. "Just remember, we're all public servants at the end of the day and our provincial government dictates we get paid absolute crap for keeping order on the streets."

My lips curled up. "How could I forget?"

The face of the current premier of British Columbia had been plastered all over the news lately, projecting balanced budgets and a plan to support families and maintain a healthy, well-educated society. She may as well have thrown in world peace with her speech. Her lies stunk even through the television.

"Tony's office is that one." Stan waved his index finger in the direction over my right shoulder.

"Thanks," I said.

"When you've reached an agreement, come back and we can get you on the schedule and put a system in place for a call out. You'll be on rotation with me. I work a lot of night shifts." He chortled.

I blinked.

"The night shift," he repeated. "Get it? You're a Shifter, we'll work the night shift... Oh never mind." Red creeped up his neck and stained his cheeks.

"Night Shift. Got it." I gave him a salute, which I'm fairly sure I butchered, and chuckled my way to Lafleur's office. My heart raced. I needed this job to stay in the Lower Mainland and close to Tristan.

Keep your cool, Andy. This is your only job prospect. Don't fuck it up.

Negotiating a contract popped up pretty low on my "Things I like to do" list. People often said one thing, then did another. Wild animals were so much easier to deal with.

My mountain lion purred and rubbed against my brain. My falcon ruffled her feathers and sank her head down into her body for a snooze. My chest hollowed out. No third response. No wolf lurking in my body to keep me straight and growl at people we didn't like. I missed her. But she missed Wick too much for me to allow her cohabitation in my mind.

My mountain lion's purr grew louder, as if trying to drown out the absence of the wolf, as if trying to distract my thoughts from thinking about the missing fera or Wick.

She had the right idea, and soon my mind tumbled into bed with Tristan and his piercing blue gaze framed with a dark mop of sleep-tussled hair.

I took a few deep breaths to settle my nerves before rapping my knuckles on Lafleur's door.

"Come in," he bellowed.

I opened the door and stuck my head in. "Stan brought me up to speed on the possibility of doing some work for you. I'm interested and would like to negotiate my salary. Is this a good time?"

Tony Lafleur grunted something that sounded like

"yes" and "no" at the same time. I hesitated at the door, but when he didn't yell at me to get out, I pulled back my shoulders and walked in. His office smelled like he did—gun oil and paper. A career cop, his steely blue eyes pierced mine, his shaved head reflected the fluorescent lights, his smushed in nose spoke of breaking up one-too-many bar fights, and his rotund belly gave credence to the cop stereotype of donut binging.

Despite his unsmiling face and rather brusque manner, I kind of liked the guy. Like I'd respect a drill-sergeant who'd make me do chin-ups until I puked.

His office was small, reflecting the exorbitant prices of downtown Vancouver real estate more than his significance. A small fan puttered away in the corner, creating a trickling breeze of pseudo-cool air, but did little to prevent my skin from warming. Lafleur sat behind a solid oak desk that would've looked nice, maybe, if it hadn't been covered with teetering stacks of files and forms. Edges of the papers fluttered in the fanned air. A smooth large rock sat atop the pile as if to stop the papers from flying away in the flickering draft. File cabinets, with partially closed drawers, appeared laden with more files and history. Perspiration and determination clung to every surface illuminated by fluorescent lights.

I'd expected a clean, almost clinical room, devoid of character, something like Agent Booth's office, when she had one, but this room spoke of a career cop who worked long hours and lived his job.

My respect for him shot up a notch.

Sergeant Lafleur waited for me to finish assessing his

personal space. When I finally turned my attention to him and took in his deep set eyes and the large bags underneath them, he nodded at me. "Ambassador McNeilly."

"Andy, is fine," I said.

He grunted again, tapped something on his keyboard and then turned his full, unwavering gaze to me. "Before we negotiate your fee, are there any factors you'd like to bring forward that will influence your decision?"

Well, straight to the point. My kind of guy. "I won't be able to work as an ambassador or as an agent with the SRD if I take this position. My fee should cover full pay, not something you'd consider a top up. I also want to be on salary, with benefits, not paid as an on-call contractor or consultant. I want to go all in and join the team." Not a lie at all, really. I couldn't work for the Vampires or the SRD because they'd both fired me.

He clasped his hands on his desk and leaned forward. "Are you sure you want to burn that bridge?"

"Have you met Agent Tucker?"

Tony guffawed, a bark of a laugh that rumbled from his belly. My respect for him automatically went up two more notches.

"Well, I s'pose I won't have to worry about your allegiance to the SRD. What about the Vampires?" Lafleur asked.

I fixed him with my best death stare. It didn't faze him at all.

"Will there be any backlash from them?" he pressed on.

It sounded like he genuinely cared about my well-being. Or maybe he worried about political ramifications. After all, I hadn't heard of this arrangement before. Maybe it had been more than prejudice preventing the VPD from knowingly hiring a supe.

"No backlash. With Lucien dead, they'd have to re-establish the relationship with my approval anyway." Feradea would be proud of my choice of words. If a Shifter or Were had been sitting beside me, they'd sniff the truth of my words.

"Name a figure," Lafleur said.

My momentary confidence faltered. My skin grew clammy as the stuffy room continued to warm my body. Crap. I hated naming a price. If he accepted the figure too easily, I'd know I could've asked for more. If I went too high, Sergeant Tony Lafleur might dismiss me altogether and find someone else. I kept my face passive, closed off from my emotions and thoughts. It would do no good to show Lafleur how much I wanted this. "I'm open to negotiation."

Lafleur paused and studied me for a half-second. "Cut the horseshit, McNeilly. Give me a number, and we'll work from there."

Gah! Sweat beaded along my nose and back as I forced my body to remain loose and my lips uncurled. "What about a salary equal to my average earnings as an agent with the SRD?"

Lafleur drummed his fingers on his desk. "And that would be…"

"Around a hundred thousand a year, but I'll accept

eighty-five thousand a year, with benefits, holiday pay... the whole shabam." I would make a lot more as a free-lance assassin, but that kind of work led down a dark path.

"Fifty-five and you pay for your own crap. We don't have the advantage of accepting *private funding* like the SRD."

He said "private funding" with a dark, clipped tone, and with an expression somewhere between a sneer and a grimace. He may as well have said, "Bribes." *Interesting.*

My face scrunched up. No point in hiding my reaction to this statement. "I wasn't aware the SRD bene-fitted from private funding. Don't both organizations fall under the government?"

Lafleur's fingers stopped tapping, and he fixed me with his steely gaze. "Let's get one thing straight, McNeilly. The SRD is corrupt. If you're going to join us at the VPD, I will not tolerate any rose-tinted glasses, if you catch what I'm throwing."

"Gotcha." I held my hands up in mock surrender. "Hey, I'm no fan of the SRD. I just didn't realize the extent of the situation." More reason to hate them.

Lafleur grunted. "Fifty-five to start and you're on one-year probation like all new recruits. Then you'll go to sixty. No benefits. You'll work regular shifts with Stan, and I'll need an updated resume and a recent criminal record check. Luckily, your SRD training is transferable and replaces the police academy requirement. You're essentially a transfer, but you're starting at the bottom, and we need to make this legit."

"What you said, with benefits. If this is going to be *legit*, I want what everyone else on the team has."

He grumbled, and his fingers started to drone on his desk again. "Deal," he barked. He straightened to his feet, and his hand snapped out in front of him.

I scrambled to my feet and shook his hand. "Deal," I said.

His hand clasped mine firmly and gave it a tight squeeze before he nodded. "Go see Stan and get caught up with our current investigation. I'll get someone to drop off the paperwork to you soon. Welcome to the team."

"Thank you." My heart picked up the pace as if I ran a sprint. I needed to get out of here before he changed his mind. I turned and walked to the door.

"And Andy?"

I paused with a hand on the doorknob. Crap. I swallowed before speaking. "Yeah?"

"Don't make me regret this."

6

T wo warm sapphires framed with porcelain skin and dark hair studied me from across the small dining table in my apartment. The dying smells of a fading summer seeped in with the coldness of the early fall, but did little to dampen the heat stirring within. Two refilled wine glasses, plates with half-eaten chicken breasts, and various cutlery covered the table. I wanted to shove everything out of the way and launch myself at Tristan, but reached for the wine instead.

Tristan smiled as if he read my inner turmoil, his cheeks dimpled and his white teeth flashed. "So, you're once again employed. I worried you'd go independent."

I choked on my wine. I bubbled down my throat with pockets of air and left it raw. What did Tristan mean by that? He'd been so calm through all my worries, which helped keep me grounded. His worry rated at the same level as my calm. I swallowed another mouthful of sweet wine. "What would you have done?"

"What do you mean?"

"If I'd gone independent, would it have changed things for you?"

Tristan frowned. "Of course not. I would've offered you a job with my company." He tilted his head. "But I suspect you would've refused me."

Got that right. My boyfriend as my boss? No, thank you.

"Even if you went independent and down that dark path, I'd be right beside you the entire way."

"I didn't want that option either. I'd rather go for an office job." A shudder spread through my body. Office job? Well, it beat the alternative. An independent contractor essentially meant a thug for hire. Plenty of ex-SRD agents went that way. What else could they do with their narrow skill set and less-than-average social skills? After slowly finding my humanity, a process that took over fifteen years from the time I walked out of the forest, the last thing I wanted to do was take a step back. De-evolution was so not my thing.

"I can't picture you in an office," Tristan said.

"No?"

"No." His lips twitched. "In a library, on the other hand... I can picture you with your hair up in a tight bun, wearing dark-rimmed glasses and giving me a death stare to be quiet."

"Hah!" I took a sip. "I wouldn't give you a death stare."

Tristan picked up his wine, reclining back in his

chair. "You're right. You'd give me something much better."

"Oh? And what's that?"

"The same come-hither naughty librarian look you just gave me a moment ago."

I bit the inside of my lip before guzzling some wine.

"I like red on you."

"You like everything on me."

He shook his head. "Not true."

"Oh?"

He gently placed his wine glass down. "I despise that shirt."

The heat in Tristan's gaze gave away his desire. I glanced down at my tight, black wrap top. It accentuated the girls and trimmed my waist. I smoothed my hands down the shirt and arched my back.

Tristan's smile grew.

"What has this shirt ever done to you?" The tension in my body roughened my voice. Low and husky, it vibrated from my chest, followed with a purr as my mountain lion pressed for control.

"You said I like everything on you. Right now, I'd prefer that shirt off." He nodded at my outfit. "Same goes for the rest of your clothing."

This time a different sensation spread over my body. Like molten honey, my blood pulsed through my veins.

Tristan raised himself out of his seat and slowly walked the step and a half to my end of the table. He held out his hand. Mine slipped into his with a mind of its own. The skin-on-skin contact tingled my fingers and palm. He smiled, took my other hand, and pulled me from my seat. It happened with acute slowness, yet my vision blurred as if I stood too fast.

I stepped into the hard edges of his physique as if he was cut from the same stone as me, yin to my yang, the icing to my cupcake. I licked my lips. I loved icing. Tristan's porcelain skin shone with vitality and permeated with his delicious scent. I leaned in and licked his neck. The taste of him coated my tongue, sweet, yet salty. Intoxicating.

A deep rumble emitted from his chest and his strong arms wrapped around me. "I'm proud of you," he whispered into my hair.

"Why?" I ran my tongue along his jaw. Like a drug, I couldn't get enough.

"You never gave up. I know you were stressed about finding a job, but you kept your head the entire time. You didn't whine or beg me to save you." He emphasized his last words by running his hands up my back and then down again to cup my ass. "Though, I wouldn't have minded playing the hero in your case."

"Kept my head? Don't you mean I kept my attitude?"

"With you, it's the same thing." He leaned down and pressed his lips against mine. Warm and pliable. His tongue slipped into my mouth and stroked. The mountain lion inside purred, compliant and content, but not calm. She wanted more. I wanted more.

"Do you think...?" I started.

Tristan kissed my neck, scraping his teeth gently

along my nerve endings and rolling his tongue in sinful circles to taste my skin. His hands slid up my back again, under my shirt, sending a wave of delicious tingles along my spine. "Do I think what?"

"We could... Oh, I don't know." My head dipped as Tristan's mouth moved lower.

"Yes, you do." He nipped my shoulder. "Just say it, Andy."

"Go further, without..." I paused again. Heat pooled between my legs. Tristan's hands moved in slow circles on my back. His mouth created a dull ache in my core, which hummed in tune with his tongue. I pushed him away. "I can't concentrate when you're doing that thing with your tongue."

"That's the point, Andy," he said. "You think entirely too much sometimes. Just feel."

"Can we...*just feel*...without bonding?"

Tristan's lips twitched. "Of course."

"How far?"

"How far what?" His hands rested on his hips, standing with his legs shoulder width apart.

"Tristan. You're being difficult, you know exactly what I'm trying to ask." Sex for power or manipulation was one thing. I'd shamelessly used my body as an assassin, but back then, I'd been a shell of who I was today, and I certainly wasn't proud of my past. Sex with a potential mate was an entirely different situation—one filled with vulnerability, a need for trust and boundaries.

"Maybe I want to hear you say the words." He

reached forward and traced a light path down my cheek with his finger.

"How far can we go?"

Tristan paused to study me, his angelic expression inviting. "As far as you want."

I hesitated. Could it be possible? Had I waited this long for no reason besides my own fear? My heart stopped. "All the way?"

"Mmhmm. All the way." He gathered me in his arms again and leaned down to kiss me.

"But, I thought..."

Tristan kept his hands on me, but drew his mouth away. "I'm glad Wick practiced restraint, for more than the obvious reason, but I'm not him. I have a couple hundred years of control on him. It's you I'm worried about. What's to stop you from gnawing on my neck halfway through? I can't promise to behave if you do that. No Were's control is that good."

Tristan probably had no qualms with me biting him. I snorted. "I chain down and contain *a beast*. You and your *hundreds of years* as a control freak have nothing on me."

"Then there's nothing to worry about." The corners of his mouth tipped up.

"Then...why..." I bit my lip and looked away. Why had he held back? Why hadn't he pushed for more? He was an Alpha and used to getting what he wanted, used to taking what he wanted.

Then again, if he had pushed, I probably wouldn't want him the way I did.

Tristan ran his finger along my jaw, gently pushing my chin back to centre so I faced him. His sapphire gaze bore into mine; intense, shining, overwhelming. "I wasn't waiting until you were ready to bond, Andy. I waited for you to be ready to go farther, period. You have a past. A dark one. I respect that. We can stop whenever you want to."

"But..." Alphas weren't exactly the epitome of self-restraint or patience, but Tristan, and Wick for that matter, had greatly changed my perception of what it meant to be truly dominant. It didn't always result in domineering or controlling behaviour, or pushing someone they cared for well past their point of comfort.

"I might be hundreds of years old, and certainly not without experience, but even I know our mating isn't going to fix everything here." He tapped my forehead.

"Or here." He tapped my chest, right over my heart. "I'll help you anyway I can, but that kind of healing has to come from within. Pressing you for more physically wouldn't have helped either of us. And as for the actual bonding, we have plenty of time for that, too. I want you to be sure, really sure, before we consider that."

His hands ran down my arms, his fingers softly entwined with my own. The subtle contact reassuring. I wanted to jump on him, stick to him like a limpet and never let go. Yet, I also yearned to continue at a slow pace, to let time and Tristan lead me as I healed from my past. I didn't want to rush the relationship we continued to build, but I also wanted the physical stuff. I wasn't a saint. Every nerve ending in my skin screamed for more.

With a gentle tug, Tristan walked backward and pulled me into the bedroom after him. My mountain lion purred—the sound vibrated through my body and settled deep in my core. Tristan's chest rumbled in answer, and my knees grew weak.

Tristan's white teeth flashed, but I stood mesmerized by the intense blue of his gaze. Heat spread across my body as his arms moved to my waist and shoulders to draw me in, snug up against his body.

Warm lips met mine. They pressed harder and when I opened my mouth, Tristan slipped his devilish tongue in. I could kiss this man forever. He could rob me of oxygen, and I'd still keep going, I'd still crave his kiss, and the taste of his skin. Right now, though, I wanted more. I pulled his body to mine, and deepened the kiss. Tristan growled, and snagged my hair tight in his grip. His strong arms crushed me to his hard chest. His body hummed with his leopard's purr, rumbling against my breasts. My mountain lion vibrated, pushing her energy against my skin to get closer to Tristan.

With my head dizzy and my heart pounding, Tristan freed his hands, grabbed the top he despised so much, and ripped it apart. My skinny jeans followed shortly after. Were strength had advantages. Although I might miss my favourite shirt tomorrow.

My hands drifted to his waist, eager to return the favour. Tristan gently pushed them away and shook his head. Feline yellow flashed across his gaze, his leopard riding him. He wanted to lead.

Oh, hell. Who was I kidding? I wanted him to lead, too. I sighed and let my arms fall to my side.

His head ducked down and with a flick of his fingers, my bra popped off to expose my breasts to his mouth. They grew heavy and burned for more. My body throbbed with need, enjoying his torment, but wanting all of him. My mountain lion's purr strengthened until my whole body vibrated in unison to the ache between my legs.

Every time my hands moved to act, to help accelerate this exquisite torture, Tristan chuckled and gently deflected my attempts. Not my turn. Not yet.

His hands grazed my body, caressing in smooth circles across my skin, making my nerves sing. As if he could hear the song, he revisited every sensitive spot that sent my pulse racing and made my breathing shallow.

I tensed, waiting for nightmares from my past to flare up like a bad case of indigestion and ruin the mood, but the horrid images never came. In Tristan's arms, safety accompanied the growing sense of belonging and the warmth in my chest. I relaxed in his embrace.

My hands drifted to his waist again to grip his hips. He let me push him back a little. I fumbled with the zipper of his jeans, but managed to yank his pants down far enough for him to step out of them without taking his mouth off me. My greedy hands moved to his shirt next, and I pulled it over his head. His skin tasted like mojitos as I ran my tongue along the contours of his body.

More. Need more. The thought so intense, it burned my skin. My mouth travelled along Tristan's sweet skin.

He grunted and responded by throwing me backward onto the bed. Before I could move, Tristan's lips were on me again, this time lower. He ripped my underwear off and tossed them to the side.

"I've waited forever to taste you." His head bent low and his hot mouth clamped onto me, taking away my breath and any comment I could form. I should've felt exposed, vulnerable, and I did, but in a good way. No memories of the past haunted my mind as Tristan's tongue explored and stirred an inferno inside me. Heat raced through my veins, flushing my skin in wave upon wave of pleasure.

Tristan's sapphire gaze met mine as I stared down the length of my body. My hands curled into his dark hair.

A tidal wave built inside me, but before the wave broke, Tristan stopped.

"No," I gasped.

He grinned and kissed his way down my inner thigh before nipping the sensitive skin on the inside of my knee. Hyper aware, my whole body jumped in response.

Tristan stood by the foot of the bed, naked and hard, and looked down at me. His defined muscles tense and ready, his dark hair mussed, his gaze speckled with leopard yellow. The absence of his body and hands created a rush of cold air. I shivered as goosebumps pebbled along my skin.

"Beautiful," Tristan murmured.

Did he mean for me to hear him? Probably not. But

his words warmed my skin from the inside out. He'd seen me naked plenty of times, and as a Were and Shifter respectively, Tristan and I were used to flaunting our birthday suits, but the bare desire burning in his gaze, called to me and my mountain lion. She continued to purr and push her energy forward.

Tristan paused and studied me, waiting. Waiting for what? Confirmation? Approval?

Pure contentment bubbled up, and I smiled.

Tristan's shoulders relaxed. He found his jeans and took a condom out of the front pocket. Supes didn't have to worry about diseases, but we did have to worry about pregnancy. Given my hesitation to complete the mate bond, the pitter-patter of little paws was definitely not on the table in the foreseeable future.

Quickly ripping the package open, Tristan rolled the condom on and then his mouth and hands were on me again. Hot lips moved over my skin as he crawled on top of me, winding his way back until his mouth met mine to delve into another heady kiss. His naked body ground against mine, an incinerator of heat, hard and hot. His erection pressed into my stomach, and his knee wedged between my thighs to nudge them apart.

I gripped his hips, and pulled him closer. My nails elongated and dug in. Tristan growled against my mouth, before returning to take my breath away with his kiss. My feras yowled and screeched indecipherable threats if we dared to stop now. Tristan shifted slightly to slip his body between my legs.

An indescribable tenderness built within my mind

and chest, something so fragile, yet strong and potent, the very idea of it expanded my chest as if my heart inflated with something other than blood.

Tristan left no room for worry or fear. The heat of him sent all thoughts, all concerns, all logic from my mind and heart, leaving only Tristan, and the indescribable, overwhelming tenderness in my chest.

His hips flexed, and he pushed into me.

He paused, and his gaze sought mine. Infinitesimal shards of sapphire gems, streaked with leopard yellow to reveal the animal simmering beneath the surface, met my gaze with a need so intense it vibrated my body, my heart, my very being down the cellular level.

Yes, yes, and yes.

My mountain lion purred in agreement.

Sensing my unspoken agreement, Tristan slid inside with deliciously slow pressure, hard and thick.

We sighed in unison. With his hips flush with mine, he paused again. His mouth twitched. He tucked a strand of my hair behind my ear and sank his weight on top of me.

"You're stunning," he said. His full lips met mine in a gentle kiss. With his arms holding me tight, he started to move.

And my world shattered.

7

The sun snuck through the gaps between the blinds and sill to caress my face. The room smelled of night blooming jasmine and japonicas. It also smelled of Tristan and me. A new smell. Earthy, and not unpleasant. Tristan's arm draped across my midsection; a welcome weight and slight discomfort. His naked body pressed into the back of mine; slightly stuck with the remnants of sweat despite having cooled down. I could lie like this forever; bathing in Tristan's heat with the dew of lovemaking clinging to my skin, the faint caress of soft sheets and the crisp smells and sounds of a calm day.

My phone chattered. I ignored it, rolled around in bed, and snuggled against Tristan so my face smushed into his neck. His honeysuckle scent engulfed my nose and I took in deep breaths, wanting to get back to the place of tranquility before technology rudely interrupted.

My phone chittered again. And again. And again. I groaned and flopped back in bed.

"Mrrmmph." Tristan's hand groped for me.

I reached over to the night stand and checked my screen. Five missed calls from Stan. *Crap!* Stan and Lafleur had told me the paperwork and red-tape would take at least a couple of weeks for approval. In the meantime, they'd only call me in as a consultant if something big came up.

I tapped in my password and hit Stan's contact information. He picked up right away.

"Andy, finally," he said. His voice sounded like it had been wrung through a cheese grater and then punched in the guts a few times.

"Sorry, late night," I said. My heart swelled with the growing closeness to Tristan and the humming contentment of my body and feras. "What's up?"

The silence on the other end droned on while I waited for Stan to make some snarky comment about my love life. It never came. Only the slight fuzzy sound of the connection. And then I heard it.

A sob.

"Stan?" I sat up in bed and pushed Tristan's roaming hands away. The dendrites in my brain sent off a cacophony of warning sirens. "Stan, is everything okay?"

Tristan rolled onto his back. His eyes popped open under furrowed brows.

Another sob, this time louder, came through, followed by a sniff. "They..."

I waited, apprehension twisting my stomach into a

62

knot. Tristan smoothed his hand down my leg and gave me a quick peck on the cheek before slipping out of bed. His footsteps padded against the laminate flooring as he made his way to the kitchen. He would've heard Stan's voice. He knew something was up. He gave me space and privacy. The coffee maker started to gurgle in the kitchen, and I sent a mental thank you to Tristan.

"Stan, are you still there?" I asked after he'd been silent for what seemed like eons.

"They killed her," he blurted out and then broke down into sobs.

"What?" I flung the sheet off and stood up. The cool morning air brushed over my naked skin and goose-bumps pebbled on my arms and legs.

"My...my wife...Lor...she's...Oh god!"

I stared at my phone, and my heart crunched in tune with the sounds of pain coming from the other end. His wife was dead? I'd never met Stan's partner in crime, but I knew the veteran cop loved her unconditionally. His face always lit up when he spoke of her. Stan emitted another sob, and I wanted to reach through my cell phone and hug him.

"Where are you?" I asked.

Stan didn't answer.

"Stan! Where are you?"

"The precinct," he mumbled. "They left me in the staffroom. They won't tell me anything that's going on. No one will talk to me. Except..." He sniffed loudly into the receiver. "...except to say they're sorry for my... Fuck!"

He drew in a long breath through his nose. "I didn't...I didn't know who else to call."

"Well, you called the right person. I'll be right there, buddy. Just...just hold on, okay?"

Tristan! I mentally called out.

I caught it all. Go. I'll lock the door on my way out, he replied.

Thank you, I replied. So much for a romantic breakfast in bed and another round of hide the sausage. Screw it. What a selfish thought. My plans were insignificant to Stan's pain. Tristan understood. We'd have plenty of mornings together later.

I threw open the window and shifted to my falcon form. The transformation would cleanse my body and soul and give me time to think during the ten minute flight to the precinct. Stan had arranged for a change of clothes and a lock box on the precinct's roof after my meeting with Lafleur. No gallivanting around naked in front of the VPD. It meant telling Stan and Lafleur about my falcon form. After they got over it, they decided it was pretty cool. Now, I was thankful I dished my secret,

Holy crap! Stan's wife. I screeched into the bright morning air. The poor man. What he must be going through right now.

Why'd he call me? Did it matter?

Not at all. But he had a whole brotherhood of police officers, male and female, to draw on. Why wasn't someone there to support him?

By the time I'd landed on the precinct's roof top, red

hot anger raged inside my bird body on Stan's behalf. I shifted quickly, threw on my stashed clothes—baggy VPD sweats and a matching long-sleeved shirt—and marched into the building.

Stan's floor was empty, aside from the office clerk, manning the front desk. Officer Gallows had deep set Slavic features and large bags under his eyes. I'd met him a number of times, usually with him sitting behind a desk. When he looked up and took in my appearance, he didn't look surprised. The creases around his eyes smoothed out, and he sighed. "Glad you're here."

"Where is everyone?" I barked.

The officer jumped in his seat. "Looking for Loretta's killer."

"Everyone?"

He nodded.

"Is that why Stan's alone right now?"

He nodded, again. "He wanted to be alone. Yelled at us to leave him and find the killer. Told the therapist to go fuck himself. Everyone's out trying to do *something*."

"Oh." My anger dissipated, and I mentally slapped myself for being such a jerk.

"No one knows what to do, so we're doing everything we can to find out what happened. We're...we've lost members of our force before. We all know it's a risk of the job, but for the perp to take one of our family members...this shit's fucked up. Everyone's on edge, and we all want to find out who did this."

I nodded, totally getting it. Stan wouldn't let them

comfort him, so they were out doing the one thing for him they knew they could do—police work.

"He still in the staffroom?"

The officer nodded. "Just Tony outside the door. Pops his head in every now and then to...you know... make sure Stan doesn't hurt himself."

Without speaking, I walked around the desk, through the secured area and made my way to the staffroom at the back of the building. A cop with a solemn expression and soft eyes, probably Tony, stood outside the staffroom. After a brief nod in his direction, I took a deep breath and pushed open the door. Stan sat at an empty table in a plastic fold out chair, elbows down and his hands cradling his head. He swayed back and forth in his seat, constantly pushing his face down to run his fingers through his sparse, but messy hair.

"Stan," I said. My voice broke.

He froze and lifted his head. Blood shot eyes, stark white complexion, dried lips. The room stank of his misery; hot metal, stiff in the air as if an invisible weight compressed everything.

I swallowed.

Stan pushed back from the table to stand. Without a word, I walked over to him, and pulled him close for a hug. With his head bent into my neck, he cried. His shoulders shook. His whole body racked with sobs, and my shirt became damp as his tears soaked through the material.

I held him tightly and whispered "shhh" into his ear. But I didn't tell him it would be okay. That was a lie. It wouldn't be. He'd lost his life partner. His mate. Norms might not have mate bonds like some of the supernatural, but that didn't mean their loss was any less significant. I'd seen Weres lose their mates. It wasn't pretty. It looked, smelled, and felt exactly like this.

I rubbed his back and kept shushing into his hair.

"They killed her," he whispered. "They killed her because of me."

8

An icy chill vibrated up my spine as his words echoed in my head. "What do you mean?"

Stan pushed away from me, swiped his nose with his sleeve and looked at his feet. "The local news ran a story about KK and named me as the lead investigator. When I got off my shift, I went home to find her..." He squeezed his eyes shut. Then his shoulders straightened, his body tensed, and he opened his blood shot eyes to fix me with his intense gaze. Cop mode switched on. "No money or jewellery was taken and a vial of KK was found on the scene. Lab results aren't back yet, but preliminary inspection... They don't think KK was in Loretta's system. Whoever shot her, did it to send me a message."

It took my brain a full minute to digest Stan's words. *How do I respond to that?* "We'll get them."

"Damn fucking straight we will." Stan's jaw

clenched, so hard his jaw would probably ache later. His body swayed.

"Should you be here?" I asked.

"Don't tell me where to go, Andy." He swiped at his running nose and sniffed. "I'll return the favour."

I held my hands up. "Stan, I'm here for you. We'll do whatever you want. I don't have to follow the rules like your fellow officers. Let's get these fuckers." Technically, as a "transfer" I did have to follow the rules like any other cop, regardless of the whereabouts of my paperwork. But I'd break the rules for Stan.

"You'll take care of it?" Stan's red-rimmed gaze remained locked on mine. Understanding smacked my brain. He wanted me here as his assassin friend. As the woman who could take out anyone, at least in his eyes.

"I'll take care of it, or I'll turn the other way if you want to do it yourself." I didn't hesitate in my answer. If anyone understood the need to mete out justice animal-style regardless of human laws, it was a Were or Shifter. No one messed with our mates without paying for it. Painfully.

Stan nodded and finally looked away. "Can you do something for me?"

"Anything."

"Can you go to my home..."

"And sniff it out?"

He nodded again.

"You bet."

Stan's body relaxed a little, and he went to the mini kitchen to fiddle with the coffee maker. "You have clearance for the crime scene, you don't have to wait for them to finish. I've already told them not to gun down any wild animals that come on the scene."

"I don't know where you live," I said.

He prattled off his address and then turned his back to me. He wanted more time alone, despite asking me to come here. A steadfast career cop, manly-man like himself would hate that I'd seen him break down. But a part of my heart softened knowing he'd trusted *me* to see him like that.

"We'll get them," I said again before walking out.

STAN LIVED JUST ACROSS THE BRIDGE FROM downtown Vancouver, and the flight to his house took less than five minutes once I launched into the air. Nestled into a cozy community cul-de-sac, his home stood two stories with a white picket fence. Stan had never mentioned children, and I always assumed he didn't have any. They'd be grown and out of the house anyway. I couldn't see Stan housing a thirty-year-old unemployed son in his basement without mentioning it at least once during our B&B sessions.

Cop cruisers took up the entire street and police tape surrounded the property. A number of cops milled around and a few sat on the curb with their heads in their hands. One of their own had been targeted. Every single one would be thinking, "What if?" What if it had been their spouse, their home? It wasn't a question enforcement officers could spend much time asking. They couldn't afford the hesitation.

With the house swarming with officers, I decided to land and shift in the park down the block behind a patch of bushes. No need for more people to witness multiple changes. Quickly shifting into my mountain lion form, I padded down the street and approached the crime scene cautiously. Just because Stan cleared me and warned his coworkers I might show up, didn't mean they wouldn't unload a magazine into my ass before they realized their mistake. The presence of a cougar tended to have that effect on people.

My ears pinged forward at every sound, and I wound around the first cruiser.

"Holy shit!" an officer exclaimed. A rustle of his uniform and the tell-tale swish sound told me he'd drawn his firearm. It took every ounce of control not to whirl and attack. Instead, I plunked my fat cat ass down and purred, as loudly as possible.

"Wait!" a female officer called out. "That's Stan's friend."

"Thought she was a wolf?" the officer shouted back.

"Nah, that was someone else," she replied and walked up to me. She had thick brown hair and kind eyes. "Look at her. She's just sitting and purring. Not feral or wild. He told us to expect a mountain lion, didn't he?"

"Dude's got connections."

"That's Stevens for you."

The officer without the drawn gun approached me slowly with her hand out. I nuzzled her hand like a fucking house cat, and her muscles relaxed.

"See?" she said.

The other officer behind me sighed and holstered his firearm. Then, and only then, I turned to him. The Asian man tensed at my approach, but copied the other officer's lead and held out his hand. His name tag read, "Chong."

I nuzzled his hand, too, before walking forward and arching my back. Bless the man, he scratched me. Maybe acting like a house cat wasn't so bad after all.

"Cindy will never believe this," he said to the other cop, the one with the kind eyes. Must be referring to his wife.

Both cops grinned and stood in front of me. I sat and waited.

"Can you understand us?" Kind Eyes asked.

I slowly nodded my head up and down.

"Good," Officer Chong said. "Follow us. We'll take you in and make sure no one else draws on you."

A man after my own heart.

With minimal yelling, a few tense moments, and one twitchy police officer, we wound our way through Stan's house to the master bedroom. The whole place was a bouquet of sweet memories. Raw emotions had a way of embedding in the walls like cigarette smoke. Stan's house smelled of love and laughter. Mountain lions couldn't cry, but my eyes stung as I padded through layers and layers of fresh cut grass, which indicated happiness. When the air turned sour, I knew we approached the location where Loretta died. The smell of Stan's apprehension rose thick, like a wall of smog, and then, once I stepped across the bedroom threshold, the power of the scents bombarded my nose and made me stagger.

I hadn't smelled the lightning strike of heartbreak since I broke it off with Wick. This was stronger. Along with tears and anger, the canned ham odour floating in waves marked despair. Underneath it all was blood and death. Stan's wife had a distinct aroma; like Stan, she smelled of soap and leather, but with a more feminine edge, as if the soap contained roses instead of an Irish spring. I'd become acquainted with it as we moved through the house.

Now at the location where she'd lost her life, the smell of her body and blood, though removed hours ago, intensified, but with a sour twist. Other scents swirled around the room. The hot metal of pain, the fierce lemon and pepper bouquet of shock, a little smoke for confusion and a lot of rust and cobwebs for regret. She'd seen her death coming, and her sadness painted the room with its aroma.

But the sour twist to her body odour and the guilt smelled wrong. Misplaced. Death never came across like a handful of daisies, but this was different. The sourness clawed at my skin. When I nosed around some more, I realized it came from the broken vial near the body outline, and blood-spattered carpet. I sniffed it again. Sour, burnt plastic, kind of like oven cleaner. This must be King's Krank.

One mystery solved.

If only the crime scene could solve who committed the murder. The room packed an olfactory punch, but the absence of the killer's scent rankled. Not the first time a Witch anti-scent charm had been used to aid an offence. The faint sweetness of the charm almost got lost, laden under all the other smells. Whomever killed Loretta wanted his or her tracks covered. The murderer's identity would have to wait.

Only one mystery remained at the scene to sleuth out.

I padded around the room, delicately avoiding the taped outline where her body had lain, where only a patch of dried blood remained, and sniffed her side of the bed. Guilt? Why would Stan's wife smell guilty? Her house reeked of happiness, love and Stan, no other man. She hadn't cheated, or at least not here and not in a way that she'd carry the other man's stench back.

Did I mess up?

Weres and Shifters tended not to outright lie about anything. We'd all smell it. Being upfront and taking an "as is" mentality tended to be a trait for both supernatural groups. It also meant I didn't often smell guilt.

I sniffed again. Parmesan cheese and musk oil, definitely guilt.

Now the question remained: what did Loretta Stevens hide from her husband that she felt guilty about?

9

The big wooden double doors of Tristan's house stared back at me. The scent of citrus and sunshine curled around my body, and the warmth of the day slipped away as I stood and waited for someone to answer the door.

Feradea, please don't let it be Angie.

After the day I'd had, I just wanted to curl up on Tristan's lap for a cuddle. My usual daily quota for sass and snark, aside from my own, was tapped out.

Nelson opened the door, and his eyes widened. "Andy."

"Hey big guy, can I come in? Tristan's expecting me."

The Wereleopard bobbed his head and stepped back to allow me entry.

I wanted to bottle this home and the smells wafting down the hallway.

"Andy." Tristan walked into the foyer with his arms wide. I walked straight into them and wrapped myself around his hard torso. His arms enclosed me, and I inhaled his citrus and sunshine. The bouquet of honeysuckles coiled around me.

My mountain lion stopped pacing, and the world slowed down for the first time today.

"Do you want to talk about it?" Tristan mumbled into my hair.

I shook my head.

"Let me put you to bed then."

My heart rate increased, and my mountain lion purred.

"For sleep, you wicked thing. You look positively exhausted." He nuzzled my neck and gave it a little nip. "But if you're a good girl, I could arrange a midnight wake-up."

"Mmhmm."

Before I had a chance to make him promise, a snort echoed down the hall. I looked up to see emotions cross Angie's face, too quick to decipher, but there was no mistaking the disgusted curl of her upper lip or the jealous scent of cat urine floating in the air.

I turned back to Tristan and mumbled into his lips. "I think I just got my second wind." I squeezed his rock-solid ass to emphasize my point.

Tristan's chest rumbled. "Staking your claim?"

"Maybe."

"Unnecessary, but I approve."

He grabbed my hand and hauled me through his beautiful home. The smells of his prowl brushed passed me, like a flicker-tape movie; emotions, identities and hierarchies packed an olfactory punch. Two things stood out to me as Tristan guided me up the stairs with no seduction, and all urgency.

One, absolute loyalty. Tristan's prowl loved and trusted him unconditionally. And two, Angie's particular brand of stench was everywhere. Embedded with lust and jealousy. Tristan's constant scent remained ambivalent throughout the house, so although Angie's desire for Tristan concerned me and meant I'd have to watch my back, at least I didn't have to worry about Tristan returning her feelings.

My mouth opened as I planned to question Tristan, but he flung me into a large master bedroom and slammed the door closed. I had little time to take in the room. A king-sized bed with reclaimed wood stained a natural blue-gray as a headboard, and a white duvet stuffed with a fluffy comforter.

"Tristan—"

His mouth on mine gave me little chance to breathe, let alone talk. He moved forward until the backs of my legs hit the elevated bed. With a glint in his gaze, he pulled back and gave me a little shove. I fell back and bounced on the pillow-top mattress a bit before coming to rest on the soft duvet and goose down comforter. Typical cat surrounding himself with bird feathers. My mountain lion purred her approval. Tristan's scent coated the entire room with his own unique spin to the leopard signature, the hint of honeysuckles on a warm day.

Plus, no Angie stench.

Something else familiar clung to the sheets, though. My eyebrows scrunched up, and I reach behind me to search under the pillows. I pulled out some clothing and brought it to my nose. My tank-top. He'd sniped my top so his bed would smell of me. I continued to hold my shirt to my face, and met Tristan's piercing gaze over the supple white material.

"It keeps my leopard calm," he said.

My mountain lion purred and preened as I re-tucked the clothing under his pillows.

Tristan remained at the foot of the bed, studying me. The familiarity of the moment triggered memories from our night together. Images flooded my mind of our naked bodies in a sweaty tangle of limbs.

Tristan's gaze twinkled as if following my mind down its dirty path. His black hair slightly mussed, contrasted sharply with his almost glowing porcelain skin. When I'd first met him, I mentally described him as angelic and had to wipe the drool off my face. Now, I knew he wasn't an angel, but the beauty of his contrasting features still struck me silly and sent heat to pool in my leopard-print panties.

Something soft replaced Tristan's wicked look.

"Speechless?" I asked.

He hesitated before saying, "I'd *as soon go kindle fire with snow, as seek to quench the fire of love with words.*"

I recognized the words of William Shakespeare, but the meaning of what Tristan said saw the return of the indescribable warmth, the one that came whenever I thought of Tristan, the one making my brain go fuzzy, quelling all my concerns and worries. I cleared my throat. "You're a poet, now?"

"No. But seeing you splayed on my bed, as I have so many times in *my* dreams, may be the inspirational spark I need to become one."

I groaned.

He smiled.

"Come here, then." I crooked a finger at him. "And *give me my sin again*."

"That's my line." Tristan pulled his shirt off and crawled on top of me. His weight sank me into the mattress, cocooning me in his scent and soft bedding.

His mouth moved wickedly over my body as fire licked my skin and fed the rising need within.

Want, my mountain lion crooned. *Want mate.*

Soon, I told her. *Soon.*

Her swirling energy nudging for the bond, abated, receding until it became imperceptible. Tristan removed my clothes with slow finesse. His gaze glinting when he discovered my underwear choice.

Staking my claim had never felt so good.

I bolted upright in bed. Tristan's muscled arm weighed heavy across my abdomen, and the slow steadiness of his breathing calmed my fast racing heart. Why the hell had I woken? Must've been another bad—

Come to me, Carus. A smooth voice slithered into my heart and cooled the fast pumping blood in my veins.

Come to me.

Another fera? Really? I'd taken two new animal familiars in the last year already. Three at fourteen and nothing for almost sixty-six years. Now they bombarded me. What the hell was going on?

My eightieth birthday approached soon. Did that have some sort of significance to Shifters or the Carus specifically? I'd spoken about my abilities to an old coyote Shifter handler at the SRD many times. Donny never mentioned anything. Not even an ominous warning, or vague threat of imminent danger, and he loved giving those.

Come to me, Carus, the unknown fera called out again. My blood thrummed with the sound, pulsating, nudging me to fling back the sheets and go to this new animal.

No, I answered back, not knowing for sure whether she could hear me. *I'm tired.*

A half-truth. I didn't know if I had it in me to accept and dispel another fera so close to my latest heartache. I'd cast out my wolf to numb the pain of losing Wick. Could I accept another fera, one cold and strange, to take her place? Even if it was temporary before dispelling?

A tear escaped and trickled down my face.

No, I repeated, not caring if anyone heard. *I'm too tired, and I'm not ready for you.*

Soon, she hissed, repeating the very word I'd told my mountain lion about mating earlier tonight.

The unknown fera continued to hiss the word like a skipping record from the past until her voice slowly faded into silence. Or maybe I drifted back to sleep. Either way, she left me alone, and slumber enveloped my tired body once again.

IO

The heavy bass vibrated the air and rocked my heart. After all these years of scoping out and preying on targets in establishments like this one, I'd learned my lesson and used earplugs. It still did little to dull the overwhelming effect of music cranked too high and drunk people yelling.

"Thank you for coming with me." Stan leaned in.

It had only been a week since Loretta's murder. I'd attended her grim funeral two days ago, and watched my friend publicly sob over her open grave. Stan shouldn't be here, dressed like a civilian and trying to play undercover cop. Despite my strongly worded attempts to tell him to stay out of the investigation, he'd insisted and told me he'd do it with or without me.

Well, damn. That had lit a torch under my ass. Stan needed me by his side. One, he should be mourning; two, he sucked at discreet. He'd never gone undercover in his career. His shoulders back with a rigid spine posture screamed career cop and for a man his age in a downtown Vancouver club, he was entirely too clean.

The only men above forty frequenting these kinds of places, chock full of drunk under-aged girls looking to make bad decisions, resembled slimy reptiles more than decent human beings.

Stan didn't fit in.

If people didn't peg him for a cop, they'd peg him for a dad out looking for his wayward daughter.

I couldn't talk him out of it though, so I found myself leather-clad and by his side on my Saturday night. No way would I let Stan do this alone.

The smell of sweat and booze clung to my nose.

"Why don't you wait here?" I said. "Work the front of the club. I'll go to the back and see what I can find out."

Stan nodded and ran his finger along the neckline of his shirt to loosen it. His gaze shifted around, and his muscles tensed.

"Just sit at the bar and order something hard to drink," I said.

He nodded and made a robot turn for the bar. "And Stan?" I called out.

"Yeah?"

"Uh...try to look more...er...less like you." I reached out, yanked his shirt out of his pants and ruffled his hair. Before he had a chance to reprimand me, I spun and sauntered to the back of the club.

The gyrating throngs of humans bounced, undulated and rubbed against me as I weaved through the crowd.

The farther in I got, the more the smells and sounds intensified.

The bar, illuminated by mirrors and black-lights, materialized like an oasis for drunks, and I sauntered up the two steps to enter the VIP lounge. The bouncer glanced at me and leaned in to cut me off. I slid my hand up his chest and smiled, letting my animal magnetism curl around him and overwhelm his norm senses. His eyes glazed a little, and he nodded before taking a step back.

Perfect.

This area of the club smelled and sounded better. Set up in lounge style and illuminated by neon-blue lighting, various people sat in black leather booths. They glanced up as I approached. The not-so famous arched their brows and gave snotty are-you-going-to-recognize-me glowers, while the men and women who probably were famous, continued on with their business. I didn't care who they were.

The man at the bar with his back to me didn't even move. His broad shoulders remained folded inward, and his head stayed bowed over what I presumed was a drink. I couldn't see what he held, not with his ridiculous shoulders...

No.

It couldn't be.

"Clint?" I asked. My voice drifted forward, and the man's shoulders tensed. Then his back straightened.

"No fucking way." I walked up and sat beside him. With slicked hair the same deep sable as mine, Clint

Behnsen had broad shoulders that made girls want to beg for a piggyback ride. Not me. I wanted to tackle and hog tie him for the market. Clint Behnsen might be a handsome man in his prime, but he was more likely to break the cow than buy one. He also happened to be the human servant to the previous Master Vampire of the Lower Mainland. He should have died with Lucien.

Should have.

When we'd first met, I'd torn his neck out with my mountain lion teeth on what I thought were SRD orders. Clint survived my attack, and a vicious sword stabbing later on by Tristan's old master. He should've died those two times as well.

Normally fastidious in his appearance, Clint looked rough. His hair disheveled, with random strands out of place, his shirt untucked and his trousers wrinkled. The smell of alcohol wafted off his breath and out of his pores.

"How are you here?" I asked.

"Taxi." He didn't look up; instead, he kept his head bowed and stared into the amber fluid in front of him.

"How are you alive?"

Clint smirked and finally glanced up. His gaze was empty and unseeing. His eyes bloodshot, his lips flat. He looked like crap after a stampede.

I sucked in my breath.

"I take it you heard?" he asked.

"Allan phoned me with the news," I said.

"You didn't do it?" he asked, his voice hollow.

"The thought crossed my mind," I said. "But, no. Not my credit to take."

Clint smirked again, but in a sad way, like his lip couldn't expend the necessary energy to scowl. He returned his gaze to his drink.

"How'd it happen?" I asked.

"Not sure, exactly. They chose a time when Lucien gave me a reprieve, and Allan was away on business. We returned to find his remains. The donors and other Vampires who'd been with him were also dead."

"So, you were down the road banging as many bottle blondes as possible while Allan got off on torturing a few random people?"

"You shouldn't judge others, *Carus.*"

I sighed and slouched a little. "Look, I'm sorry for your loss. Lucien was...well, he was a dick. He treated me poorly and threatened those I lo...cared about. I don't forgive easily. But what I can say is he treated those loyal to him well. Very well."

Clint hesitated. "I think he sent me away on purpose. Like he knew what was to come."

"Did he say anything to you before you left?"

Clint turned to me again. He leaned forward with pinched brows and a tense mouth. His lips parted to speak. He tensed. His gaze darted to the side, and we both turned to watch Stan stalk toward us. His shirt now sported a large dark patch on the chest. Stan flicked liquid off his hands.

"Why's your shirt wet?" I asked.

"Fucking chicks. Like I'd hit on any of the hot messes

in this place. Like I'd..." His voice cut off with a strangled noise. The glimmer in his gaze spoke of Loretta. My heart clenched and I wanted to reach out and comfort him, but he wouldn't want me to. Not here. Stan met Clint's piercing gaze and nodded before turning back to me. His eyes steeled over, and his body straightened. Back to police business. "I saw one of the known dealers in the area go to the back of the club near the stairs."

"You want to follow him into the bathroom?" I'd seen the signs. "There's less intrusive ways to discover whether he's a lefty."

Stan glowered. "Do you have any better ideas?"

I bit back a snarky response. Stan didn't deserve my sass. I held up a finger to Stan and turned to Clint.

"Do you know anything about King's Krank?"

"It's a new street drug."

Not the informative answer I'd hoped for. I pursed my lips and looked around. More than one girl show-cased jiggling breasts in low cut tops while prancing around.

"Why did you come to this bar?"

"Closest place to drink where I'm left relatively alone." His massive shoulders shrugged.

"Could drink at home."

"That's just sad and there's no tits and ass to look at there."

"Well, uh. See you later." God that sounded lame. Did I even care if I talked to this douchebag again, ever, in my life? The man grated my nerves and had some serious perversions, namely breaking women as a hobby.

Clint smirked again and went back to contemplating life on the surface of his premium whiskey. Stan tugged on my arm, and I walked away from the sad, former human servant.

"What was that about?" Stan asked.

"Nothing. What's the dealer's name?" I asked Stan as we walked out of the VIP area and rounded the corner to the back of the club.

"Aahil."

"South asian?"

"I guess." Stan shrugged and then peered over the side to view the landing. When he looked back his mouth twisted down. "What?"

"You're a cop in *Vancouver*—one of the most multicultural cities in existence, or at least in Canada. How do you not know?"

Stan sighed. "Because we honestly don't know. We have no background on this guy, and it's not like he wears a sign around his fucking neck stating his ethnic background, or his affiliations. It *is* Vancouver. That means there's so many options to choose from, and with only a street name and physical appearance to go on, it makes his ethnicity near impossible to determine. Besides, Aahil is a Muslim name, which doesn't pinpoint a geographical area so much as his faith."

I opened a mouth, but stopped when Stan held his hand out.

"And before you ask, no. He doesn't hang with a certain crowd, and his English is fluent without accent. And even if we pinpointed his ethnicity, what the fuck would it matter? It doesn't change his actions. God, you're so annoying sometimes." He glanced around, but we stood alone at the top of the stairs. The nearest couple appeared too busy dry humping to pay us any attention. "Let's go."

I nodded and followed him down the stairs. Sometimes, my best behaviour involved keeping my mouth shut. When we reached the landing, the place opened up to a small lounge with bench seats, a small bar and a hallway leading to the bathrooms, and what I assumed was the emergency exit.

One sniff of the air nearly had me whimpering on the ground. The smell of urine, fecal matter, and alcohol-laced vomit permeated the air, so strong I wanted to puke.

A group of men wearing more bling than the entire female population in the club turned at our approach. Black hair, dark brown eyes, various skin tones ranging from light cream to dark beige. They appeared almost like clones, all stood around six feet tall with massive necks, shoulders, and arms. Obviously, they never got the memo about skipping leg days.

One of the men stepped away from the group and squared off.

"Hey handsome," I crooned. "Could I have a word?"

He started and then his gaze slid to Stan. "Got no time for cops."

It was a mistake to bring Stan. I should've prepped him better for what was to come. With Stan's inability to blend, I'd expected the dealer's response. Only one way around it. Bluff.

"Who, this guy?" I jerked my thumb at Stan and snorted. "He's not a cop! Runs security at the nearby shopping centre." I walked a little closer and watched the man's shoulders drop. The action so minute, I might've missed it. With all the muscle this guy packed, his relaxed stance almost mirrored his tense one.

"A mall cop?" The man squinted Stan.

"Yeah."

Stan's outrage rolled off him in waves of burnt cinnamon, but I didn't care; at least he went along with it. With a room full of norms, they'd have no way to detect our lies with their noses.

Some cops were so snobby when it came to security guards. Never understood why. Half of them started in the profession before joining the force.

"Why'd you bring him?"

I shrugged and closed the distance. "I like 'em old and vanilla. More fun to break. But..."

"But?"

I trailed a finger along the dealer's chest, and released the magnetism. "But if you're offering something more... intriguing..."

The dealer peered down at me. The hardness of his eyes softened as my scent coiled around him and my animalistic mojo magic did its thing. His lips widened to show off his gold grill.

"Johnny!" One of the other dealers barked.

The dealer straightened and took a step back. "Yeah?" he asked over his shoulders.

"What does she want?"

Johnny turned back to me. "What do you want?"

Not you. Not this entire situation. And certainly not the sweaty ass these leather pants gave me. "I heard you're the guys to speak to if I wanted something new and hot."

Vaguely aware Stan shuffled up behind me, I kept my body loose and went for the seduction face I used on targets when I was an SRD assassin. When my energy coiled around the other dealer, though, the one who'd barked, his expression remained unfazed. Huh. Normally, my magnetism was enough to rope in the norms.

Another man, most likely the thug-on-call, stepped forward at my approach, but the Barker held his hand out to stop him. My gaze flicked briefly to Barker's beefy arms. He had full tattoo sleeves with intricate line work. Below the Egyptian hieroglyph on the inside of his wrist, he wore a number of leather cuffs and bracelets. My eyes narrowed as I stepped in close, only a few feet from him. Wafts of vanilla and honey spiralled from his wrist.

Witch charm.

Well, fuck me sideways. This operation just got more difficult. I might be pretty, but no way could my looks seduce this man alone, not with Stan giving them all the stink eye behind my back. I should've left him upstairs.

The Barker narrowed his eyes at me. "It's not going to work."

"Excuse me?"

"I hadn't realized the VPD had grown desperate enough to hire call girls for their dirty work. You're not my type, lady." His gaze flicked to my chest before he sneered. "Go back to the vamp bar and suck some dead wood."

The beds of my fingernails stung as my nails shifted to claws. I clenched my jaw and squeezed my fists to hide the partial change. This guy had already pegged Stan and nothing I said or did would convince him otherwise. Worse, he knew my face now, so I couldn't come back later.

"I think it's time you and your stiff cop left." The Barker's face transformed as he flashed even, sparkling white teeth at me.

I could knock a few of those veneers out of his mouth.

Where would that get us?

"Your loss," I said and stepped back. I didn't like the expression on the guy's face. It had changed from disgusted to thoughtful. Nope, never liked that look on the opposition.

"No sweetheart, it's yours." He snapped his fingers.

My eyes narrowed, and I sensed more than saw two more beefcake thugs move to block our exit up the stairs.

"I wanted to have a word with the VPD." He turned to Stan. "Did you think I wouldn't recognize you, Stevens? Your ugly mug's been plastered on the front page for weeks now. First, to take on the...how'd you put it? The scum of Vancouver. And then because someone killed your pretty, li—"

Barker didn't finish his words. A high-pitched wail emitted from Stan before he dove at the group of dealers, fists flying. One of the other meatheads stepped forward and attempted to intercept Stan, but the career cop had a few moves left in him. He stepped to the side like a professional rugby player and weaved around the other man. Stan threw a massive clobber fist at the back of the guy's head and knocked him to the ground.

"Here's fifty bucks. Get out of here." The Barker stuffed a red bill down the centre of my cleavage and smacked my ass.

He still thought I was a call girl.

"See, you made one mistake," I said, drawing the Barker's attention away from the grunting men trying to take Stan down as the cop's hammer-fists flew around and made contact.

The Barker's eyes narrowed.

"You assumed I was unimportant."

A slight tingling radiated through my eyes as they shifted to reflect the animals caged within.

The dealer's dark brows arched. He barked out another order and one of the other thugs whipped out a gun and pointed it at my head.

"Should've taken the fifty bucks." He plucked the bill out of my cleavage before I could stop him, and stuffed it in his back jean pocket. With a gun pointed at my head, I had to choose my next actions carefully. Fifty dollars and a boob grazing rated pretty low on the importance scale. Stan grunted behind me as the three muscle-heads managed to smack him to the ground.

"Should've taken my warning," I said and pulled at the beast locked up inside, not enough to shift, but enough to gain some of her strength. I let her roar rip from my throat. The men around me yelled and stepped back. I ducked away from the gun holder's arm, grabbed his wrist and yanked him down over my bent knee. When I pulled, his arm made a sickening crack, and he bellowed in pain. The gun dropped to the floor. Another dealer dove for it, but I stomped down on the dangerous metal and kicked it across the room where it slid into a grate.

Three dealers, including the Barker straightened and squared off with me.

"Bring it," I said.

They lunged in unison. I blocked, countered and kicked myself into a better position. Despite staying in human form, my supe-fast reflexes, beast strength, and martial arts background gave me more than enough advantage over the skilled fighters. When I rounded to where the other men stomped on Stan, I turned and threw one of them off the cop. I struck Johnny in the face with the base of my palm. His nose snapped and blood spurted across his face. His hand instantly flew to cover his nose, and I used the opportunity to deliver a series of blows to his solar plexus. One. Two. Three.

Out.

The man crumpled to the floor and groaned beside Stan's feet.

With the other men behind me, regrouping, limping, and nursing injuries, I snatched Stan by the shirt and hauled him to his feet.

"Time to go," I said.

He nodded.

"Can you walk?"

"Yes."

"Run?"

"Yes."

"Good. Go!" I pushed him toward the exit and turned in time to get a fist in the face. My vision exploded into stars, and I staggered to the side.

When my vision cleared, I caught Stan hobble-running up the stairs out of the corner of my eye. Another fist connected with my face. Stan needed more time to clear the building.

The Barker and two others attempted to surround me. Time to play Pig in the Middle, but they wouldn't like my rules. With a nod from the Barker, they attacked in unison. I blocked a punch to the head as I side kicked another in the gut. The Barker got a shot in, but I used the momentum to spin around. My legs swung up and connected with his face, and he crashed to the ground.

The Puncher renewed his attack as the other one regained his breath from the kick. With a fury of blocks, I batted his well-aimed strikes away with little effort. My heartbeat thudded in my ears as searing hot adrenaline raced through my veins.

The other man moved around to my back, but before I could kick him again, he lunged and crushed me in a barrel hug. The Puncher lived up to his name and struck me. Pain exploded in my face, and lanced up my nose to the back of my skull. The Puncher moved in close, and delivered a liver-staggering blow to my stomach.

I kneed him in the balls.

As he doubled over in pain, I flicked my heel back and kicked in the Hugger's knee, raked his shin and stomped on his foot. He shouted in pain, and his hold loosened. I flung my arms up and dropped, driving my elbow into his gut. Free from his crushing hug, I delivered another swift elbow, this time to his crotch. He doubled over and groaned in my ear. Perfectly within reach. I grabbed his head and hurled him over my shoulder. His body impacted with the Puncher's before sliding off. I gave a nice chop to the Hugger's throat to make sure he stayed out.

"You!" the Barker yelled from across the room. He staggered to his feet and flung a tattooed arm out to point his index finger at me.

I winked.

He reached into his jacket.

I turned and bolted up the steps. The bricks behind me shattered as a shot rang out.

Stan's steely cop scent led me to the back alley. I threw open the doors and the cooler, fresher night air greeted me. A silent alarm probably went off somewhere. I slipped into the alley and let the heavy metallic doors close behind me, shutting out the stench and heat of the club.

About halfway from me to the main street, Stan hobbled like a lame donkey. I sprinted to catch up. Our slapping feet echoed off the cement alleyway and the sides of the building. The distant sounds of laughter and nightlife beckoned ahead.

A dark shadow spread out to cover the alleyway, blocking the moonlit path. A large object with wings.

Bola?

With tense muscles constricting my chest, I drew in a shaky breath and spun around. Nothing but the empty alley and night sky.

"Come on." Stan grabbed my arm and tugged.

"Relax. They're not following us," I said, staring down the empty alley. "Besides, I can be pretty badass if I need to be."

Despite using the strength and roar of the beast, Stan didn't know about my most dangerous form, and I'd prefer it to stay that way. Still, I could, and did, hold my own against a handful of drug dealers.

"Badass enough to stop a speeding bullet?"

Then again, maybe not. Weres benefitted from speedy healing. Shifters...not so much. Even with accelerated capabilities, a bullet to the head was a bullet to the head. I had no idea if the beast form had other supernatural skills besides extra strength, fire-breathing, and a prickly attitude. Frankly, I hoped to never test out death-avoidance.

"Good point," I said. "Let's go."

We walked out of the alley and into Vancouver night life, Stan limping at my side. I tried to offer help, but he shoved my hand away and grunted. We made it to Granville Street to find a bunch of wide-eyed norms.

"What the fuck was that?" a man in disheveled clothes said as he pointed to the building to our left.

"An angel?" A woman said. With smeared makeup and a sweaty complexion reeking of booze, she clearly enjoyed a night of drinking.

"No way, man...a Valkyrie," one of the homeless said before launching into a story of ancient Viking mythology. The clubbers became distracted and engrossed with the man's tale.

So I hadn't imagined it.

Something with wings had flown over us.

The sense of foreboding prickled my skin like a light rain.

II

After putting Stan in a cab, I looked around the downtown core of Vancouver. Turned out "the Barker" was Aahil. Made sense. After web searching his name on my phone, I discovered it meant "Prince." He certainly acted like one.

The sea breeze whistled through the dark streets as club music blared from various clubs. I loved this city. It was a dichotomy of senses; the lush evergreen forests; snow-capped mountains and crisp ocean contrasted with the cityscape, with its modern buildings of glass, slabs of concrete and bustling businesses.

A coastal seaport city, nestled in the Lower Mainland of British Columbia, Vancouver was by far the most ethnically and linguistically diverse urban centre in Canada and the third largest metropolitan area in the country. It was consistently named one of the top world-wide cities for livability, quality of life, and natural beauty. Not bad for a city that grew from a sawmill and a nearby tavern.

But not all that glitters is gold. The natural beauty of the city shone through during the day, full of spandex-clad yoga practitioners and outdoorsmen, but the city held darkness as well. It was built on the unceded territories of the Squamish, Musqueam and Tsleil-Waututh First Nations and currently had the largest population of homeless people in Canada, a renowned serial killer, infamous strip clubs, overdosing celebrities, rundown buildings, greasy bars, dark alleyways, a buzzing night life...

And the Vampire club called Hell.

Two blocks away from Lucien's club, I decided to pay his heir a visit. If anyone would have tabs on mysterious creatures or the drug culture of the Vancouver underground, it would be Luci...Allan's Vampire horde.

And thanks to Stan, I was already dressed for the club.

After sending a quick text to Tristan to outline my plans, I sashayed to the vamp bar.

Situated in the heart of Gastown, the nice part, the ground level entrance to Hell consisted of double doors and a foyer at the bottom of an all-window building. Two intimidating Vampire bouncers stood at the doors leading to a spiral staircase in the foyer. Justin and Dmitri, the same guards from the last time I came here looking for answers.

The steps behind the bouncers led to the basement where the Vamps and vamp-tramps rubbed against each other. Deep bass resonated from the club and travelled up to the street level.

Last time I'd been here, I stood in line for all of ten minutes before throwing my reputation at the guards to butt ahead. This time, I didn't bother with the line at all. I walked right up to the doors and fixed Dmitri and Justin with my best let-me-in-or-I'll-bite-you stare.

Dmitri, with his Slavic good looks, mumbled into his radio. "The Shifter Bitch is coming down."

Lovely.

After a garbled response, both guards stood aside to let me through. I didn't bother correcting them on my actual name. Shifter Bitch would do.

By walking through the doors, I accepted the rules of the establishment. They were simple—don't fuck around with the Vampires. For me, I avoided prolonged eye contact, exposed necks, going into the private enclaves or down to the dungeons, and I sure as fuck wouldn't agree to anything proposed by a Vampire, no matter how innocent it sounded.

Two cookie-cutter bouncers stood at the bottom of the stairwell and opened the doors when I reached the landing. I took a deep breath before stepping into the dark, dank realm of the Vampires. The music thumped heavy and low red lighting gave the place a monochromatic vibe. Not much had changed. The place still smelled of musky coconut, crayons, and sweet sweat— lust, excitement, and fear. The last overpowered the rest.

I found Allan sitting at the bar, his gaze darting around the room, calculating and assessing. His suit remained impeccable, but his hair looked a little mussed since the first time I'd seen him.

May as well get this over with. I straightened my shoulders and stomped my way to the new Master Vampire of the Lower Mainland.

"Allan," I said.

"Andrea." His eyes narrowed. "To what do I owe this honour?"

"I need information." Although I tried to keep my mind on the forest, this guy could read my mind, and would probably pluck out my intentions at any time, so I cut to the point.

"What makes you think I have what you need?"

"You're Allan. Master Vampire of the Greater Vancouver Vampire horde. And your special skill is mind reading. You probably have exactly what I need." To anyone else, this conversation might sound sexual, but there was no desire on either of our parts to bump uglies. Allan liked to dominate in a way that put BDSM practitioners to shame. I'd never be submissive enough for him, and I...well, I didn't like him that way.

He was handsome enough, and he'd been nice to me, to a point, but no, not kindling a little fire for Allan.

He snorted, probably reading my mind and finding my thoughts amusing, but he didn't comment on them. "You're right, Andy. I probably have the information. Let me rephrase. What makes you think I'll give it to you?"

"Because you're a nice guy?" Lie.

He shook his head.

"Because you like my prickly personality?"

Again, he shook his head.

"Because...because it would be for the greater good? Clean up Vancouver, and all that?"

Allan barked out a laugh. "I like it dirty."

"Seriously? You're not going to help me?"

"I see nothing in it for me. I don't want to bang you, I don't want you to dance for me, and I certainly don't want you as a mate. The only thing you have to offer is your tasty blood, but I know you'll never give that up."

He got that right. "Can I at least ask?"

"Fine." He placed his forearm on countertop and leaned into the bar.

"Was Lucien investigating King's Krank?"

Allan stilled. His pupils dilated to the point his irises disappeared and two black orbs stared back at me. No breathing, no moving, nothing.

I waited. And waited.

He continued to sit like a statue doing a fairly decent Lucien impersonation. He didn't appear too ready to answer my question. Not that I needed him to do so. His reaction said it all. Maybe I should try another one.

"Is Glasya Labolas connected to the drug somehow?" I may have defeated the dog Demon with the help of the goddess Feradea and Sid the Seducer, but Bola's ticket back to hell wasn't one way. He could easily be re-summoned to the mortal realm.

A muscle in his cheek twitched, and his eyes refocused on my face. "Careful, kitten. I admire your sass, but questions like these will get you killed."

I waited and tapped my foot. Allan's face remained

impassive porcelain, only his eyes gave away his internal calculating. The irises around his pupils contracted, shifting back and forth in minute degrees. His hands remained relaxed on the armrests and his body statue-still. His scent, still carrion-esque, carried none of his emotions to me.

"Well?" I asked, shattering the silence between us.

"Well, what?"

"Are you going to answer?" *Do I need him to?*

"No. I think not. This is not a concern for the Vampire court. Lucien's attempt to meddle in every pocket in the community led to his demise. I have no wish to follow him. You are on your own, kitten."

A few Vampires paused and studied us before Allan sent them away with a glare, and a flick of his wrist. Ideas flashed through my head, but none of my reactions would get me the answers I sought.

Allan barked out a laugh. "Punching me in the face will only serve to piss me off. You better go. Now."

Squaring my shoulders and clenching my fists, I nodded. "Goodbye."

I turned and stalked toward the exit. When I made it to the doorway that led to the stairs, Allan's voice called out across the club. Not yelling, but loud enough for my Shifter hearing to pick it out from the deep pounding bass. "Oh, kitten?"

I turned and fixed my death stare on him. "What?"

He stood and moved with Vampire grace to stand a few feet away. The gliding motion so fast, my eyes crossed to track his progress. "Your Kappa is missing. You better find him before he goes on another bender."

12

The Kappa, an abnormally massive turtle-like Japanese supe who sucked living energy and slaughtered hundreds roamed free. In addition to that potential hot mess, Loretta's killer was still on the loose, drug addicts still indulged and died on King's Krank, the connections of the Vampire court were lost to me, and Wick and his Werewolf pack hated me.

At least I had Tristan. Right?

Then why the heck wasn't he answering his phone or replying to my text messages? I took a deep breath and refocused. The calm dissipated almost immediately. *Oh no.* I refused to become the bunny-boiling, stalker girlfriend.

My heart thumped in my ears, and my skin prickled. Why wasn't he responding? He normally replied right away. I checked my watch. Well, maybe he was sleeping. Not everyone stayed up this late, although there was a lot of night left before dawn.

I dragged my tired, pinched toes, and sweaty thighs back to my apartment. My disappointment hung heavy in my chest. I'd secretly hoped Tristan had gone incommunicado because he used his key to wait for me at my place. Naked.

A pleasurable bolt of lightning struck my crotch at the thought.

Unfortunately, no naked Tristan. When I walked in, the air was stale and bereft of his delicious scent. Something else slithered through the apartment. Something I couldn't quite place, but drew me forward into the room. I sniffed around like a bloodhound, but the smell evaded my detection, slipping away from my reach. I should be creeped out, but no malice hung in the air. Another fera, maybe? The one who rudely interrupted my sleep?

My phone vibrated, and I pounced on it. Ben, not Tristan. I sighed, and picked it up.

"Why are you calling me? You live next door," I said. Ben and his coven were home, too. No way could I mistake the screeching and bickering travelling through the thin walls.

"Who knows what you're up to," Ben grumbled. "You Shifters are way too comfortable running around naked for me to ever consider a surprise visit."

He had a point. "What do you want?"

"You're on speaker phone. Can you settle an argument I'm having with Patty?"

"Seriously?"

He ignored the snark in my tone, and launched into a

speech. "If a vamp tramp got a tramp stamp, would you call it a vamp tramp tramp stamp, or a vamp tramp stamp?"

"I'm hanging up now."

"Noooo! Please don't. You know Patty. He'll peck away at me like a deranged leprechaun until we get someone to break the tie. It's two and two."

I laughed, and the tension flowed from my shoulders and neck. "My vote is for the latter. Vamp tramp stamp. I think it's safe to cut out the redundancy."

"I told you!" Ben bellowed, presumably at Patty. A thump followed and I envisioned Ben throwing one of his poorly-aimed, poorly-formed punches at Patty's shoulder.

"No fair. Of course she'd side with you," Patty muttered, his voice growing more distant until someone punctuated it with a door slam. He probably wouldn't appreciate me pointing out I didn't know whose side was whose when I answered.

"I feel like there should be a tongue twister poem in here somewhere," Ben said.

"How many stamps can a vamp tramp stamp, if a vamp tramp could stamp stamps?"

"Yeah, like that, but better," he replied.

"Ungrateful bastard."

"Good night to you, too, sweetheart," Ben crooned.

This time, I didn't announce my intentions. I hung up on his laughter.

After a bit of cursing, I managed to peel off the leather pants with minimal skin loss, and hopped into the shower. Unfortunately, the fifteen minute reprieve did little to slow my racing brain, or wipe away the feeling of grime from the clubs.

After the shower, I dried my hair and checked the clock. Way too late to call Donny and ask about any SRD investigations into King's Krank. While the VPD was the acting enforcement agency for the Lower Mainland, the SRD handled all supe on supe crimes and tended to act more behind the scenes. They sent out killers, like me, to take out the culprits. They were the judge, jury, and executioner all in one.

My head hit the pillow, and my mind easily slid into slumber.

Instead of sinking into nothingness, I walked through a moonlit path in the middle of a forest, clothed in some long translucent nightgown probably dating back to the 1800s. Fog blanketed the ground and parted majestically as I walked. Warning bells chimed in my head instead of birds. The forest had no scent. No pine aroma laden with summer flowers. No crunching of branches or snapping of twigs as animals roamed through the dense, moss-coated floor. No rustling leaves in the wind. My bare feet padded along the rough rock and grass path without a sound and without any pinched nerves.

An artificial forest.

Only one person...thing...would muck around with my mind like this.

I rounded a large evergreen, and the path opened up into a large clearing. A man stood in the middle. Naked skin glowed in the moon light.

Sid.

"If this is how you seduce a girl, it's not working."

His lips twitched and thankfully only that. I closed the distance between us and came to a stop three feet away. No need to get too close.

"Relax Carus, I have no wish to make you mine."

"Good."

"No more than you already are..." Sid winked.

I clenched the cotton material in my fists and squeezed. Attacking Sid in this realm, one under his control, would not be a good idea, and wouldn't get me the answers I sought.

Smashing my fist into his kidneys would feel pretty good though.

"Are you still pissed?" Sid wiped at his washboard abs.

"Of course I'm still pissed." I crossed my arms.

"And why do you have me dressed like a historical damsel in distress?"

Sid's eyebrow rose, but he didn't snap his fingers and change my outfit. "Are you pissed about the bond or that night a week or two ago?"

Although he didn't trick or force me into the bond, it metaphysically dug into my heart like a bird of prey clutching a field mouse. In addition to this bond, he'd incited an intimate dream the other night with Tristan and Wick. What was I pissed off about? "Both, you sick pervert."

Sid tsked at me.

Maybe I should attack him anyway. Get a few good

shots in before he gained control and altered the world, or kicked my ass. The dream from the other night still made my blood boil. "Why the heck would you play with my mind like that? It was messed up."

"I was hungry."

I gaped at him. "Hungry?"

"Haven't you ever gone back for seconds?" He held his hands out in a supplicating gesture. Like it should make me hate him less.

I pursed my lips. "That wasn't going back for more, that was...a double helping."

The Demon's smile grew. "Why, yes, that's a fitting analogy."

"Again. What the fuck are you playing at?" The wind caressed my nightgown and rustled the leaves in the forest, but nothing could break my death stare on Sid.

Sid held up both his hands and shifted his stance. "Calm down. I won't do it again."

"Then what do you want?" I stomped on the path and the rocks dug into the sensitive skin on my soles. I winced. Now he decided to make the dream more realistic?

"I want to warn you," Sid said.

"Warn me?"

"Yes."

I tapped my foot.

"The new moon is three nights away. Do you know what that means, little one?" He cocked his head and gave me a patronizing smile.

"That you can count to three?"

111

He grunted. "Guess again."

"All the feline Weres are forced to shift and will run rampant through the forests?" The wind picked up and wound around the dense tree trunks to press against my body.

"They will, but that's not what I'm getting at."

"Witches are at their strongest and will do a lot of hocus pocus bullcrap?"

Sid sighed. "Are you really this naive?"

"No. I'm still pissed. Get to your point, Demon. I'd like to get some normal sleep."

"In three days' time, the new moon will bring the demonic realm closer to the mortal one, close enough for me to use a blood bond as an anchor."

Ice chilled my boiling blood, sending shivers of simmering warmth through my veins. What the hell did he mean by that? He could do more than invade my dreams? "Aren't you using it now?"

"Not to its fullest extent."

"There's been one new moon since you got my blood. Why didn't you use me as an anchor then?"

Sid tilted his head. "I needed to test the strength of the tether first."

The warmth seeped from my body, replaced by a frigid stream of ice. "I thought you didn't feed on fear."

"I don't." His dark browns furrowed.

"Then why are you trying to scare me?"

"I'm not."

I gave him a pointed look.

Sid's shoulders drooped, and he took a step forward.

112

"I want you to be prepared. In three days' time, I will use our bond to gain access to the mortal realm. You're my little anchor, after all."

My scalp prickled, and my stomach clenched. His anchor? Fuck that. I didn't want to be anything to the Seducer Demon. "Why tell me? Surely, you know I could try to set something up to harm you."

"You could try."

My pulse sped up as options flashed through my mind. Things I could do to hurt Sid, closely followed by things he could do to me in retaliation. My body tensed, and I balled my fists as heat flushed through my veins once more.

"That's why I wish to warn you," Sid continued. "If I appear and scare you, and somehow you manage to smite me, which I highly doubt, I'll return to the demonic realm."

"Good," I spat.

"And I'll have a whole month in which to make you pay for your actions."

I gulped down my breath to stay quiet. Could he sense my thoughts? Did he know the deranged ideas running through my distraught brain? Could he read my mind like Allan?

Sid cocked his head. "Although I prefer other emotions, if you cause me harm, I will exact payment of equal nature. I'd prefer to avoid those unpleasantries altogether."

"There's another option."

"I'm using you as an anchor, Andy, so don't suggest I

don't."

"That wasn't it."

"What brilliant option have you concocted then?"

With a deep breath, I turned my attention internal and sought the Demon's bond. It centred in my chest with ferocious attachment, as if it drove steely talons into the tender muscles of my beating heart. I rounded up the Demon's taint. Surely, it would work now that he was right here with me.

"I dispel you."

Nothing happened.

I yanked harder and put a forcible command behind my voice, making it come out deeper, more gravelly, as if embedded with jib rock. "I dispel you."

Nothing happened.

Sid tsked. "Silly Carus. I'm not a simple Vampire or fera for you to cast away. I'm a Demon."

A slice of ice shot up my spine as the hair on my arms lifted off prickled skin. Slowly, my unease faded, leaching out of my blood as my thoughts drifted. Sid no longer occupied my brain, and I drifted into true sleep.

13

My phone blared and shook me from my deep slumber. Last night's conversation with Sid resurfaced as a distant memory, but true to his word, Sid had let me sleep the rest of the night without any more of his perverted influence. I reached out and snatched the phone from my nightstand on the third attempt. All the while the piece of plastic continued its shrill call. I'd given up assigning song ringtones to the people in my life. Too many weird dreams happened when I got a call during the go-the-fuck-away hours of the morning. I received these types of calls more often than I'd like.

I tapped the phone and put it to my ear in time to hear Stan bark out, "Carleton and Frances."

Click.

Well, I guess I should be a good doggy and come when called. Except, I wouldn't show up as a wolf. With that form too painful to consider, I'd show up as a mountain lion again and sniff whatever Stan pointed out.

Time to earn my government-sized paycheque.

I scrolled through my phone. Still no message from Tristan. I sent him a quick text to let him know where I went, waited for a whole minute for a response, got none, ripped off my clothes and stalked to the nearest window. Then I paused. Carleton and Frances? Where the heck was that?

I groaned, retrieved new clothes, grabbed my keys and phone, and stalked out the door.

THE BLUE DOT ON MY GPS BLINKED BACK AT ME. Surely, I got the address wrong. Stan had rattled it off quickly, but his words had been crisp and clear. Carleton and Frances.

When I turned the corner, the red and blue flashing lights of police cruisers beckoned me. In the middle of suburban Burnaby, where Italian families staked a claim in Little Italy a few blocks away, and large homes sat with two-point-five children and white picket fences, this area hardly hit the crime radar often.

When I first started helping Stan out with crime scenes, we'd gone to other areas outside of the city of Vancouver as well. Around a decade ago, the local municipalities had merged, making two giant police departments, instead of numerous smaller ones. The provincial government tried to sell it as a way to "save on administration costs," but everyone knew it was a last ditch effort by the local police forces to deal with the constant budget cuts and underfunding.

Sadly, the treatment of law enforcement paled in comparison to how the government butchered public education.

The VPD took everything north of the Fraser River and West of Coquitlam River, and the Surrey Police Department took everything else within the Lower Mainland. Things had changed a lot since the Purge.

I pulled up to a two-story, terracotta Italian stucco house. Tuscan-style, or something. The brakes of my poor excuse of a car screeched, and the heads of the nearby police officers monitoring the taped line snapped in my direction. Squinting, wary eyes studied my movement as I put the car in park and clambered out. The rusty hinges groaned as I exited and a number of cops winced. Some snickered.

Stan stalked out as I approached the yellow tape, clad in civvies with two other surly-looking detectives behind him.

"Thought you'd come in animal," he said when I drew close.

"I was going to, but I had no idea where this place was and prefer driving to unknown locations. I can use my phone and it's easier to stop for directions, if needed." Try asking a gas attendant for directions while naked...it doesn't work. Been there, done that.

Stan grunted. "Do you need to..."

"Change? No. Not if it's fresh." I tapped my nose.

Stan pursed his lips and exchanged looks with the nameless detectives at his side. Maybe I shouldn't have referred to the dead body as fresh.

"Homicide detectives Edwards and Liu," Stan said, nodding at each detective. Edwards, middle-aged Caucasian norm with deeply embedded frown lines, and Liu, also middle-aged with graying hair at his temples, nodded at me.

I dipped my chin and waited. When it appeared we'd stand around giving each other googly eyes, I let the tension flow from my body. "Shall we?"

Stan grunted again and waved me forward. We left the detectives behind and walked into the immaculate house with freshly vacuumed carpet, smooth hardwood flooring, and Italian tiles. Death clung to the air and drifted to meet me at the entranceway.

"What's the story?" I asked Stan's broad back as he continued forward.

"Housewife's habit gone bad."

"Seriously?"

"Addicts come in all shapes and sizes. After twenty years on the force, nothing really surprises me anymore." His tone came out even and matter of fact, but his scent said so much more. Not a surprise. No lemon and pepper sprinkled the air around Stan. No. Simple sadness mired his scent with a stiff weight, and something else. Sickly sweet sweat called out to the predators cohabitating my mind. They liked Stan, but sensing fear brought forth their most primal nature.

"Why do you smell off?" I leaned in and asked. I'd never accuse him of smelling like fear in front of his comrades, but something about this crime scene had spooked him.

Must be why he called me in. I *still* awaited approval on my paperwork.

"You'll see," Stan said.

I huffed at his back, but he ignored me and kept leading me farther into the house until we turned a corner and walked into a large master bedroom with a king-sized bed. A door on the far side of the room let in more light from what must be the en suite bathroom.

A woman in a white negligee lay sprawled on the rumpled covers of the bed, smelling of recent sex, vomit, death...and something else...something off. Not like Stan's fear, something different. Like sour, burnt plastic, like the vial found near Loretta's lifeless body. "King's Krank," I said as I walked up to stand beside Stan and observe the crime scene.

Stan's gaze flicked to me before he nodded. "We're waiting on the tox screen and test results from the lab to confirm, but we found a vial similar to..."

To the one found near his dead wife.

"What about the lover?" I asked, cutting him off from the words he couldn't say.

He took little time to recover. "How'd you know?"

"Everything leaves a trace. The husband's scent is ingrained on every piece of furniture, flooring, wall, and ceiling in this place, but it's not the one fresh on the bed or her skin."

Stan's lips snarled up.

"Not a surprise, either?"

He shook his head.

"We got anything on the lover?"

"He's the one who called it in." Stan pulled out his notebook and leafed through the small pages. "Charles de Jong. No record. Not even a speeding ticket. Married. Two kids. Lives three streets over and met the victim at church over a year ago. They've been having an affair for the last five months. Says he came here around nineteen-hundred after the husband left for a work trip. He was intimate with the deceased and then Suzy..." Stan pointed at the dead woman with the butt of his pen, "Wanted to try something new. She drank from the vial first and apparently the effect was immediate. She started vomiting and foaming at the mouth. That's when Charles called it in. Nine-one-one took the call at oh-two-hundred. She went into cardiac arrest shortly after and died before paramedics arrived. Liu and Edwards took the case, but called me in this morning due to the potential KK link."

"Who supplied them with the drug?"

"That would be convenient, wouldn't it?" Stan snorted. "Charles claims Suzy supplied the drug, and he didn't know what it was. She never said where she got it, and he never asked. He couldn't even confirm whether it was KK."

I pursed my lips and thought about the details for a

bit, trying to fit them together in a way that made sense. "If my lover pulled a vial of mystery drug out to share with me post-coital, I'd ask a lot of questions. Like what it was and where it came from."

"My take on it as well."

"And?"

"And without his consent, or a warrant with just cause, we can't strap a lie detector to him."

My lips curled up. "You don't need to."

"Don't need to..." He turned to me with pinched eyebrows, but understanding spread across his face, and his features relaxed. "Ah...I see. Let's go question him, again, shall we?"

"Let me finish in here first." I approached the bed, careful to avoid disrupting the strewn clothes, a condom wrapper, and rumpled sheets. I leaned over the bed and started breathing through my mouth. Her scent up close couldn't give me anything it hadn't already ten feet away, save a nasty headache.

And there it was, the reason this crime scene creeped out the veteran cop.

Horns.

Little nubby horns had punctured through Suzy's forehead near the hairline. Blood had trickled down her face to dry in a cobweb pattern. The skin around the protrusions looked raw and fresh.

Stan stepped up to the bed. "There's no evidence she was a supe and lover-boy denies any knowledge. The husband is on a plane and won't touchdown for another three hours, but once we get hold of him, we might get a better picture."

"She must've hid it well." I sniffed her skin. "Doesn't smell like a Were or Shifter, there's no animal scent on her. Not sure what kind of supe she is...was... but she must've wanted it kept a secret. She probably masked her scent with a Witch charm. Her skin smells like a norm's."

"Can you detect the charms?"

I shook my head. "Not always. The really expensive ones will mask even the Witch's scent. The one the dealer Aahil wore smelled faintly of Witches, more of a transfer scent, if anything. I can't detect a Witch's involvement with this deceased in any way."

Stan's shoulders drooped.

"But I know someone who can."

BEN STRAIGHTENED UP FROM HIS CROUCH NEAR the corner. He'd been resting his face in his hands with his elbows braced on his knees. His skin had paled at least three shades and dark bags under his eyes had appeared. "Lover give you anything?" he asked as we walked into the bedroom.

I glanced over my shoulder at Stan. He shook his head.

"I can't give you the details of an ongoing investigation, but yeah. He gave us a little." The lover had taken one look at my animal shifted eyes after he told his first lie and decided honesty was the best policy. We had confirmation the drug in the vial was King's Krank, not that we needed it, and the name of a street level dealer.

"That's fine. I don't need to know any details," Ben said. "Glad you got something out of him. Can you tell me if he did it?"

"He may be scum, but he's not a drug addict, dealer or a killer," I said.

Ben nodded. His gaze slid to the bed before he quickly looked away. Maybe I shouldn't have asked him to help. He may be my best guy friend, but he wasn't a crime scene investigator, and the only harm he'd ever caused anyone, to my knowledge, was an earache from his midnight karaoke crooning.

Well, not entirely true. He had blasted me with a wicked spell once to stop me from gutting his coven member.

"Thanks again for coming," I said. "I know this isn't your thing."

He nodded, then gulped.

"Did you find anything?" I asked.

Ben wiped his hands on his jeans. "Nope. She wasn't a Witch and the nearest charm is three houses over on the left-hand side to mask a grow-op."

Stan's eyes narrowed. He pulled his phone out, punched some numbers in, and when someone picked up, he prattled off a series of number codes. The VPD probably expected me to learn those. *Crap.*

"Any idea what she is?" I asked Ben, nodding my head toward the bed.

He shook his head. "My magic reacted to her as if she was a norm."

"A norm with horns," I said. *What the heck is going on?* "Can I call you for future crime scenes? If we get another like this one? You don't have to come into the actual room next time. I didn't know you could detect things that far away."

Ben's lips pursed and his gaze cut away, not in a way that made any sense for this situation. "I need to go. My shift at the SRD starts soon."

"Ben?"

He dropped his head.

"Ben, what's going on?"

"I've been summoned to the Elders. Me and my coven. We have until midnight tomorrow to present ourselves, or they'll..."

"Retrieve you?" Despite my calm tone, my brain fired millions of signals to comprehend Ben's words, and my heart went into full panic-attack mode.

Ben nodded.

"Because of Bola?" I whispered. Ben had said there'd be backlash for his den's actions. I should've known this was coming. Over a month ago, Ben's mentorees—Christopher, Patty and Matt—summoned the sadistic Demon without Ben's knowledge or consent, in a desperate attempt to get Christopher's voice back. He'd lost it from a spell gone wrong and figured Bola could help with his science background and Demon skills.

Christopher did get his voice back, but the Witches forgot to specify the length of time Bola could possess Christopher's body, and Bola used the opportunity to wreak slaughter and mayhem across the Lower Mainland.

Now, the Witch Elders wanted to speak to Ben and his coven, most likely to exact punishment.

"Yeah," Ben said, interrupting my thoughts. "Because of Bola."

"No," I snarled, in a voice more animal than my own. The beast roared inside my core. My feras growled in agreement.

Ben snapped straight and took a step back.

I cleared my throat. "Sorry. My feras really like you. They don't want anything bad to happen to you any more than I do."

Ben frowned. "Define *really like*. You're not exactly my type and I don't want to fight Tristan for you."

I groaned and punched him in the arm. "Not like that."

Ben's sad face brightened as his lips twisted up. "I know."

"Don't try to distract me with your lame jokes. If anything happens, Ben, I'll come for you." I meant every word. In this life, I was short on friends. Living as a mountain lion for over three decades to emotionally heal from an abusive relationship tended to put a kink in the social life. As one of my close friends, one of my only friends, I'd defend Ben any way possible. Even if it meant going against the all-mighty Witch Elders.

He reached out and squeezed my hand. His tone dropped into a more somber one. "I know."

14

The old man dodged my calls. Without any leads on the street-level dealer named Patty Cake, I used my precious spare time after helping Stan with the crime scene to drop by the SRD Vancouver headquarters and track down Agent Donny O'Donnell, fellow Shifter, former handler, and wily old coyote.

Ben and Matt winked at me as I skipped the sign-in desk and headed straight to the elevators. They'd cut the security tape feed with a little magical interference on my behalf. Not that I couldn't enter the building, I'd just prefer not to deal with ATF unless necessary. Sadness punched my heart at seeing Ben and Matt on their last shift before facing the Elders. They'd be okay, though. They had to be. Ben promised.

Maybe I should take Tucker out as a going away present for my Witch bros.

My finger hovered over the button for the tenth floor where Tucker's office sat.

No. Too obvious.

Besides, it would be a total abuse of the trust the Witches gave me. Not that they didn't owe me, because they totally did. I'd spared their insufferable buddy from being put down as a rampaging Demon host, but they had enough on their plate. I hit the button for the fifth floor instead.

I found the old man exactly where I expected. Stooped over an old book in the resource library on the fifth floor.

The double swinging doors opened to a large room. It always surprised me the SRD valued the reference books enough to house them in their downtown head-quarters in a space the size of ten offices. Real estate didn't come cheap in this area, and the media preference these days skewed toward the digital format. Regardless, someone in the SRD knew these books couldn't be scanned and retain their value. Amazingly insightful for the SRD.

Two long tables with plastic chairs were placed in an open area and on the far side ten tall, solid wood book-shelves stood floor to ceiling. Books of all shapes and sizes adorned the units, giving the room that studious, dusty smell I loved. It reminded me of school.

Donny sat at the end of the far table, hunched over a large odorous book. His coyote familiar, Ma'ii, curled up on his feet, legs straight out and eyes closed. A soft snoring sound vibrated from his chest.

When the doors swung shut behind me, the air blew

forward, announcing my entrance. The old man ignored me, but Ma'ii stopped snoring and popped one eye open.

Don't stress him out, Ma'ii warned.

I ignored the ankle-biting familiar and took in Donny's appearance as I walked toward him. Slight and wiry, his white hair hung long and curled around his ears. The wrinkles on his face spoke of a long life lived well, full of humour and sunshine.

"Carus." The old man's voice travelled softly through the air.

"Is the SRD investigating King's Krank?" I asked. No need for preamble. This guy could evade answering me like a pro-boxer dodged and weaved. I needed to pin him down with straight to-the-point questions.

"That's an odd question to ask right away. Normally, 'hello' and 'how are you?' are more typical conversation starters. It's good to see you, Carus. How are you?"

"Annoyed. Is the SRD doing anything about KK?"

"Like what? Enforcement?" A small smile danced on the old man's face as he turned to me.

I nodded.

"It's a street drug, not a supe-on-supe crime. Not necessarily, at least."

"What exactly does the SRD do, then? Aside from ordering hits on supes?" I closed the distance between us and took the seat opposite Donny.

He opened his mouth, but I talked over his response.

"I mean, I get that King's Krank might not be on their radar because it lacks a supe connection, but it just highlights their lack of initiative. They were completely useless in the Kappa and the Demon incidences. They'd labelled me rogue, but couldn't track me down in their own backyard. Didn't appear like they even tried. It's like they've completely given up on having an enforcement or investigatory presence for current crimes."

Donny's eyes darted left and right before settling on the book in front of him. "I cannot speak on that. But, you're starting to ask the right questions."

I stared at him blankly. Once again, old man O'Donnell went cryptic on me.

"This is good," he added, as if he made all the sense in the world.

Silence settled over the room as Donny pretended to read the book in front of him. The air laden with dust, parchment, and old bindings hung stagnant around us, yet oddly it comforted my irritated nerves.

"Is the SRD investigating King's Krank?" I asked again. "There's something odd about it, and I can't help feel there's a supe connection."

Donny nodded, slowly, and pried his gaze away from the book. "They sent Agent Nagato to discern rumour from truth."

"And?"

"He's missing."

I shut my eyes and let my head drop back for some deep breathing. Why couldn't I get a break, just once? "What happened?"

"They're not sure. His last correspondence indicated he planned to visit the Vampire court and then he disappeared. The SRD director has officially labelled Nagato rogue, and there's a bounty on his head."

Wow. A bounty on Nagato's head for going rogue without a proper investigation. Seemed uncomfortably close to my personal history with the agency.

"Sound familiar?" O'Donnell arched a shaggy brow. If we walked outside, Donny probably would've spat to the side. His face scrunched up with evident disgust, and he shifted in his seat, giving off wave after wave of agitation.

"You know it does," I said. My legs started to heat against the plastic chair. "I take it you don't believe Nagato went rogue?"

Donny snorted and relaxed a little in his chair. "No."

"Yea, me neither."

"Nagato was a rule follower," Donny said. "Compliant. He never would've turned his back on the agency."

"This is the second time the SRD has labelled an agent rogue without an investigation, and I'm assuming little follow up or an attempt to retrieve him?" I drummed my fingers on the wood table.

"None. Just the open bounty."

"And no one's asking questions?"

"Not out loud." Donny cast his gaze around the room again. "And you should be careful of which questions you voice in this building."

"This room bugged?"

"No. Probably the only one that's not. Tucker never felt the library held much significance. Once he discovers you've visited here post-employment, though, I doubt it will stay that way."

"Well, if you answered your phone—"

"They tapped it last week."

My mouth clamped shut.

Donny smirked and continued to read. I wanted to haul the massive book away from him and throw it out the window. The five-story fall would probably do little to harm the ancient relic, which reeked of old magic, but I didn't want to touch it. My experience with ancient texts made me apprehensive of any unnecessary skin-on-skin contact.

"Is there any connection between KK and Demons?" I asked, going for a new angle.

Donny's head snapped up so fast it cracked. "Why in Feradea's name would you think that?"

I shrugged. "Saw the shadow of something with wings following us."

"Do you think Bola is involved?" Donny knew the painful history I had with the Demon.

I nodded.

"That's a big leap. There's lots of supernaturals with wings, you know. Maybe you gained a guardian angel."

"Doubt it." I snorted. "If I have a guardian angel, I'm pretty sure she drinks...heavily."

"You're right. You're a mess." Donny shook his head, shaggy white hair brushed against his wrinkled face. He peered at me and stilled. His shaggy, white mono-brow dipped severely in the middle, his eyes squinted and his lips compressed as he studied me from across the table.

"Something's different about you," he said. Like I'd tell him I finally got laid. I bit my lip. "Something new."

I shrugged, trying to ignore my quickening heartbeat and clammy skin.

"Any new calls in the night? Another fera beckoning you to the deep forest?"

I froze. My skin tingled as if a ghost tried to give me a full body massage. After a silent three-count, I glared at the old man. "I swear to Feradea, if you're keeping tabs on my nocturnal habits with some pagan, hoo-doo, voodoo Witchery, I'll hurt you."

"No, you won't."

Ma'ii's teeth sank into my ankle, but I'd expected it. My shoulders sank and some of the tension flowed from my muscles. I found the coyote's familiar gnawing on my leg oddly comforting. "No, I won't. But I'll be extremely pissed off. How do you always know what's going on in my life?"

Ma'ii released my ankle without saying anything, flopped back onto the floor by Donny's feet, and resumed his snoring.

Donny smiled, a small, knowing twitch of his lips before he leaned back to rest in his plastic chair. "Well, what is it?"

"What's what?"

Donny's eye roll made him appear ten years younger. "What type of animal is your new fera?"

"I don't know."

"You resisted the call. Again?" He chuckled and

shook his head. "You're as stubborn as my daughter. What did it feel like?"

"Cold. It feels different from my other feras."

"Cold?"

I nodded.

"Like a reptile?"

I thought about it. The ice slithering through my veins, the cool detachment of the call, the tin-like quality of the fera's voice. It fit.

"Snake," I said. "I think."

The trench between Donny's brows deepened.

"That worries you?" I leaned forward until the edge of the table pressed uncomfortably into my abdomen.

"The snake is powerfully connected to primal energy and represents the source of life, but it also signifies important transitions in your life."

"Can you elaborate?" I asked.

"Something's building, something behind the scenes, like all the puzzle pieces falling into place..."

Donny's voice trailed off and his gaze turned vacant. Maybe he did practice some pagan stuff.

"And?" I prodded.

"And you're either at, or soon arriving at, a major precipice in your life. You're going to face a crossroad."

"You got all that from *cold*?" My question sounded flippant, but inside, my mind reeled. More difficult decisions? Had letting Wick go not been hard enough? Did my heart and body not ache from his loss, even as I developed a relationship with Tristan?

Donny nodded. "The snake also represents healing and spiritual guidance."

"That's good, right?" I held my breath.

"Depends on how you look at it."

"What do you mean?"

"Your feras appear when you need them most."

My chest tightened, and I grimaced. Donny always had a way of delivering knowledge bombs that blew me out of the water. Did I even want to know? Yes. Yes, I did. "Please, explain."

"You'll be in need of healing and spiritual guidance."

At first, my thoughts froze, as if ice travelled through my neurons. My heartbeat picked up its pace and warm blood flushed through my body. In need of healing? That meant I'd get hurt. Call me a wimp, but I preferred to stay pain free as often as possible.

"It's good the snake will be present to heal and guide you," Donny continued, "but you will be hurt, Carus, and maybe not in the physical sense."

Acid gnawed at my gut, as if a pack of rats needed to get out. Would it be Tristan who hurt me? Ben?

"Well, that sucks."

Donny nodded. "Remember, Carus. When darkness descends on your soul, you're not alone."

"Thanks." *I think.*

Donny went back to reading the ancient manuscript in front of him, and this time, his body language told me the conversation was over. I would get no more information from him. Not sure I wanted to. My limbs went slack, and my chest ached. I mumbled a goodbye and left the library, Donny and his sleeping fera.

After closing the door to the library quietly behind me, I walked down the hall to the elevator. I pressed the button to go down. My phone vibrated against my thigh. I dug it out of my pocket, and accepted the call from Stan.

"Hey, Stan," I said. "What's up?"

"I found Patty Cake."

15

My breathing hitched as my brain desperately groped for a witty reply to match Stan's statement. Did Stan find him in a bakery? Patty Cake and the baker's man? No, too obvious, and lame. There had to be a good one-liner in there, somewhere, but the words escaped me. Stan had found the street dealer of King's Krank. Finally, some good news.

"Where?" I asked.

"Central City Morgue."

And just like that, excitement seeped from my bones, leaving my limbs heavy. My shoulders dropped, and my posture drooped. *Dangit.*

"Guess we won't get any answers from him," I said.

"Not unless you're a necromancer or know one."

"Screw that. Necros creep me out." Reason number one why I never used them and didn't seek their help during the Supe Slayer or the Dog Demon cases.

"Why?"

"They require sacrifice. And I'm not talking chickens."

A pause. "Yeah. Fuck that. Well, Patty Cake may still tell us something useful."

"How?"

Stan tsked.

My fingers pressed against the phone as I waited for him to enlighten me.

"His possessions, you amateur. His cause of death, location of death, all these things can be valuable clues or lead us to some."

"Or lead us to more dead ends."

"Who made you Ms. Pissy Pants? We have to start somewhere."

"I know that. I just hate investigating shit."

"That's because you suck at it."

Jerk! He was totally right, but he didn't have to say it. "I wasn't trained to investigate. I trained to kill supes."

Stan cleared his throat. "Meet me at the morgue?"

"Yeah, sure."

Stan hung up and left me staring at the closed silver doors of the elevator. They dinged and opened. There, on my right, stood Agent Tucker, fixing a stray hair in his reflection of the shiny metal while making an epic trout pout. He jumped when the doors slid open and turned to face me. His gaze narrowed.

"What are you doing here?" he demanded.

I should've taken the stairs.

Agent Tucker fixed me with a condescending sneer, making my mountain lion hiss and my falcon urge me to peck out his eyes. He had no idea what I could do to him. Take the stairs?

Nah, this would be more fun.

Tucker's eyes widened when I stepped into the elevator.

"You shouldn't be here," he said, voice cracking.

"Is there a rule against civilians entering the SRD headquarters?"

He sputtered. "Ex-employees are not permitted on the premises. Security should've detained you."

Oops. Didn't want to get my Witch-boys in trouble. "I made sure they were distracted. And the ex-employee thing only applies when the employee is fired. Technically, you laid me off. I received a wonderfully articulate letter to prove it."

Tucker's glower had no effect on me.

I stepped closer. "Are you worried?"

Tucker tensed, and a sweet, sweaty scent rolled off his lips. "No."

His lie stunk up the elevator.

I took another step forward, my face within head-butting range to his. "You should be."

The elevator stopped on the third floor, and the doors dinged open. I spun to stand shoulder to shoulder with a frozen Tucker as two women stepped inside, most likely accountants from their shapeless skirt-suits and stern expressions. The elevator filled with the aroma of computers, paper, and pencils. The women turned their backs to us without a second thought or glance. Not even a polite greeting.

My mountain lion paced in my head and hissed at me. *Take them out. No witnesses.*

My falcon squawked her agreement.

Silence followed. A silence that would've been filled with my wolf's growling...if she still lurked inside.

The other two feras started up again, as if sensing my sadness. I shushed them and enjoyed the smell of Tucker's fear filled the elevator.

Why hadn't he run off when he had the chance?

Pride?

Did his arrogance overpower his fear that much? He certainly didn't possess any common sense, but that was nothing new.

The elevator stopped on the next floor, and the women walked off without a word. Again. Instead of using the stop as an opportunity to escape, Tucker stood like a statue in the corner of the elevator with his knees locked and posture stiff. When the doors closed, I turned to him.

"You can't kill me," he said.

I had no intention of harming Tucker where videotape and witnesses could lock me up. But it sure as hell was fun to fuck with his mind. I leaned in. My mountain lion purred and urged me to rake my claws down his face.

"They'll catch you. I have cameras everywhere," he rambled.

"But," I paused for effect, "you'll still be dead."

His lip trembled before he sucked it in and clenched his jaw. Arrogant, proud, and stubborn, apparently.

The elevator slowed for the ground floor.

"You're right, though," I said. "I have more finesse than an elevator mauling. You can relax."

His stance loosened. Within seconds, his smug expression returned to his smarmy face, and my mountain lion nudged my brain again.

Rake, she said.

I spoke again, before he could. "I've been too busy to plot your demise. But one day, I'll find the time. One day, I'll circle back to you."

I enjoyed another waft of fear before the doors opened and I walked out, giving Tucker my back.

16

Central City Morgue sat attached to the new hospital on Sixth Street and Royal Avenue in New Westminster, the original capital city of British Columbia before Victoria stole the honour. With rundown parliamentary buildings and a healthy dose of street skids who could rip a stereo system out of your car in under three minutes, this municipality, dubbed Royal City, still held its head high with picturesque views of the Fraser River and easy access to surrounding areas.

After the Royal Columbian Hospital burnt down from malfunctioning equipment way past expiry date, the city rebuilt the medical facilities here. Sixth Street dipped with a steep decline to the heart of New West's downtown. Standing on the precipice, the view offered was breathtaking. I took a moment to enjoy the misty Fraser River, and bustling city below before steeling myself for what was to come. I pulled open the thick double-paned glass doors leading to one of the outer wings of the hospital, and followed the stairs down to the cold, drafty basement.

I hated morgues. Not because they smelled bad. They didn't, really. The clinical environment and chemicals overpowered the decay, and they kept the decomposition minimal with their body sized cold storage spaces.

No, I hated morgues for another reason. They creeped me out.

Central City Morgue specialized in storing the deceased for autopsy. After researching the morgue on my smart phone, I discovered it prided itself on providing a clean and isolated environment for autopsies. It made me wonder what other morgues were doing that "clean and isolated" environments became a selling feature for Central City.

I walked up to the receptionist's desk and provided my details. The young woman in scrubs nodded and pointed at the swinging side door with the "authorized personnel only" sign in big, red block letters.

"They're waiting for you in the back," she said.

Great.

I managed a smile, and then pushed through the door, which led to a hallway, lined with what looked like autopsy rooms. I followed the path and signs like Dorothy following the yellow brick road and took a deep breath before entering the storage room. Floor to ceiling stainless steel gleamed back at me. The air hung light and crisp, flowing gently through the well-ventilated and fluorescent-lighted room. The decay odour minimal, but present.

The coroner and Stan turned at my entrance, but my senses remained preoccupied by the deathly horrors confronting me.

The large metal, cold storage spaces where they stored the bodies lined an entire wall. More than a few bodies had been pulled out, white sheets covering their bodies.

So many.

"Andy?" Stan's voice yanked my mind away from the dead. "You okay?"

"Huh? Yeah, yeah...I'm good." I turned to face the career cop and coroner. Rarely did I deal with the aftermath of death, I just caused it. Feradea, how did Stan do this on a regular basis? Scrap that. How'd he appear calm and collected now, after his wife's death? This had to cut him emotionally, yet he asked if I was okay. My eyes tingled.

Suck it up, buttercup, I told myself.

Stan studied me for a few ticks of the clock and then nodded. He pointed to one of the bodies. This one had the sheet folded down to reveal the face and upper body. "Patty Cake is over here."

I nodded at the coroner. "I'm Andy."

"Dr. Cohen. You can call me Greg," he replied. Wearing a crisp white lab coat and thicker round lenses to magnify his large brown eyes, the man with a curly fro looked like the classic geek. Nothing wrong with that.

Geeks were my people, but this guy's appearance was so stereotypical it was almost comical.

"We find out anything?" I turned to Stan.

He shook his head. "Real name is Dwight Lancaster, twenty-two, in and out of foster homes. Alcoholic mother, absentee father, stereotypical path to self-destruction."

I grunted. Some people started life with a few strikes already against them, and faced an uphill battle out of depravity. Reality sucked. Often, the apple didn't fall far from the tree. Growing up, I'd hated that expression, but a number of life experiences taught me there was more than a bit of truth in the statement. I commended those people who stopped the negative cycle and broke out of their preformed mold.

"Cause of death?" I asked as I leaned over the deceased body. With a lean, long frame, Dwight's sunken features and scar-riddled forearms spoke of chronic drug abuse. He would've been handsome, had he been clean and given a chance at a good life. Another soul our society's system failed.

"Overdose," Greg said. "We're waiting for the lab to confirm, but we suspect it was King's Krank. There were several glass vials, some full, some empty, on his person."

"Anything else interesting in his possession?"

"No," Stan grunted. "His wallet had been cleaned out. Only his licence and the vials."

"Huh."

"Yeah. Can you get...anything more from the body?"

Stan asked, shifting his weight on the sterile metal flooring.

Greg's eyebrows pinched together as he turned to me, but I ignored him and leaned closer to Dwight's body. The smell of oven cleaner lingered on his skin—King's Krank, all right. But nothing else. No grease on his hands from a chicken finger dinner, or perfume from a midnight liaison, not coffee or cigarettes, not that many people smoked these days, but still. Nothing. This man must've recently bathed. And by bathed, he must've scoured the first couple layers of skin off.

"He's been cleaned," I said. "But I can confirm the KK."

Greg's face twisted up in a skeptical what-the-fuck-do-you-know face.

I shrugged. Stan grunted.

"Will that be all, officers?" Greg asked. He shifted back and forth on his feet.

"Yeah, we're done here," Stan said.

We walked in silence together down the hall, leaving Greg to his room of corpses. My mind ran through all the possibilities. Most street level dealers weren't known for their personal hygiene. They certainly wouldn't go to such measures to remove all scent traces unless they expected an interrogation by the SRD, or a supe with a sensitive nose. Someone in contact with Patty Cake wished to remain anonymous.

"Do you get the feeling someone's cleaning up?" I asked Stan as we stepped out of the building and into wonderfully fresh air.

"Definitely."

17

The hot air in my car hung heavy and stagnant, with a side of pizza. I rummaged through the contents on the backseat and found an old cardboard triangular container from last week that had held some to-go pizza slices with pepperoni and green pepper. Hooker slices, I used to joke, because they cost only a dollar per slice. I climbed out of the car and threw the cardboard in the nearest recycling bin.

My cheeks heated. Last week, I picked up a bunch of pizza and drove Tristan to one of the only drive-in movie theatres left in the Lower Mainland. We'd ended up making out like lusty teenagers in the backseat of my four-wheel junker instead. I still had no idea what happened in the movie, but half of Richmond knew what went on in my backseat. Oh well.

Once in the car, I maneuvered away from the curb and into traffic. Sweat dripped down my face and lower back. Even with all the windows rolled down, I couldn't drive fast enough to get much airflow. I sat in a sauna until I made it to the highway.

The reprieve didn't last long. Rush hour gridlock left me sitting in a boiler pot. The exhaust fumes radiated off the sweltering pavement and filled the interior of my car. Should've taken Kingsway instead of Canada Way. My falcon squawked for release. The clear skies called to me. If I didn't have to worry about leaving my vehicle stranded in the middle of the Trans-Canada Highway and showing up at my ex's naked, I would've gladly flown to my destination.

My heart sank.

With Allan unwilling to help, in any capacity, I had only one option left to ask about horde business. Technically two, but I'd rather peel off my fingernails than approach Clint again. That left one person who might help me.

Wick.

My body became one large beating, nauseated ball of nerves the entire drive to his place. All forty-two minutes of it.

Luckily, when I pulled up to Wick's house, only three vehicles sat in his driveway. The full moon wasn't for another couple of weeks, but pack houses tended to be revolving doors of Weres.

I didn't have the heart, or the patience, to play nice with others right now.

Sitting in the heart of trendy Kitsilano, only blocks from the beach, Wick's house was quintessential Kits. Probably worth well over three million dollars, since housing prices for this area were ridiculous, it had multiple levels and a covered front patio I adored. Painted Parisian blue with bold white trim, the house fit in with the other heritage-styled buildings on the street. On the inside, everything had been upgraded and modernized and Were-proofed. Wick did well in the building development profession.

Tourists might see a beautiful home with a handsome owner, but few knew what went on inside. When I'd been held captive here, I'd fought for dominance with the leading pack-bitch and won, I'd sprayed dog repellant in Wick's second-in-command's face to escape, and I'd fallen in love with the Alpha. Not once were the cops called, nor did the neighbours call to complain about the racket.

I hadn't seen or heard from Wick since I broke his heart and denied his mate claim over me.

Maybe I should put the VPD investigation off, and look for the missing Kappa instead. No bodies had turned up floating on the river, so wherever Tamotsu hid, he kept a low profile. There'd been no signs indicating he'd started on another supe sucking bender. Maybe he left for Japan. Maybe whomever killed Lucien captured him.

I drummed my fingers on the steering wheel and mulled the idea over. As much as I would love to procrastinate when it came to contacting Wick, it would give Loretta's killer more time to walk free, and Stan's vengeance put on hold. My feelings regarding Wick were inconsequential. *Dang it!* I had to do this now. The

Kappa could wait so long as he didn't start rampaging again, and under my control with orders to not kill anyone, I found that unlikely. Could Tamotsu be involved with my current investigation?

If there's a will, there's a way around orders.

I shook my head and wrenched open the door of my car. Tamotsu could wait. A loud grating sound erupted from the hinges and I winced. If the Weres didn't know I was here before, they certainly knew now.

Maybe I should've called instead.

No. I wanted, needed, to see Wick and know he was okay. That and no one from this pack, Wick included, was likely to take my call.

Now, with his house looming over me... Maybe my choice for a face-to-face conversation inflicted unnecessary cruelty on both of us.

I took a deep breath, shoved the door closed and walked up the wood steps to Wick's house. The twin oak doors stared back at me. Large, ominous, and thick. With a straight spine, I rapped my knuckles on the smooth surface.

After a minute or two, the door swung open to reveal a tall redhead—Wick's second-in-command. Ryan's ice-blue eyes glared down at me, and his mouth compressed into a thin line. When I'd been held captive by Wick, we'd formed a fast friendship. Well, friendship on my part; Ryan made no secret of his wish for more. I'd used his desire for me to escape and ever since we've been not-so-friendly. Not for my lack of trying. I couldn't blame the guy either. My attack had been a low blow.

"Hi," I said, rather meekly.

His eyes narrowed. "Haven't you done enough?"

Before I could reply, he slammed the door in my face.

I stared at the wood panelling with a gaping mouth. Did I expect a warm welcome, full of rainbows and unicorns? No, absolutely not. But a door in the face? Well, that was just rude.

Hunt, my mountain lion suggested, and my falcon squawked her agreement.

Once again, silence greeted me where my wolf normally piped up. She would've growled at the cat. But my body no longer housed the wolf. I didn't just lose Wick with my decision. I lost my wolf, too.

Destroy, my beast demanded, stirring from where she rested, shackled in my core.

All of you, shut-up! I hissed before turning my thoughts outward again. *Do I text? Do I knock again? Do I keep standing here until someone comes out?* Ryan hadn't flicked the deadbolt, so I could walk straight in.

I leaned forward. The doors were thick for more than weathering harsh West Coast storms. They dulled the transmission of sound. Ryan probably stood on the other side of the door, watching me through the peep-hole and wishing a lightning bolt would strike me down. Barging through the door probably wouldn't work, either. Even if it did, it would piss the pack off, not encourage them to help me.

Wick! I mind-spoke to the Alpha. *We need to talk. Let me in.*

Silence. More silence.

Sweat dripped down my back. Children laughed and squealed at the nearby park and impatient motorists honked and swore at each other along the busy street a few blocks over.

Andy? Wick's reply sounded hesitant.

Yes. I'm at the front door. Ryan won't let me in, I said.

I waited, unable to listen through the tight seals of the door, or solid panelling. My hearing was no match for the Werewolves. After five minutes, a soft murmur of raised voices trickled through.

The door swung open again without warning. I jumped back, my body crouched and my hands flew up in a fighting stance.

"Are you here to fight?" Wick asked, with one eyebrow raised.

The sight of him sucked the breath out of my lungs. Dangerously tall and well-muscled, Wick resembled a present day Norse God, with blond hair cut short, a straight, thin nose and a chiseled jaw. But instead of ice-blue eyes, Wick's gaze was molten brown, so dark I could melt in their chocolate depths.

"Andy?" Wick frowned at me.

"No, I'm not here to fight." I straightened and shoved my hands in my pockets. Who knew what they'd do if given free rein. Wick might be total eye-candy, but I'd turned him down a month ago and chose Tristan.

"What are you here for then?" he asked, his voice chilled whiskey over warm cream. His expression turned soft, then hard, then soft again—a war on his face between hurt and hope. The sight of both emotions weakened my knees and turned my stomach inside out, as if a heavyweight boxer punched me in the gut.

Oh Feradea. I shouldn't have come here.

"I'm...we're free now," Wick said. "Free of Lucien."

"I heard."

He nodded.

I nodded.

He waited.

I wanted a hole to open and swallow me up. "Congrats on your release," I said, and mentally face-palmed. *Really?* Just rip the bandage off and get to the point. The longer this went on the more awkward and uncomfortable it would get.

"Yeah, uh..." Wick rubbed a hand back and forth in his short hair. He didn't do the gesture often, only when nervous. Alphas rarely experienced that emotion. "It's good you removed his blood bond when you did," he continued.

Heck yeah, it was. I would've died otherwise. I nodded, again.

He nodded, again.

Maybe Ryan would get his wish and lightning would strike me down. At this moment, I'd gladly welcome it.

"Andy?"

"Yeah?" I asked my feet.

"Why are you here? Have you...have you changed your mind?"

My stomach dropped to my feet. I gulped. "No...I... sorry...I needed help... Ah fuck! I shouldn't have come.

I'm so sorry." I whirled around and walked to my car as fast as possible without running.

"Andy," Wick called out.

My hand froze on the door handle. My spine straightened. My muscles tensed.

"Don't go. I'll help you if I can."

I turned slowly.

"Come in."

18

Nothing appearance-wise had changed. Wick's house still flaunted the tasteful light-taupe painted walls and dark espresso accents. When we walked inside, the familiar scents coiled around me in greeting. His place smelled of rosemary and sugar, of Wick, laced with the intricacies of the pack and constant visitors. One smell, though, burned my nasal passages.

Christine.

As a member of Wick's pack, Christine's stench had always been present, but not to this degree. When I'd been held prisoner by Wick, at Lucien's behest, the stick-insect had challenged me to a dominance battle. I won. Barely. If I'd shifted into my mountain lion or beast, things might've been more decisive, but the bitch had claimed that wouldn't be fair and her comment still rankled my pride. So I fought her as a wolf.

And won.

Christine also wanted Wick, but he'd wanted me and she'd hated me since the day we met.

Things had changed, apparently. With her scent more present and ingrained, it meant Wick had been passing this last month in her company.

A sharp jab stabbed at my heart, sucking the air out of my lungs.

Wick and Christine.

I had no right to be jealous. But...Wick and Christine?

Another pang sliced my chest, and I wheezed to get enough air in. *Get it together, woman! You can't let him see you this way. Or smell it.*

When we rounded the corner, I went to throw my purse on the kitchen counter, as I used to do, only to find another purse already staking claim on the space. I stared at the peacock blue and green contraption, probably designer. Waves of Christine's stench wafted from the sleek leather shell and gold-link chain straps.

The house opened up to a large living area where large bay windows allowed natural light to flood the area, and contradicted the wild nature of the resident.

"Hello, Andrea." Christine's nasally voice fractured the silence, and I turned slowly to see the shewolf sprawled comfortably on Wick's large L-shaped couch. An attractive, skinny, model-type woman, with thick dirty-blonde hair and a ski-slope nose, she wore designer everything, at least as far as I could tell. Never been a brand name kind of girl. What was the point? Half my clothes ended up in shreds.

Ryan took his place by the front doors and folded his arms. He kept a disgusted expression plastered to his face, just in case I misunderstood how much he despised me.

When Wick entered the living room, Christine unfurled, and gracefully stood, all lanky arms and legs.

Break them, my beast growled. *Like twigs.*

Well, that was unexpected. The beast hated Wick for what she unrealistically perceived as a betrayal, but I guess she hated Christine even more.

"Wick, darling," Christine drawled as she sashayed non-existent hips to him. "I know you feel...a bit responsible for this...woman, but should the pack really get involved with her business? We just won our freedom, we should focus our attention elsewhere." Her body pressing against Wick's gave little doubt as to what she thought Wick should focus on.

I waited, clenching my fists at my side, so hard my nails partially shifted and claws sank into the flesh of my palm.

"Let me decide what's best for the pack," Wick said, his whiskey and cream voice gruff, but not rebuffing. He turned to me, without detaching Christine. The sight of her latched onto him like an oversized accessory, made me want to break every limb of hers as the beast suggested, then run from the house crying.

"Andrea?" Wick said. "What can the pack do for you?"

I tried to ignore his torn expression, one mixed with smugness and pain. I had no right to judge him, no right to be jealous, no right to wish him ill. The pain and betrayal he caused me were not his fault, but that of Lucien's. I chose the other man. I chose the easier and safer path.

And I'd hurt Wick, deeply.

Still proving himself a good man, he was willing to help me, despite my faults and despite our past.

"Andy?" Wick asked, taking a half step forward. He faltered when Christine's body remained clung to his torso.

"Uh, yeah," I said. "Sorry."

Christine's lip curled up into an ugly sneer.

"I wanted to know about King's Krank, Lucien's possible involvement with it, and whether you knew of SRD agent Nagato's visit to the horde."

Wick nodded, his expression shuttered. "To my knowledge, Lucien had no involvement with King's Krank, although I heard mutterings he planned to look into the supply chain. He didn't like someone slipping into the drug scene within his territory without his permission, or without getting a cut. As for Nagato, he came to ask Lucien similar questions, namely his involvement with KK and whether Lucien knew who was behind the drug. I wasn't privy to the whole interview because Lucien took him into his private chambers for further discussion. Nagato left in one piece, though. I saw him leave. No harm came to him from his visit."

"Ah. Okay." I stashed the information in part of my brain while another part struggled to figure out what this information meant. What else did I need to know? Nagato met with Lucien, then left for another meeting, then Allan and Clint were sent away and Lucien was killed. Connection? Probably.

"Does that help?" Wick asked, interrupting my processing.

"Yes, sort of. Nagato is my only lead on a case, and he's gone missing. No idea where he headed to after Lucien's?"

Wick shook his head. "No, but he kept checking his watch. He must've had another appointment."

"Is that all?" Christine's nasally voice punctured the room.

Ryan snorted from his guard post.

My skin itched to shift. "Um, no, actually. How soon after Nagato's visit were Allan and Clint sent away?"

Wick frowned. "Not long. Lucien sent them off the next night."

So Lucien was definitely involved somehow with KK, but Wick had spoken true when he said he knew nothing about it. A lie would've stunk up the room. What had Nagato and Lucien discussed to result in Lucien's death? "Thanks for helping. That's all my questions."

Christine pushed off Wick and folded her arms. "You could've phoned for this information."

I nodded and started toward the exit. "True, but I didn't think anyone would take my call."

Wick turned as I passed him, eyebrows scrunched.

"Thank you for your help," I said. "I'm glad you're well."

Wellness is a relative term, Wick said, using mind

speech for privacy. *It would be best if you kept your distance from now on.*

Another stab to the heart. I nodded and sucked back the sob threatening to bubble up my throat. *I understand. Take care.*

You too, Carus. The formality of his tone and words cinched the moment and acted as the death knell for our relationship.

19

Exhaustion normally reared its ugly head in many ways: sore muscles after a workout, a weird buzzing sensation as if I consumed one cocktail too many, slower, slurred speech, or droopy eyes. With drained energy after a long day, I wanted either a nap or an extra-strength cup of coffee. Usually, I pushed through fatigue and allowed my supernatural glands time to pump out more adrenaline to pull me over the proverbial finish line.

Not today.

Maybe it was the emotionally draining conversation with Donny, maybe the charged banter with Tucker, maybe the high of Stan finding Patty Cake, followed by the low of discovering Stan found him in the morgue, maybe it was the memory of Patty Cake's lifeless eyes, maybe seeing Wick, or maybe seeing him move on with a woman I hated.

"Tired" did not cover it. Nor did exhausted, or

fatigued. What plagued every cement-block step of mine as I plodded up the walkway to my apartment needed its own category, something not cured with caffeine or a snooze on the couch.

The night lights on the street flickered on as the sun set and darkness shrouded the neighbourhood. I unlocked the door to the building and then, shortly after, the one to my apartment. The familiar smells of my home wrapped around me as I closed the door and rested my head against it. Crippling exhaustion left my muscles beyond sore, and turned them into pudding, so boneless, they no longer seemed functional.

I dropped my purse and staggered into my apartment. My place opened to the dining and living room. A Wereleopard Alpha lounged on my couch. The sight gave me the energy boost required to complete the final steps and close the distance.

"Hey," Tristan said.

Without a word, I flopped on top of him. My body sagged and tension flowed from my muscles as weightlessness consumed every cell of my being. I sank into Tristan and the soft sapphire blue T-shirt matching his eyes. My attention drifted into a dark haze, fogging over any conscious thoughts, and sleep slid through my veins. Moving right now would take a Herculean feat.

A trickle of energy teased my neurons, the mist slipped from my mind, and my body began to hum with vitality. My eyes fluttered open.

"How are you doing that?" I mumbled into Tristan's chest.

"As a feline Alpha, my leopard can call your mountain lion, to heal, to link, to command, not that I would choose the latter."

"Leopards and mountain lions are hardly the same species."

"No, and your exhaustion would be an easier fix if they were, but they're both feline. I can do similar things for Werelions and Weretigers. Any feline Shifter, really."

"Oh." I didn't like the idea of him helping other women like this.

Tristan chuckled. "There's nothing sexual about it, Andy. That's just the nature between you and me. A normal link, like a pack link, doesn't have any sexual physicality to it."

"Oh," I breathed and snuggled into his chest. His arms came around to hold me against his hard muscles. "Where were you? Why didn't you answer my texts?"

His heartbeat sped up a little, but his voice came out smooth and calm. "I was investigating something and had my phone off. Sorry. I would've texted a few hours ago, but apologies are better in person."

"You could've just let me sleep and apologized later."

Tristan took a deep breath. "I could have, but I also wanted to talk."

My body stiffened.

"Not that kind of talk," he quickly added.

"What kind, then?" I clambered off Tristan, and we both straightened to sit side by side on the couch.

His nose twitched and he hesitated, opening his mouth, only to shut it again. An intense sapphire gaze scrutinized my face and the tension from Tristan's shoulders eased away. "You saw Wick?"

Not what I expected. Not even sure if Tristan had intended this subject as his talk. He read me so well, unlike any person I'd met.

"It's all over your face and your scent." He pulled his shoulders back. "Are you having second thoughts?"

My head jerked up, and my stomach lurched. How could he think that?

"We haven't bonded, yet, Andy. But when we do, I want you to be sure. There's no room for a third person in a mate bond."

Definitely not the time to mention Sid's enforced dream. "I'm not indecisive, Tristan. I chose you. I want to be with you. Hell, I have been with you."

Tristan's serious face cracked and a small smile tugged at his lips. His chest rumbled with a purr. "Yes, you have."

I nodded and scooted closer on the couch so our thighs touched.

Tristan leaned in and twined his fingers with mine. "Why do you look so pensive, then? Do thoughts of Wick plague your mind?"

I swallowed and looked at our clasped hands. "It was hard to see Wick. To see the pain I caused, but also to see him moving on, and which direction he's chosen to move toward."

"You don't approve?"

"Absolutely not."

A pause. A squeeze of my hand. "Would the woman make any difference?"

"What do you mean?" I frowned.

"You know exactly what I mean. This woman, she could be anyone, maybe even someone you'd like and be friends with under different circumstances, but she's going to be Wick's, and the quality of the woman matters little, it's that she exists." His hand continued to hold mine, but his grip slacked a little.

"I know, but—"

"Let it go, Andy." Despite his words, his tone was soft, gentle.

"Huh?"

"Let it go. Let him go. Let him rebound with whatever woman, or women, he wants. If you meant it when you said you chose me, it means you have no say in Wick's life. He needs to move on just as much as you do."

I sighed. What he said made sense. I still didn't like it, but Wick deserved happiness, even if I didn't agree with the happiness he sought. My muscles grew weak, and my heart dropped in my chest. I'd made my decision a month ago. Tristan was right. I had to let Wick go.

"Was this what you wanted to talk about?" I released his hand to hold my own on my lap.

Tension tightened his shoulders again. "No..."

"Did you cheat on me, do you want to cheat on me, or do you plan to leave me?" May as well throw it out there. I held my breath and waited for his response.

"Never." He looked appalled. After sitting with his mouth gaped open for a silent second, he reached out and grasped my hands, squeezing them a little too hard. "Never."

Truth. Thank Feradea! My shoulders relaxed. I liked direct questioning, and I liked that Tristan never tried to evade answering, either. "Then whatever you want to talk about can wait."

"Andy—"

I pushed my finger against his full lips to stop whatever he planned to say. I probably wouldn't like this talk he planned to have, but frankly, if he wasn't cheating or leaving, I didn't care. Not right now. I wanted his skin on mine—to feel the heat of his body as he thrust into me, to see his loving eyes close as he found a rhythm belonging only to us.

My gaze drifted down to his chest. The blue shirt fit him well, but not like a glove. I dragged my finger from his mouth. He nipped at it, but let my finger go. I slipped my hands up his shirt and along his smooth skin, exploring each divot and curve of his muscled torso.

Tristan sucked in a breath. "Your fingers are cold, woman."

I smiled and kept exploring. Heat emanated off Tristan. He leaned forward and trailed kisses along my neck. When he started to push forward, I straightened.

I waggled my forefinger at him before using it to push him back. "My turn."

Tristan's sapphire gaze sparkled as he reclined in the sofa and drew me down on top of him. "Have your way with me, then."

"I plan to." With a gentle tug, I pulled off Tristan's

shirt before he fully relaxed into the cushions. When I yanked on his form-fitting jeans, he quirked an eyebrow at me.

"Impatient."

"Stop talking. Get naked."

He laughed and lifted his hips so I could slide his jeans off and get a nice view of his bulging briefs.

Very nice.

"You going to stare at it all night?"

I licked my lips. "Maybe."

Tristan grabbed my hand and tugged. I sprawled out on him. His warmth seeped into mine as I found his soft lips. My heartbeat pounded in my ears as he deepened the kiss. Heat radiated through me and the energy of my mountain lion rose to mingle with Tristan's leopard, yearning, straining to join. Instead of caving to the call, I embraced it, enjoying the extra dimension of pleasure as it wound around me.

I ran my fingers along Tristan's sides, but I wanted more, I needed to touch more. My head grew light, and my heart fluttered in my chest.

Tristan groaned and pushed up.

I shoved him back. With one swift motion, I pulled my shirt off. Tristan snaked his hands up to quickly remove my bra. His hot mouth claimed a nipple. I lost focus. My breath quickened.

Pants. Off. Now. As my nerve endings tingled and called for more, I squirmed and wiggled out of my jeans. I grabbed a condom from Tristan's pocket and tore open the package.

Tristan ripped off my panties. The cold air hit my body. I reached down and returned the favour, shredding Tristan's boxer-briefs from his hard body.

Tristan purred.

My pulse raced, beating, thumping, hammering to the point of pain. I rolled on the condom, and with weak knees, rose above him to guide him in. My mountain lion yowled as I sank down and our bodies joined.

Tristan groaned and sat up to hold me close.

Molten heat spread through me as we moved together in our own dance, making our own time and rhythm. Tristan's talented mouth played with my senses and nerve endings. The room filled with his delicious scent, musky coconut, and our lovemaking. The heady dose made my mind swim as a rising tide consumed my core, breaking waves over and over again on my senses. My canines elongated, and my mountain lion's energy pushed to complete the bond, to claim Tristan as mine, truly and forever. My heart pounded in my chest, as my last orgasm rocked through my body. I bit down on his shoulder and yowled.

Aftershocks rippled through me. Pleasuring tingles raced along my nerves as my heart attempted to recuperate.

Tristan's canines sank into my collarbone, and he growled his release. I sagged into him, consumed with a satisfied warmth, and a sense of belonging.

"You bit me," I mumbled into his neck, after a long quiet moment of pure contentment passed.

"You bit me," he whispered into my hair. "Pretty hard to resist."

He meant the mate bond. It involved biting each other's necks during orgasm, and I'd come pretty close to claiming him. Heck, a few inches over and I would have. As Tristan pulsed inside me, questions clanked around in my mind. Why did I hold off with the mate bond? Why did I wait?

The answer slapped my brain. I needed to fix me, first. The Bola incident had brought to light a lot of baggage I needed to confront and conquer. Tristan was a million times more a man than Dylan. A million times more a mate. I knew that. My heart knew that. But I still hesitated. A mate bond wouldn't heal my trauma. Nor should it. When the time was right, it would happen.

"I want to make sure I'm ready," I said. I wanted to be whole. To be a good mate. To be worthy of Tristan's love.

Tristan's neck twitched under my mouth as he shrugged. "I'm enjoying the practice. Take your time, I'm patient."

"Like a cat?"

"Exactly."

I drifted to sleep with the soft sound of his chuckle.

20

The chirping beside my head woke my mountain lion before the rest of my brain could gather a cohesive thought.

Hunt, she whined.

Sleep slipped from my mind, and my eyes fluttered open. Daylight streamed into the bedroom through the slats of the blinds, reflecting off the stark white of my bed linens. The mussed spot beside me, where Tristan had drifted to sleep holding me, was now empty, and something pinged in my heart. He must've been called to work again. I inhaled his lingering sunshine and citrus scent, cloaked with honeysuckles, and fell back against the soft pillows.

The chirping started again.

Kill! My mountain lion demanded.

Relax. It's my phone, not a bird to eat.

She huffed and raked her claws against my thoughts

before flopping down somewhere. My falcon cackled with glee.

I ignored them both and reached over for my cell phone.

"McNeilly," I barked.

"Morning sunshine," Stan's voice replied. "Are you still in bed? It's almost noon."

"Don't judge me. Night shifts are draining."

A pause. "We worked a day shift yesterday."

My falcon puffed her feathers to sink her head down for more sleep. "Maybe you worked a day shift, but I kept going. Besides, I hate shift work."

"Shit work, or shift work?"

"Both."

Stan sighed. "Did you discover anything?"

"Well, what I told you earlier about Nagato has been confirmed by the Werewolf Alpha previously under Lucien's control."

"That your ex?"

His words stung, but I doubted he meant them to. "Yes. He said Nagato came to visit Lucien and had a private meeting with him. Allan and Clint were sent away shortly after, and Lucien met his ultimate death soon after that."

"And Nagato?"

"Apparently left the horde house hale and hearty."

Stan grunted.

"So Nagato's gone in the wind, either going rogue or he became another loose end to tie up, our one known street-level KK dealer is in the morgue, Allan's unwilling to help in any capacity…" I let my voice trail off.

"What are you getting at?"

Not sure, actually. Good question. "I hate this investigation shit."

"Clearly."

I drummed my fingers along my duvet cover. "Can we put trackers on Nagato's work phone and bank cards?"

"Already done. Though I doubt he'd be stupid enough to use either."

"So we've got nothing?" I sat up and pulled my sheets with me to cover my naked body.

"*Au contraire, mon amie.*"

I cringed. "Stan, your French sucks about as much as my investigation skills."

"Ouch."

"Friends don't let friends spout off clichés in bad French." I stretched my neck by tilting my head side to side. The wounds from Tristan's canines had already scabbed over and the slight twinge of pain brought a smile to my face. The bone numbing weariness from last night had disappeared, replaced with relaxed contentment.

Tristan had worked magic on me in more ways than one.

After the first round, he'd taken control and worked my body until the wee hours of the morning. He'd loved every inch of skin, making me pant, beg and practically sing with delight. The contracting muscles of his toned body had glistened with...

"I thought friends don't let friends skip leg day?" Stan interrupted.

Flustered, I fanned my face and ignored my mountain lion hissing for me to swipe at Stan through the phone. "That too."

I waited for Stan to fill me in, but silence consumed the phone connection instead.

My phone indicated the call hadn't been dropped, and I had full bars.

"Loretta had a storage room," Stan whispered.

"What?" I heard him, but I didn't understand the significance.

"She had a storage room I didn't know about."

"Where, when, why? How'd you find out?"

"An employee from Premium Storage called Loretta's phone to say they hadn't received payment for the next month. I went through her previous credit card statements already and there was nothing on them for this storage facility, but when I went back to the bank statements, I discovered she made regular monthly withdrawals for almost the same amount as the storage employee mentioned."

"Huh." *Crap.* Loretta did have a secret, and it would explain the guilt I smelled from her. "What could she possibly hide? She was an administrative assistant for a pharmaceutical company, right?" Did we even need to unearth her secrets? She'd been killed because of Stan's position with the drug force. Her secrets wouldn't help our investigation so much as they would hurt Stan.

"Maybe she was having an affair," Stan whispered again. His voice caught.

I gripped my phone and spoke as clearly and factually as possible. "No, Stan. She loved you."

"How would you know?" he barked back.

"I smelled it…and more importantly, I didn't smell anything or anyone else. I would've caught another man's scent, either in the house or residual trace amounts from her skin or clothes if she was having an affair. She wasn't, Stan. She loved you."

Silence again, broken by a muffled sob. I squeezed my eyes shut.

"Where's Premium Storage?" I asked. Distraction 101.

"Kingsway Avenue and Mary Hill Bypass," he said. "PoCo."

I checked my clock. Sure enough it was almost noon and traffic always picked up at this time. I lived in Port Coquitlam, or PoCo, one of the municipalities that made up the Tri-Cities, but Stan didn't, it would take him at least forty-five minutes to get here. "Meet you there in an hour?"

"Yeah," he gruffed before hanging up.

When I pulled up to the intersection across from the orange and beige storage buildings, a five minute drive from my place, my mind reeled with possibilities.

What the heck would we find? How badly would it hurt Stan?

I'd purposely arrived early to get an advanced showing, so I'd discover what to prepare Stan for, or in case I needed to burn down the entire complex to save Stan from more heartache.

On my way to the storage facility, I called Stan and suggested letting the forensics team go through the contents first. Technically, the location might hold evidence for an ongoing investigation. Protocol dictated we wait for forensics.

Stan had replied with a single word. "No."

When I tried to push it, he'd barked into the phone. "I asked for *your* help so I wouldn't have to do things by the book. Fuck, Andy!"

My mouth had clamped shut after that. Guess he was anxious about what the room would reveal as well.

If Loretta hurt this man...even her position beyond the living realm wouldn't save her. I'd find a way to make her pay. But somehow that didn't fit. I was missing something. A feeling kept eating at my brain, much like little fish pecking at the food floating on the surface of water. I didn't think Loretta was into anything that would hurt Stan, not in the emotional sense. That didn't sit right in my gut. But why had she kept secrets from Stan. Had she become addicted to drugs? Didn't smell like it. A life of crime? Again, didn't *feel* right.

Whatever the reason, I hoped we'd discover it soon and Stan would get some closure. He might appear to hold it together, and he definitely succeeded to a certain extent, but his despair leaked from every pore.

The storage facility sat on the outskirts of PoCo before the bridge to Maple Ridge. Spanning one city block, it held orange-coloured garage doors and a black wrought iron security gate.

When I pulled past the gate and into the parking lot, I blew out a bunch of air. Stan had beat me here. Guess I'd have to kiss the advanced viewing goodbye. I maneuvered the Poo-Lude into the guest parking spot beside Stan's car. He drove like a maniac, so it shouldn't really surprise me he made good time. But it did.

As I wrenched open the driver's side door, and clambered out, Stan appeared by my side with an owly-looking, middle-aged woman with skinny legs and dyed orange hair. Her mane frizzed out in a mullet-esque fro. Did she dye her hair to match the company colours? I tilted my head, but bit back the snarky words.

"About time!" Stan growled.

My mountain lion perked up and mentally swatted at him.

I grimaced and slammed the door shut, trying to ignore the loud shriek of rusted hinges. "If I'd realized you'd break every speed limit and traffic law on your way here, I would've left sooner. As it is, I'm fifteen minutes early. Bite me."

"Is that what you say to your Vampire friends?"

The owl lady shuffled her feet.

I glared at Stan.

He narrowed his gaze.

Silence.

Stan grunted and nodded at the owl lady. "This is Mrs. Smith. She runs the place. She's going to show us Loretta's storage room."

I jerked my chin as a hello. "Were you present when Loretta opened an account to rent the space?"

Stan rolled his eyes, and Mrs. Smith cast him a wary glance before shuffling her feet again. Nervous fumes wafted off her skin.

"Easy there, Ace," Stan grumbled at me. "I've already asked Mrs. Smith questions. Including that one."

"Oh," I said. How much sooner had he arrived? From Mrs. Smith's shaky limbs, it looked like she'd received a full interrogation. I squinted at Stan, and he puffed his chest out. So he'd intentionally arrived early to ask questions. Ones he wanted to hear the answers to alone. He must've been in PoCo when he called me. Rat bastard.

His mate, my falcon squawked.

Fair enough. The bird had a point. I'd be a mess if anything... My eyes tingled, and I squeezed them shut. If something happened to Tristan, I'd be a mess. But after I recovered, I'd turn over every rock, burn every bridge, and break any rule necessary to get answers.

"Have you already checked the room, too?" I sighed.

"If I got dressed for no reason, I'm going to be supremely pissed."

"No," Stan barked and turned toward the facility. "This way."

We walked to the pedestrian door beside the security gate for vehicles, and Mrs. Smith keyed in four numbers —0814—before the security pad buzzed and the lock released. Loretta's storage compartment was located at the far corner of the complex. As a small storage option, it sat beside six identical doors in the room. To access it, Loretta could drive up to the main room's door, but she had to get out and walk into the main room to access her compartment. She paid $47.50 a month in cash and had never missed a payment during the last eleven months.

On her insurance form, she claimed the room stored personal items.

Mrs. Smith talked and talked, with a nervous quiver in her tone, but the truth of her words rolled over me. She might look cagey, but she hadn't lied the entire time she walked us to Loretta's storage room.

When we reached compartment 102, Mrs. Smith turned to us and handed Stan a plain gold key.

"I'll leave you to go through your wife's belongings." Though she spoke to Stan, she stared at the floor. "My condolences for your loss."

Stan grunted and gingerly plucked the key from the woman's hands. "Thank you."

Mrs. Smith nodded and ducked around us to scurry away.

Stan turned toward me. "What if it's rigged?"

"Loretta's storage compartment?"

Stan nodded.

I glanced at the orange door. "She was an administrative assistant, not an international spy. What the heck would she booby trap it with?"

Stan shrugged. "Loretta is...was...fuck!"

He cleared his throat and looked away. His hands bunched into fists at his waist. "Loretta was always resourceful."

I hesitated. Maybe I was closer to the truth than I realized. What if Loretta was a spy? I glanced at Stan's expression as it closed off, but not before the same painful thought flashed across his face.

"Well, let's get this done," Stan grumbled before stepping forward.

I flung my arm out and stopped him. "Let me."

With my nose pressed to the seams of the door, I inhaled long drags of air, followed with short successive ones. I took in the scents and emotional traces left behind.

Loretta. Guilt. Fear.

No one else, and certainly no explosives. I snatched the key from Stan. As I turned the lock, my fera-heightened senses strained to pick up anything extra. Falcons and mountain lions lacked in the smelling department, but they had considerably better hearing. Other than the lock flipping into place, turning the key resulted in nothing suspicious. Clean. No triggers.

With a glance and a shrug at Stan, I stepped in front of him and pulled the door open.

Nothing happened.

Not sure what I expected, but last I checked, human shield wasn't a Carus ability. I had bullet scars on my arm and ass to prove it.

A gust of stale air flowed from the room, and an old two-drawer filing cabinet and one storage box greeted us.

"A box?" Stan choked out behind me. "A box?"

His pissed off scent flowed around me, and I turned to see his face twist up.

"Mean anything?" I asked.

"She went to an awful lot of trouble to hide this box from me. There's got to be three dozen in the attic, and I never fucking touch those. She knew that."

We turned to the small room, and I hesitated to walk in farther. This was Stan's business.

"You first," I said. Despite wanting to discover Loretta's secret, find her killer, and get to the bottom of the possible KK link, Stan needed to unearth this mystery.

Stan pulled surgical gloves out of his pocket and tossed a pair at me before putting on his own. I mimicked his actions. Guess he wasn't completely throwing out the book.

Stan cleared his throat and stalked past me. His shoulders bumped mine, but the small space made body checking inevitable. He didn't do it on purpose. I think.

After squatting beside the mysterious box for a few minutes, Stan took a deep breath and flipped the lid off with a stiff index finger. His shoulders tightened, and his back straightened. He growled.

My mountain lion pushed forward, wanting to shift

and protect. I shushed her, but she refused to settle, instead, she paced back and forth, put on edge by Stan's aggressive posture and angry scent.

He dipped his hand in the box and pulled out a wad of white shredded paper.

"Are you kidding me?" I lunged forward and looked in the box. Sure enough. Stuffed full of machine-shredded office paper. The smell of bulk toner lingered in the box.

"She always liked puzzles," Stan grumbled.

We exchanged a glance and then went back to staring at the tangle of paper.

"A bit extreme for a hobby," I said. "It will take days to piece this crap together."

Stan nodded and shoved the lid back on. "I'll give it to the forensics department. There's a few puzzle geeks on the team who'll get a hard-on trying to put this back together." He straightened and turned to me. "What does it smell like?"

I shrugged. "Nothing of note. Smells like an office. Paper, pens, and whatnot. A few people, other than Loretta, but no one I know, and no emotional imprint. Either the shredders are sociopaths, or they had no idea what was being disposed."

"Or they wore gloves."

My mouth clamped shut, and I nodded. If they'd been really emotional, their scents would still linger on the paper, but no point in debating the finer aspects of blood hound-ery to Stan.

"What about my wife?" Stan asked.

"Loretta's scent is the freshest, and she was scared when she collected it."

"Afraid of getting caught." Stan's voice remained factual, but his jaw clenched, and his hands balled into fists again.

"Where'd she work again? In an office, right? Tancher Pharmaceuticals?"

Stan froze and turned to me.

"The more we learn, the more I think Loretta's death had nothing to do with you as a cop and everything to do with what she hid from you."

Stan's gaze cut away. "The thought crossed my mind as well."

"But?"

"But, it doesn't shake this...feeling. Her... What happened to her is on me. She should've told me. She should've confided in me,"

"Maybe she wanted to protect you."

"I SHOULD'VE PROTECTED HER!" Stan bellowed. "Me!" He thumbed his chest and then his voice cut off in a strangled cry. "Me..."

His shoulders shook as he turned around and stomped out of the storage room. I let him go. He needed some time. I ached to take his pain away, but a hug from me, no matter how well intended, wouldn't go down well right now.

What the heck was the point of being the big bad Carus if I couldn't help my friends?

I squared my shoulders, took a deep breath and

turned to the filing cabinet. One yank and the drawer flung open, nearly knocking me on my ass.

Empty. Fucking hell.

After shutting the cabinet gently, I opened the bottom drawer.

Also empty.

"Fuck!" I jumped to my feet and threw my foot forward, booting the cabinet across the small space and into the wall.

Sharp pain radiated from my toe, and I bit my lip to prevent howling. The cabinet dented the drywall, and the front end fell heavy against the floor.

Then something metal slid inside the cabinet.

My eyes narrowed.

With supe strength, I hauled the cabinet to me and wrenched open the drawers, while holding it on an angle. Still empty.

I tilted the cabinet. Swish...

Again, metal sliding on metal. I tiled the cabinet forward.

Swish...

My heartbeat thudded in my ears. Could this be it? The key to solving everything? Hoisting the cabinet to head level, I planted my ear against the cool metal and repeated the process.

"What the fuck are you doing?" Stan demanded.

I yelped and almost dropped the cabinet. Taking a deep breath, I ignored him and repeated the tilting process.

Bottom drawer.

I set the cabinet down and ripped out the bottom drawer. When I flipped the drawer over, the fluorescent light above revealed no second compartment. No room for any false bottoms. My heart hammered in my chest. I wanted to find something. For Stan.

Loretta's scent clung heavily to the drawer. After I flung it to the side, I turned to sniff out the rest of the cabinet and froze.

A black object reflected light from a cut out groove on the bottom of the compartment, the one used to house the bottom drawer.

A phone.

An ultra thin one. I reached in, picked it up, and rocked back on my heels. The plastic of my gloves stuck to the sleek surface like super-grip dish gloves. The phone smelled of Loretta and no one else. I powered it on and after the brand logo, a password screen appeared.

I glanced over at Stan, expecting him to be leaning over my shoulder, mouth-breathing on my neck, but he squatted a few feet away, rummaging through the shredded paper box.

"Look at this," he said, before I had a chance to announce my find.

How could he miss it? I'd been dancing the salsa with his deceased wife's filing cabinet. I held my breath, clutched the phone and closed the distance to hover beside my friend.

He'd pieced together a few strands of paper to make out a header, or some sort of logo.

It looked familiar.

An oval with two feather-like drawings separated by two crude parallel lines and a company name. It resembled an Egyptian hieroglyph.

My stomach sank.

A hieroglyph much like the one tattooed on the inside of Aahil's wrist.

"Interesting..." I said. Good thing Stan couldn't detect the waves of unease leaking out my pores. Maybe there was a connection between Loretta's death and the KK dealers after all...But what? Had Loretta's death been caused by Stan's involvement with the KK investigation, or because of something Loretta had been up to?

"It's the logo for Tancher Pharmaceuticals."

Huh. My mind reeled to connect the dots with the new information. The logo was from the company Loretta worked for, not the KK dealer. Many hieroglyphs had a similar appearance, and Tancher Pharmaceuticals was a company in the Lower Mainland. Maybe that's why the logo looked familiar.

My brain convulsed as the niggling feeling from earlier returned.

Did Aahil have some sort of connection with the pharmaceutical company?

I pursed my lips and racked my brain for a mental image of the dealer's tattoo. But the harder I tried to focus on the memory, the blurrier it became until the image slipped away.

Stupid brain.

I'd kill for an upgrade to an eidetic memory right now.

Stan looked up at me, the tattered shred of paper delicately held in his two upturned palms. With wide eyes and upturned brows, Stan's expression morphed into one of almost hope. The best thing I'd seen on his face since Loretta's death.

Maybe I'd keep my mouth shut and pay Mr. Aahil the dealer a visit to confirm or dismiss my suspicions. Stan teetered so close to the edge right now, I didn't want to push him over with a shoddy memory, not when it might incite a cop versus gang shoot out.

"Why would she keep shredded documents from her work in a personal storage locker?" I asked.

Stan's shoulders drooped. "I don't know. Do you have anything better?"

I held Loretta's secret phone up and waved it a little. "You bet I do."

21

The rush of adrenaline and motivation quickly seeped from my veins with each attempt and failure of Stan's to unlock Loretta's phone. He tried birthdays and anniversaries, but nothing worked, and his momentary reprieve from doom and gloom crashed back, physically weighing down his shoulders. I watched his body language slump and finally ripped the phone from his hands.

"There's nothing special about this phone," I said. "Let your tech group handle this. It won't take long for them to crack it."

Stan nodded, took the phone back, and bagged it. After we moved out of the storage room, he taped up the door with official crime scene tape he grabbed from his car. We walked in silence to the entrance of the storage compound. Stan said a gruff goodbye before flopping into his vehicle and driving away.

With no reason to hang around, I stuck my head in

the office to thank Mrs. Smith. "We're leaving now," I said. "Thank you for letting us in."

Her owly face popped up from behind the counter. "You're welcome, dear. Any idea when the VPD will release the storage locker?"

"No idea, but I wouldn't count on it happening any time soon."

She bobbed her head and turned to shuffle some papers on her desk.

I let myself out, hopped in the car, and drove home. The stale smell of my empty apartment greeted me. Only one way to make it better. I put on a pot of coffee and got out my laptop. Time to investigate Loretta's employer—Tancher Pharmaceuticals.

I checked the VPD database with my remote access. Nothing.

I checked the SRD database with my remote access, and thanked the inefficiency of my former employer. They hadn't denied my access yet. Someone in IT missed the memo, but the access did me little good. Still nothing.

I checked the Tancher website. Founded by a rich American by the name of Tancher Isis, the pharmaceutical company was one of North America's most prominent and successful companies for research and prescription drug production. They had a bunch of fancy badges on their website and declarations of their integrity from customers and industry experts.

I didn't buy it.

A drug dealer with the same or similar tattoo to a

drug company? The same drug company Loretta worked for, the same dealer of the drug found with Loretta's body? Too coincidental for me to ignore. But I was missing the pieces for the whole centre of a puzzle.

First, I needed to confirm Aahil's tattoo was the same as the logo.

I needed to hit the streets to do that.

WHEN I WALKED INTO THE SIXTH TATTOO parlour of the day, the smells of green soap, A&D ointment, and cleaning supplies rushed my nose like an angry mob. On a flattened chair, a muscular man in his late twenties lay on his side with his arm draped over his face. He successfully hid his expression, but wafts of hot metal and canned ham gave away his pain. A female artist hunched over his ribs, dreadlocks held back with a bandanna and what looked like macramé rope.

On another chair, a young woman sat back with her earbuds in, humming along to a song, while another artist with shaggy hair and a dense brown beard worked on her full sleeve. Mesmerized by the colours, I stepped closer. The piece depicted an ocean scene with swirls of blues ranging from shallow water to deep angry ocean. Seagulls glided in bands of wind while the Sleeping Beauty mountain range from up north sat behind mist to watch it all.

Beautiful.

Before I discovered my inherent Shifter skills, I'd dreamed with my high school girlfriends of potential tattoos, coming up with different ideas of what we wanted to get once we came of age.

After discovering I was a Shifter, my tattoo dreams faded. Ink didn't stick around when shifting from one form to another. After any transformation, all that remained was clear, clean, unblemished skin and a distant memory of how awesome the tattoo looked. Even my bullet scars would fade over time until they disappeared.

If I'd been tattooed prior to bonding with my feras, I might've kept the permanent ink.

Now standing in a tattoo parlour and gazing on the beautifully intricate design, I wished again I'd acted on those dreams and rebelled against my parents all those years ago.

Then again, maybe not. One of my not-so-great ideas had been to get a stamp tattoo on my ass that read, "Canadian Grade-A Beef."

Dodged a bullet there.

Still, I loved tattoos. I got one once to go undercover, and if I wasn't a Shifter, I'd probably be covered in them. But the voices of my feras calling me into the woods when I turned fourteen changed a lot of things for me, not just my dreams of inked skin.

"Can I help you?" the receptionist asked.

I turned to the young woman I'd noted when I entered the shop. She had thick, jet black hair, cut into a blunt bob with straight bangs, and styled like a pin-up girl. Her dark, penciled-in eyebrows rose almost theatrically in an arch over her black-brown eyes. Powdered white skin made her brightly-painted red lips stand out. She looked like the slutty version of Snow White. Maybe the troubled younger sibling.

"Yeah, you can help me," I said. "Can I talk to one of the artists?"

Her dark lined eyes narrowed and a hand went to her well-rounded hip. "You looking to get some ink?"

Her voice conveyed skepticism. What the hell?

Maybe I should've worn something different, but all sorts of people got tattoos nowadays. Sure, I wasn't trying to go deep undercover, but what made me so unbelievable?

"Yes," I said.

She snorted. "You look like a cop."

Well, fuck me sideways. I'd lost my game. I'd never been pegged faster in my entire career with the SRD. Then again, Tristan read me like a naughty tabloid magazine. My friend Mel sometimes knew my thoughts before I did, and even Stan and Ben picked up on some of my facial cues now. Having a readable expression was apparently some kind of nasty side effect of regaining my humanity and becoming more open to relationships. Well, crap. Opening up to my friends and Tristan was one thing, but strangers? Heck no. Not happening.

Now aware of my deteriorating *condition*, I'd have to readjust.

With a blank expression, I replied to the receptionist. "No, actually, not a cop." Not yet anyway. "But I am helping them with an investigation." Truth. The paperwork still hadn't gone through, and although I wasn't working pro-bono, payment as a consultant was significantly lower than working as an officer. Go figure.

Her full lips twitched, twisting her expression into something so smug I wanted to punch it off her face.

The beast rumbled her approval, but I shook away the idea of punching her. She read me once, she wouldn't read me again.

"So, can I speak with one of the artists?" Without moving, I loosened control on my animal magnetism. Even with it tightly coiled, it leached out and attracted norms, but sometimes I purposely let go to get my way. It made things go a lot faster.

The receptionist's eyes softened and her body lost its stiff posture. "Ken and Barbie are both busy right now. They don't like to be interrupted." She lifted her chin toward the two artists I'd already noticed.

Ken and Barbie? Really? How'd she say that line without cracking up?

"But..." She licked her lips. "Butch is taking his lunch right now. Had a no show. Let me go ask him."

I nodded and waited as she sashayed down the hallway at the back of the main room. She turned the corner, and I followed the conversation from the short distance with my heightened Shifter hearing.

Butch. The receptionist's voice turned from hard and sarcastic to sweet honey. My back straightened at the abrupt change, and I took a few steps forward to hear better, errantly flipping through some workbooks.

Back for more? Butch asked. His voice came off deep and growly. Kind of like a masculine version of Baloo, my bear fera. *I would've thought after I bent you over my drawing table earlier, you'd had enough.*

The receptionist made the same "mmmm" sound I did when I saw specialty cupcakes. If only my hearing had an off button, or volume control. Not sure I wanted to hear how this conversation slipped into the gutter, but they might reveal something—

No, but I'm getting hot just thinking about it. She continued describing just how *hot* she got.

Err...Gross.

Then what do you want? Butch asked.

Besides your thick...

I quickly turned away and walked to the small sitting area to look outside. Eavesdropping sometimes went in unexpected directions. It didn't mean I'd tune out, it just meant my ears would burn.

...some woman wants to talk to you.

To me? His tone turned skeptical.

Well, she purred, *she wants to talk to a tattoo artist. Says she's with the police.*

Fuck that.

She has a nice rack. Maybe we could, you know...invite her to join us. You said I could pick the next one.

Butch growled and what followed was wet and sloppy.

Join them? Not likely. Not ever. Images of my Sid-induced dream spiralled into my memory, and I squeezed my eyes shut. I needed to run away with Tristan to a tropical beach with whiskey.

The receptionist sauntered back ten minutes later with a satisfied grin on her face. Her lipstick bright, shiny, and re-applied. "Butch agreed to answer your questions. Please follow me."

I nodded and followed her into the back room where a large, over-muscled man waited. The receptionist's perfume coated his skin along with other, less pleasant, smells. He perched with his butt on the edge of his drawing table, arms crossed. A black T-shirt hugged his bodybuilder frame, accentuating his lack of a neck, and biceps that could probably twist off beer caps. His bald head shone under the fluorescent lights and every inch of exposed skin had ink, with the exception of his face and head.

His eyebrows bunched together, and his lips turned down when he first took me in. Confusion flittered across his face.

Probably wondering what the receptionist saw in me.

The instant my animal magnetism hit him, his eyes widened and his mouth twisted into a smile.

"How can I help you?" he asked, his tone pleasant with a side of flirty.

"I wanted to ask you about a tattoo."

He nodded and pushed off the table to close the distance between us. "Okay."

"Your website said this tattoo shop specializes in hieroglyphics, among other things. Do all the artists here do them, or is there one in particular I should speak to?"

"Ken specializes in fine-line black and gray and photorealism. Barbie does a lot of Japanese and colour. You're talking to the hieroglyphics guy. I also do traditional and tribal."

"You must have a real steady hand." I groaned on the inside. My game had seriously deteriorated. A steady hand? Really? That wouldn't exactly have the man swooning at my feet and offering up all his information.

Butch's eyes shuttered, and his lips twitched. "I'm very good with my hands."

The receptionist let out a little moan behind me.

Then again, maybe it didn't matter what I said. I had my beast mojo on my side. Relief washed through my body. "If I showed you a hieroglyph, would you recognize the tattoo and remember who got it?"

"Maybe. Depends. Some are very unique and intricate, some are super common. Some are off the wall." He jerked his chin toward the wall plastered with pictures of generic tattoos.

I nodded and pulled out the letterhead from Loretta's shredded files. When I flipped it around, Butch's expression closed instantly. His eyes narrowed, and his posture stiffened.

"You need to leave." Butch's voice deepened and developed a cold edge.

"Excuse me?"

"Leave," he demanded.

"You can't tell me who you tattooed this on?"

Butch's shoulders rounded, and he took a step forward. I sensed, more than saw, the receptionist close in behind me. I could easily take out both of them. Fear didn't grip my heart. Annoyance did. The room developed a honeyed vanilla scent.

They'd been spelled.

I could gyrate on this guy's face or shove a million dollars at him, and I still wouldn't get any answers—not from him or anyone else in the shop.

But I didn't need to.

Their silence and spelled behaviour answered for me.

The logo matched the tattoo. And not just anyone's, someone scary and rich enough to hire a Witch to spell the artists.

Aahil was linked to Tancher Pharmaceuticals, and I'd bet my entire stash of chocolate Easter eggs, Aahil was connected to Loretta's death.

B-i-n-g-o.

22

The tattoo parlour left me feeling dirty. Although I held another piece to the puzzle, I lacked solid evidence. My beast growled for me to tear into something, or someone; my mountain lion paced and whined for Tristan like some wanton harlot with nothing better to do; and my falcon kept sending images of the moon-lit night sky with a gentle breeze. If things kept going downhill, one of my feras would get her wish.

I had money on the falcon.

As the sun set and the world dulled under the dusk lighting, I stalked down Granville Street, and passed a familiar bar.

And stopped.

Why the hell not? Invisible grime already coated my skin. Maybe the man sitting at the bar could tell me more than Wick. I squared my shoulders, pivoted and walked into the establishment. Hopefully, Aahil and his gang wouldn't be here. If they popped by, I'd have to get out quickly.

No thugs greeted me on entry, and after surveying the area, I deemed it safe enough to seek out Clint. The human servant's familiar frame stood out amongst the other patrons, and I headed straight for him.

Broad shoulders hunched over the bar and presumably a stiff drink. A redhead with a killer body and giant knockers sat to his right, leaning into him. She batted her eyelashes and murmured in his ear. Absolute smut. She probably didn't intend for others to hear, but with Shifter senses, I couldn't help it.

The rumours were true, redheads were feisty. I'd never again look at a jar of petroleum jelly and a papaya the same way.

I walked up to Clint and sat down on the seat beside him without saying a word.

His glass was empty.

The red-head leaned forward and speared me with a green-eyed death stare.

"You're wasting your time, honey," I said, moving my fingers in a circle in front of me and Clint to signal the bartender. He straightened, and I held up two fingers.

"Excuse me?" Jessica Rabbit sneered, using the opportunity to press her ample boobs into Clint's arm.

"He prefers blondes."

Clint snorted and accepted the new drink from the bartender when he slid it to him. Clint lifted the amber fluid in a silent salute to me. I returned the gesture with my own drink before sliding a fifty on the counter for the bartender.

Jessica's mouth gaped open, and her beautiful face contorted into something ugly.

Clint turned to her. "She's right. But if you want a pity screw later, I'll take you up on it."

She gasped before slapping Clint across the face. The angle was weird and her form terrible, but Clint took it without a word. She paused to see if she'd get a reaction and when she didn't, she grabbed her pink martini and stalked off.

"What do you want?" Clint said, his tone dark and unwelcoming.

"I've been thinking," I started.

"I'm not a medical professional. If you've hurt yourself, go to the fucking emergency room."

I ignored his barb, and took it as a good sign he'd perked up a little. "You can survive a torn out neck, getting skewered with a sword and the death of a Master Vampire you're blood bound and sworn to. I think you're some kind of immortal yourself."

Clint peered at me over the rim of his glass and took a deep swig of the amber fluid. "Is that so?"

"That or you're part jellyfish."

Clint coughed, choking a little and glared at me before setting his glass down.

"Sid called you *neo-bhàsmhor* a number of times. I searched it on the internet and found out it's Gaelic for immortal. At the time, it made no sense. Of course, you're immortal. You were a Master Vampire's bonded human servant. But now...now...I think you're immortal all on your own."

He drummed his fingers along the bar, gaze going distant. After I figured he'd remain mute on the subject, he spoke up. "Took you long enough. It's a good thing we never needed your skill as an investigator."

I snorted. He obviously had a terrible memory. Lucien ordered me to investigate a number of things. I just sucked at it. "So you're immortal?"

"Yes."

Something clicked. My neurons fired on all cylinders. "Wait a minute. *The* immortal? Like the movie with the television spin-off series? The one from the 80s with the Scottish Highlander in a kilt?" I surveyed Clint. "Can't picture you in the get-up."

"You'd fucking hump my leg if you saw me in a kilt."

"Gross." My face twisted. People turned and stared, but I ignored them and leaned away from Clint. "Why are you such a pervert?"

Clint shrugged his massive shoulders. "Passes the time."

Strangely, I believed him. Half the time, I got the impression his twisted words were an act, put on to fill his role or hide his true self. The other half... Well, the bruised, although consenting, women leaving his hotel room, and some of the hateful things he'd said to me made sure no one got close to Clint. "How'd your secret get out?"

He drummed his fingers along the bar again as he

contemplated his answer. "A few decades ago, a woman discovered my true nature."

"Would this be the woman fifty years ago you were nice to?" A while ago, I'd asked if he ever tried to play nice, instead of his mean, perverted self, and he'd admitted to an attempt. When I'd asked him how it went, he'd said "not well," and the conversation went downhill from there.

Clint speared me with an icy look.

"Sorry. Carry on."

"Later on in her life, she had a son with another man and told him all about me."

"I think I know where this is going."

Clint nodded. "The prick wrote a screenplay on it for his writing class project, and it turned into a whole fucking franchise. I had to deal with Lucien bellowing, 'There can be only one!' for years."

I laughed.

"Asshole made me dress in a kilt every Robbie Burns day and recite lines from the movie." His wording may have been harsh, but his shoulders sank and his tone softened when he mentioned Lucien.

"You miss him."

"Fuck off."

Silence stretched across the bar. What would make a man, already immortal by his birthright, sign up as Lucien's human servant? There was more to this story, but gauging from Clint's flattened mouth, slightly turned down at the corners, I doubted he'd tell me more about Lucien. "So how much of the movie was based on truth? Is beheading really the only way to kill you?"

"Like I'd tell you."

"Well, I could always test out my theories until one of them works."

"By all means, kitten, you could try."

I smiled. He smiled. Neither one of us joking.

23

Clint had a whole lot of attitude for me, but little in the way of new information. He confirmed what I'd already learned from Wick. I left Clint to his whiskey and made my way home.

Or at least started to.

As I drove home cranking Metallica from my car stereo, another thought crossed my mind. I glanced at the clock. Late afternoon. May as well. I took the exit that led me up a winding mountain road. I parked, got out of the hunk of junk car, and found the nearest dispenser of caffeine.

The university campus smelled of paper, sweat, and lusty youth. A gentle breeze rolled up the small mountain, carrying the tang of pine, spruce, and alder in the cool, salt-laden air. Warm frothy milk from my cinnamon-sprinkled cappuccino coated my tongue as I walked from the coffee shop to the West Mall Complex.

The internet research, the tattoo-artist angle, and the

Clint interrogation had been a bit of a bust as far as concrete evidence went. With no desire to track down the drug dealer and ask to look at his ink for a direct comparison to the pharmaceutical company's logo, I needed to find another avenue for my investigation.

Maybe the gang squad at the VPD had a record of Aahil's tattoos. That would give me the confirmation I wanted. I had no plans whatsoever to allow the norm judicial system to take care of Loretta's murderer, but if I ripped off some guys head or turned my back to let Stan do whatever he wished, I wanted to know beyond a doubt the person we picked up was the right one. No more acting like the SRD assassin and asking no questions.

Mental note: ask Stan tomorrow about the gang squad.

I'd call him now, but he was off duty, and he needed the rest and shuteye more than I did—assuming he managed to do either.

Instead, I took a detour on my way home and ended up at my alma-matter, looking for a rake-like Demon named Takkenmann. Here, everyone knew him as Professor Westman, and, although the university was aware of his Demon status and responsible for his presence, it wasn't clear whether the students had any inkling to his supernatural essence. Given Takkenmann's efforts to hide his Demon scent, the student body probably had no clue.

The Demon's unnaturally strong, and fake, Witch

scent coated the hallway as I made my way to Professor Westman's office.

When a sadistic Demon named Bola had rampaged through the Lower Mainland over a month ago, I'd attempted to slip into a fourth year Demonology class to see if I could learn anything helpful. I discovered another Demon instead.

Takkenmann.

As one of Bola's associates, he tried to rend my flesh like one of his animal carcasses. I'd shifted into a bear and bashed his head repeatedly into the cement flooring. Carus, one; Nether realm being, zero.

We made a deal: I stopped bashing his head into the ground, and he promised to tell me everything he could. He also had an agreement with the university for his services as a professor in demonic studies. One of their stipulations prevented Takkenmann from leaving campus, so not only did Takkenmann have to answer all my questions, he couldn't avoid me either.

I definitely preferred this method of Demon info-sourcing to the alternative. I no longer had to dance naked for Sid the Seducer.

Holding my breath, I rapped my knuckles on the solid door and waited in a cloud of Witch stink. Takkenmann wore a charm to mask his demonic almond scent. It worked, but it was a bit overkill. My nose continued to shrivel as I waited. He was in there.

I knocked harder.

Wafts of vanilla and honey, tainted with Demonic almond, leaked through the door seals. No need to question whether he knew who stood on the other side of the wooden slab.

Should I kick the door in?

No. Way too dramatic.

I reached forward and turned the knob. Open-sesame. The cold metal turned easily, and I opened the door, wincing as the hinges creaked.

Takkenmann's long frame folded in a chair behind his large wooden desk. His angular, sunken features, no less disturbing than the first time I saw them, remained stiff as he glared at me. His long limbs stretched out across his desk to where he laced his long fingers together. I watched the skin around his knuckles turn pale as each footstep brought me closer to his desk.

"Carus," he hissed between clenched teeth. "To what do I owe this *honour*?"

His tone implied it was anything but. I smiled and pulled the guest chair away from his desk and plopped down on the dilapidated faded green cushion.

"I have some questions," I said.

Takkenmann tensed and his eyes darted to the side. "Why should I provide any answers for you?"

"If you answer my questions, I promise not to beat you soundly in your own office."

Takkenmann's lips compressed, and his knuckles turned stark white. If he squeezed his fingers any harder, he'd probably break a few.

"Ask," he said.

A smile spread across my face. He had few options to deny me and nowhere to run. He already swore to answer my questions, too, so his defiance was unnecessary.

"What do you know of King's Krank?" I asked.

The Demon flinched. "It's a street drug."

I tsked and shook my head. "You know more than that, and I seem to recall a promise of yours to answer my questions fully."

"It's a street drug that has the ability to change the genetic makeup of the user."

I stilled. I'd expected him to name Tancher Pharmaceuticals, or Aahil, or even Bola, as much as I dreaded that possibility. But changing the genetic makeup? That hadn't entered the scope of my mental processing at all. "What do you mean?"

"Some case studies have shown norms develop supernatural features or abilities."

"What case studies?"

Takkenmann shrugged. "They're unpublished. Case studies need to be peer moderated before they are published in an acclaimed scientific journal. A few have crossed my desk, but I don't know the researchers named on the document. The names seemed fake, and they used a scientific name for KK. After reading the news headlines, I made the connection."

Huh.

"Do you have the case study still? Why would they send the paper to a professor of demonology?"

"They wanted my input on the supernatural aspect. Although I teach demonology, I'm also the professor for a number of more general supernatural courses. Regardless, I provided my comments and sent the research paper back." He hesitated before clamping his mouth shut.

"Answer fully," I reminded him.

"I don't think they intend to publish the article. The phrasing in their letter gave me the impression they distributed the article for feedback on how to improve. But this is conjecture."

"Do you have the address or names recorded anywhere?"

Takkenmann glanced around his office. I followed suit. His desk and shelves were covered in stacks of folders and loose leaf papers. My shoulders sank with my stomach.

"Somewhere..." Takkenmann trailed off.

"Do you have an assistant?"

"Yes." Takkenmann's lips twitched up. He had an assistant all right, and I doubted she helped him with any research or office organization, so much as his physical needs. Demon pervert.

"Well, get her to look for the information. In the meantime, please summarize the research."

"They found in one percent of trials, norms took on supernatural abilities or features, and not just a little. A lot."

"They became super supes?"

Takkenmann's smile was slow, and dark. I wanted to scratch it off his face. "Yes."

So someone could create their own personal super supernatural army. Ice flowed up my spine and settled at the base of my skull. I shivered. The last thing this city needed was another douchebag epidemic where someone or something went on a rampage.

Takkenmann eased back in his chair and re-laced his fingers across his lap. "Is there anything else I can help you with, Carus?"

"What happened to the other ninety-nine percent of the trials?"

"Some died. Most survived and remained useless norms."

I stared at Takkenmann and willed him to elaborate.

"Around fourteen percent of the trials exhibited supernatural abilities or features before overdosing, twenty-five percent experienced a mind-debilitating high before overdosing and the remaining sixty percent experienced 'the best high ever' without any adverse side effects."

Huh. That explained why addicts continued to use the drug. Anything to get that next great high, consequences be damned.

"Thank you for your time, Takkenmann."

The Demon nodded and made a sweeping gesture at the door. "The pleasure was all yours, Carus. I hope to never see you again."

I stood, flipped the Demon the bird and walked to the door. "Trust me, you're not on my Christmas card list, either."

24

My apartment was empty. Again.

No Tristan. Again.

My shoulder's drooped and a long sigh escaped my lungs.

Whatever. I might want to jump him every second, but I refused to become a needy girl obsessed with her boyfriend's every move and whereabouts twenty-four-seven. As much as I wanted to text him to get his sexy feline ass over here, I also didn't want to lose myself in him. I made that mistake with Dylan a long time ago, and I refused to make it again. Space was good for personal growth.

I sighed and flopped on the couch. Nothing on the television.

No new emails or posts on social media.

Ben and his coven were still away for their meeting with the Elders. Ben had warned me there'd be backlash for him and his coven for the Bola incident. Sure, Christopher, Patty, and Matt had summoned the destructive Demon behind Ben's back, but as their mentor, Ben was responsible for all their actions.

He promised to call when it was over and made me promise not to interfere. He'd failed the Witch community and needed to make restitution. I hoped the meeting didn't last much longer and the punishments doled out were fair, but not too extreme. I missed singing with that brat pack for karaoke night, and my mind thought up awful possibilities when left on its own. Ben promised the Elders wouldn't kill him or his coven. I hoped for everyone's sake Ben was right. If they harmed my boy, I wouldn't hold back the beast. I'd make them pay.

The beast rumbled her approval and stretched.

Simmer down, I told her. *They haven't been gone long.*

Ben said to give it at least a month or two before panicking. He'd taken a leave from work, along with the rest of his coven. Apparently, the Elders believed in long-lasting punishments.

The beast huffed and relaxed, leaving me again to my thoughts.

But rarely did my thoughts get much alone time. A cold shudder racked my body as if a sheet of death rolled over me—my peace and quiet shattered.

It is time, a voice slithered in my head. *Come to me.*

My body shook as wave after glacial wave washed through me, urging me toward the window—to take flight and leave humanity behind.

Well, why not? I didn't have any plans for tonight anyway. May as well go out and tempt crazy.

With the compulsion riding me as liquid ice in my veins, I stumbled toward open air. With each step, movement became easier and within seconds I shifted to the falcon and was aloft in the fall night sky, heading in the direction of the summons.

The flight was short. The call came from the west side of Pitt River, near Widgeon Creek. I used to canoe here to find isolation and run through the mountain forest.

Near the mouth of Widgeon Creek, the grass grew tall and the marsh-like land fed the loamy scent in the air. As soon as I touched down, I shifted back to human and waited. The wind sifted through the tall blades of grass. Probably home to a gazillion deer ticks.

Grass brushed against my shins, flicking sharp edges against smooth skin. The bushes rustled and the leaves on nearby trees swished in the breeze. The cold shakes returned, and I crossed my arms over my naked chest to stay warm. Goosebumps pebbled up along my skin.

Anytime now.

Patience, Carus, the reptilian voice replied. The wind picked up speed and howled through the long grass and reeds. The foul musky scent I associated with snakes during hot summers on the Sunshine Coast floated in the air. I blanched. The fera smelled like mink poop.

Something slithered over my bare foot.

"Gah!" I jumped two feet in the air and turned. A

garter snake studied me. She coiled into a tight ball near my right foot. She could touch me all she wanted, but one touch of my forefinger, and I'd absorb her into my body.

"A garter snake?" Really? Not exactly helping my street cred, or my badass image as the Carus.

The snake tongued the air, probably tasting my disappointment. *Be faithful in small things because it is in them that your strength lies.*

Did this fera seriously just quote Mother Teresa to me? Well, damn. I sighed and sat down. She slid onto my outstretched arm, and wound around my wrist.

It is time, Carus.

I know. I reached out and touched her nubby snout with my forefinger. The moment my skin contacted hers, ice flowed through my veins. She lost her brown and soft yellow colouring, and faded into ghost white before my energy hoovered her into my body like a dust cloud.

Inside, the effect was instantaneous. My mountain lion and falcon screeched with rage and defiance at her cold-blooded presence.

Food! the falcon squawked.

Pest, the mountain lion roared.

The beast stirred, and my head pounded.

Settle, I told them all, adding command to my voice, like an Alpha badass. No more putting up with their infighting. That shit hurt.

Snake, I said. *I shall call you Kaa.*

May as well keep with the *Jungle Book* theme I started with Baloo the bear.

The snake flicked her tongue out to caress my brain's nerve cells.

I shivered.

I am you, you are me, we—

Yeah, yeah. You still need a name.

We are one, Kaa finished with a hiss.

Kaa, I dispel you.

My body shook with more cold energy as Kaa wrenched from my essence. Her little ghost body appeared coiled on my thigh. She flicked her tongue out again and reached up to butt her tiny face into mine. She really was cute for a nope rope.

I am you, you are me, we are one. Approval and an odd warmth accompanied her reptilian voice.

I know, Kaa. Please dematerialize.

Kaa's mouth twitched up into what probably passed as a reptilian smile, if even possible, and her tongue snaked out one last time to caress my cheek before she shrunk into nothing and disappeared.

See you soon, her last thought floated through my mind, before leaving it empty. In the space she vanished, I caught a glimpse of something more. The other side? Gone too fast, my brain had no time to process the flicker of an image.

The mountain lion and falcon, who'd remained quiet through the exchange—thoughtful, and entirely out of character—now cuddled up together and sent a calming warmth through my body.

The beast grumbled and called me a wuss before settling down.

I wiped an errant tear from my cheek and stood up. I dabbed at my nose. No blood this time, and my headache had almost disappeared. Weird, but my fera acquiring skills seemed to be improving.

Time to go home. I groped for the falcon. *We'll take our time and play in the air flows.*

She screeched in agreement.

Just me and my empty apartment. No Tristan. No pack or prowl. No Witches. Solitude never bothered me before, but now it tugged at my heart. Just months out of the assassination game, and I was already getting soft.

Red? I called out. *Red, come here, please.*

My ghost fox fera materialized on the couch beside me.

Run? she asked.

No. Just lonely. I want company.

You're weird.

Shut up and cuddle me.

Okay. She curled up in my lap, and I stroked her soft, fine fur. Only I could see or touch her, but her presence made the emptiness of my apartment drift away. If only I'd been born a normal Shifter. I'd have a physical fera with me all the time.

My phone pinged and I pulled free the device to read the message. My friend, Mel, had texted to arrange a coffee date for tomorrow. Most insistent. That couldn't be good. I agreed to meet her, stashed away my phone and let my head fall back on the plush pillow.

The night sounds of light traffic and distant coyotes howling filtered through my apartment. The couch softened under my weight, cushioning my tired limbs and embracing me like a lover. I closed my eyes. My muscles slackened and a deadening weight spread through my body as sleep seeped through my bones.

Someone gently rapped on my door. Whatever, they could call or text. Sleepy time. My mountain lion and fox yawned.

My falcon puffed out her feathers and nestled her beak under a wing.

The beast snored.

The knocking came again. One eye popped open.

Maybe it's Ben.

Ben!

Energy zapped my body. Oh my Feradea! Maybe it *is* Ben. He better be okay.

I opened my eyes and leapt up. Red jumped from the bed and dematerialized. A wave of dizziness travelled up my body from the quick motion, and I gripped the wall to avoid toppling over.

"Coming," I bellowed.

When I walked down the hallway, streams of Witch scent met me. But it wasn't Ben. The scent didn't belong to any of my Witch neighbours. I halted and sniffed the air.

A charm. Fuuuuuuuuuuck!

I pivoted on my heel as my apartment's door burst open. A hailstorm of bullets rained down the hallway as I dove around the corner. The rat-a-tat-tat of machine gun fire echoed through my apartment.

Not wanting to test my beast against bullets, I sprinted to the bedroom as the intruders entered the apartment. Their heavy breathing and careful footsteps on the throw rugs the only hint of their progress.

The soft smell of night blossoms flowed in through my opened bedroom window. I ripped off my shirt, called the falcon and shifted as I launched into the air. I pumped my wings hard as the would-be-killers burst into the bedroom. More gunfire echoed into the night. I careened sharply to the right and then up and over the building.

Out of sight and out of reach of the shooters, I circled back to my apartment. My tiny bird heart pumped hard, punching against my breast bone. The sound of sirens ricocheted through the night air and drew closer to my apartment. I angled through the neighbouring buildings and perched on a nearby rooftop.

The men exited the building carrying guns by their sides. A gray van with no plates parked around the corner jostled as someone from the inside slid open the side door. The men, dressed in black fatigues and balaclavas, jumped in. The door slid shut and the van peeled away, leaving one man alone in the street. He watched the vehicle turn the corner and then walked gun-less to a black SUV with tinted windows and also no plates. He unlocked it by remote, opened the door, hopped in, and after a minute of rummaging around started the vehicle. He didn't appear rushed or concerned with the encroaching sirens or possibility of witnesses.

When his vehicle pulled away from the curb, I followed him.

He didn't drive far; around the corner, down a few blocks, then into one of the deserted parking lots for the river. No witnesses around here except for the homeless living in the woods.

The man hopped out. He'd taken off his balaclava and changed into a red shirt somehow while driving. He left the SUV and walked into the forest.

I knew this section of the PoCo trail. A bridge connected the banks of the PoCo River, and was one of the few places to cross from the west side of Port Coquitlam to the east side of Coquitlam without getting my feet wet. Swallowing a screech of delight, I pumped my wings and flew ahead of my assailant. I'd meet him on the other side of the bridge and cut him off.

SWEET PINE AND THE SMELL OF A COOLING cedar grove wrapped around my mountain lion form as I quivered and waited. A gentle breeze combed through my coarse feline fur, and my paws sank into the soft soil.

The man approached. No longer taking heed with his step, his boots fell heavy and thoughtless against the forest trail.

"No, we didn't get her. You didn't tell us she could shift into a bird," the man said, his voice surprisingly high and squeaky.

Another voice, scratchy and indiscernible replied, presumably on the other end of the phone.

"You didn't pay us enough to go back."

The voice intensified, but garbled and too far away, I couldn't make it out.

"Whatever. We'll deal with it. Goodbye." The man swore under his breath and continued to plod along. His heavy footsteps hit the concrete of the newer path, which led from the bridge. The cool night air whistled along the river and rustled his shirt and pants.

When he reached the other side, I moved. Weaving around the trees, I exited the forest right in front of the bridge landing. The man froze.

With wavy, deep brown locks, strong eyebrows and a straight nose, the man would've caught my attention if we stood together in a line for coffee. But tonight, he caught my attention for another reason. He'd tried to kill me on someone else's orders. Mercenary. My fate, had Stan and the VPD not pulled through with a job offer.

I needed to find out who hired him and why. Then I needed to kick some ass.

"Hey, kitty," the man crooned. He took both hands

out of his pockets and held them out in front of his body. He moved them up and down as if the gesture would soothe me. I tracked the movement, and he stopped.

Kill, my mountain lion hissed in my head.

Let me out, the beast demanded. *I'll make him talk.*

My falcon yawned.

With my body crouched low, I advanced and ignored the voices in my head.

"Hey, kitty." The man moved backward slowly with each step I took forward. "Nice, kitty."

Hah! He had no idea.

His hand disappeared into his back pocket and a shiny knife made an appearance. "Go the other way, kitty."

I continued to approach. Like a four inch knife would deter me.

The man cursed again. He used colourful language. If we'd been friends, I would've complimented him on his word choice.

"Go away!" the man yelled. Sweat oozed from his pores and trickled down his face. The sickly sweet smell of it saturated the air. He continued to step backward as I herded him onto the bridge. The one-way fifty metre long bridge.

I barred my teeth and gave a good yowl. The piercing sound filled the night air. The hairs raising on the man's arms and his quickening heartbeat pleased my mountain lion and delighted the beast.

"Nice—"

I pounced. A thick paw slammed his knife hand

against the bridge's pavement. The sharp knife clattered against the stonework before falling over the side into the water below. With recent rainfall, the water level had risen enough to allow the river a faster pace.

With his arms pinned back and his face inches from my own, the man screamed.

I let my teeth talk for me, and he stilled under my furry body. His screams became whimpers.

"Please," he begged.

Well, hopefully I instilled enough fear.

With a deep breath and a moment to focus, I started to shift back when a shot rang out in the night. A blast of pain shattered out from my left hip. I yowled into the night.

"I got it! I got it!" a man yelled from up the river. His voice broke on the second sentence. A young man. A teenager, maybe.

"Keep shooting," an older man yelled. "It has someone pinned."

Fuck!

I raked a claw against the man's chest before taking off down the bridge. My lungs constricted as I pushed my feline body to sprint. Sharp shooting pains laced up my leg and jolted down my back with each stride. What the hell were hunters doing on the river? This was in the middle of a residential zone. The gun fired again, and the metal railing behind me rattled as the bullet struck.

As soon as I hit the forest, I shifted into a falcon and flew off into the night. Intense aching radiated from my hind quarters. Shot, again. Three times in one year. My badass-ery skills needed work.

At least the hitman also screamed in pain. He'd survive his wounds. I didn't rake him deep enough to be fatal, but one check for a man admitted to the hospital for mountain lion injuries, and I'd find him again.

I screeched into the night and let the cool wind carry me away to heal.

25

"How many times can someone get shot in the ass?" Stan asked as he handed me a new bandage.

We sat in his cheap hotel room surrounded by a dozen empty liquor bottles as I waited for my sluggish Shifter healing to kick in and take some of the pain away. Not as fast at healing as a Were, and certainly not as fast at healing when I was blood bound to a Master Vampire, this wound would take a while to mend.

As I'd beat my wings in the strengthening winds, I realized I had few places to turn. I didn't trust going home. Tristan was away, and shooting the shit with Angie in his absence had as much appeal as shooting my other butt cheek. Ben and his coven were also away, and Wick's place was definitely off-limits. That left Stan.

Holed up in a VPD-paid room at a hotel near the

downtown Vancouver precinct, this wouldn't have been my first choice. I liked Stan, but the room reeked of misery and despair. With no solution to make his suffering go away, his emotions cut deep. Even if I helped find Loretta's killer, Stan's healing process would be a long, lonely road.

Well, I'd seen his pain, maybe it was only fair he got to see mine, even though it paled in comparison and was a completely different type.

He hadn't been phased when I'd tapped on his balcony screen door at way-too-fucking-early in the morning, butt-naked and gushing blood.

How many times can someone shoot me in the ass?

Two too many.

"Yeah, this time it hurts way more." I snatched the bandage from his hand and pulled up the towel to apply it to my cheek. With a few successive changes, the bullet dislodged and the wound had begun to heal, but the frequency of shifting had left me drained and short on patience. With the new moon in less than twenty-four hours and Sid's promise to visit looming in the back of my mind, I cursed the timing of events.

Last time I'd been shot in the ass, I'd been blood bonded to a Master Vampire and the wound had healed in under an hour. The time before that, it had been a shot to the arm and took a couple weeks. This time, the injury appeared to heal with a rate somewhere in between.

Huh.

Did my bond to Sid have something to do with that?

Or was it because I'd embraced my beast recently? Why would that make a difference?

Again, I wished for a Carus Operating Manual—*Beast for Dummies*. Maybe I should write one for the next Carus. Five hundred years in the future, they might appreciate my effort. Or maybe my manuscript would prove useless as future generations might only speak in hashtags.

"Here." Stan handed me another bar-fridge beverage.

I took it, we silently saluted each other, and I drank the burning fluid in one swallow. Ugh. I glanced at the label. Sherry. Who even drank this stuff anymore? An image of me and Stan, gray and wrinkled, sitting around a doily-covered table as we sipped sherry and played cribbage flashed in my mind. Total nonsense. Stan would be long in his grave before I saw a gray hair.

My heart sank. An extended lifetime kind of sucked sometimes.

I cleared my throat and blinked back unexpected tears. Before Stan noticed, I flapped my open palm in the air. "Can I use your phone?"

Stan scrunched his face.

"So I can text Tristan and warn him about my place? Even if you called it in, I don't want him there."

"No sexting." Stan slapped his phone into my open palm. "Anything else?"

"Got any clothes I can wear?" I asked, clutching my towel outfit around me.

"Yeah. Hang on." Stan stumbled to his feet and shuffled to the bedroom.

While he rummaged through his dresser, I sent a quick text to Tristan explaining the attack and warning him off my place. No immediate response. Stan would mock the crap out of me if I clutched the phone all night waiting for my boyfriend's response, so I placed it on the coffee table where I could see the screen if a message popped up.

When Stan walked back out, he threw a ratty pair of jogging pants and an old T-shirt at me. They smelled of Stan. "This do?"

"Perfect."

Stan nodded and sat down, sprawling his legs out as he leaned back and reached for the remote control. "What do you want to do?"

"Let's get our drink on," I said. Alcohol metabolized fast in a Shifter body, but it helped to momentarily numb the pain radiating from my butt.

"Perfect."

Before Stan could grab us another round of disgusting and expensive liquor, his phone rang. I glanced at the screen as it vibrated on the coffee table beside me.

"The Flower," I said.

"Sergeant Lafleur?"

"Yeah, him." I yanked on the jogging pants under the towel and pulled the drawstring tight before they could slip down my ass.

"What's your problem with him?" Stan asked.

"Problem? None."

Stan's eyebrows pinched in as he grabbed his phone and hit the accept button. "Stevens," he grumbled.

"Got another one," Lafleur's low voice carried through the speakers to my sensitive ears.

Stan nodded. "Where?"

"At 109th Avenue and 130th Street."

"Isn't that Surrey?"

"Yeah, Surrey PD is letting us view the scene as a courtesy."

Stan checked his cheap wristwatch. "Be there in thirty minutes."

"Bring the Shifter," Lafleur gruffed before hanging up.

I pulled the shirt on and threw the bloody towel on the bathroom floor. Maybe I did have a problem with Lafleur. He'd just spoiled a night of bonding with Stan. Nothing said besties better than projectile vomiting over the same toilet.

WHEN WE ARRIVED AT THE INTERSECTION OF 109th Avenue and 130th Street, it took little time for my nose to tell me why we got the call. Sour, burnt plastic and decaying flesh clung to the air and barrelled down the street to where I parked Stan's car. King's Krank and death.

With only one drink in my system, and a supernatural metabolism, I drove. Each bump and jiggle of the vehicle on the uneven roads sent a little power punch of pain through my body.

Looking down 130th Street gave a glimpse of the Fraser River and the mountains behind it as the sun peeked over the horizon. Such a beautiful dawn landscape scene. It contrasted sharply with the death in the air.

"Here." Stan slapped a pair of gloves in my hand, grunted and turned toward the crime scene. I hadn't told him what I'd discovered at the tattoo shop or from Westman yet. I liked to verify things before I acted, and if I told Stan anything, he'd jump on it. His body vibrated beside me, the alcohol long gone from his breath. His hands balled into fists as he adjusted his shirt. Even though he mostly walked around in plain clothes now, I still envisioned him in his uniform and marked police cruiser. Couldn't break the habit.

Stan got us past the yellow tape by signing in with the officer in charge of maintaining the crime scene. They exchanged stiff nodes and *voila*, we were in. We entered a standard Surrey home. With at least three floors and more than two suites, this place either housed a multiple generation family or the home owners had tenants to help with their exorbitant mortgage.

We walked into one of two basement suites. Well, Stan walked, I hobbled and tried not to wince with each step.

The door separating this place from the rest of the house was open and voices carried from the main floor upstairs. Waves of grief carried in the flowing air, along with unconditional love. Multiple generations, then.

A couple lay on the queen-sized bed in the main bedroom. Surrounded by framed pictures of family and minimal furnishings, they remained sprawled on their backs, blank eyes staring at the ceiling. Dried foam laid a path from their mouths to the sheets beneath them.

Another overdose. Two victims this time.

The sour, burnt plastic hit my face right away, but also something else. Something different. Something "other." I limped forward, ignoring the alarm bells in my head chiming along with my feras.

Wrong, growled my mountain lion.

Leave, my falcon screeched.

Destroy, rumbled the beast.

Shut up, all of you! I hissed at the feras and leaned over the female victim. South Asian, mid-twenties, beautiful. With horns. I pulled on the gloves Stan gave me. I reached out and gently pushed the tip of the horn on the left side of the woman's temple. Solid, cold. Yup. Horns.

Repeating the gesture for the other horn didn't give me any more information, but my OCD kicked in, and I couldn't prod one and not the other.

I moved to the male victim. Also South Asian, mid-twenties, attractive, and sadly, also very dead. No horns.

The medical examiner finished taking notes on his observations, or lack thereof, and turned to me. His eyebrows pinched in as his gaze travelled down my body to take in Stan's old clothes and probably my limp. His mouth scrunched up before he nodded at the victim. "Check his mouth."

With a steady finger belying the unease flittering around in my stomach, I lifted the deceased's full upper lip. His canines were considerably longer than the rest of his teeth. Long and pointy. I pushed his upper lip farther to look at the gums. Dried blood crusted around the base of both canines.

"See anything?" The ME asked.

"He was left handed?"

The ME grunted.

I grunted.

He left me alone after that. I had the cop lingo down thanks to Stan.

I straightened and turned to my partner. He raised his shoulders and ducked his head as if to ask, "Anything?" He kept his hands deep in his pockets.

I tilted my head toward the exit. Stan nodded, and we walked out together into the fresh night air. My limp drew the attention of a few officers, but they wisely chose not to comment. The pain continued to radiate down my leg, but knowing it would go away soon acted like a calming salve for my mind.

Upwind from the house, I inhaled long drags of the cool air and let it flow through my system as a natural cleanser.

Stan stood beside me and remained silent until I opened my eyes.

"So?" Stan asked.

"Horns and fangs. Definitely Kings Krank. No other

familiar scents. No one else had recently been in the room, other than family members." Takkenmann's words replayed through my head. One percent of trials experienced extraordinary supernatural abilities. Had Loretta made the connection between her employer and the new street drug? Is that where the KK came from? Is that why someone took her out?

Stan nodded. "Doesn't really give us anything new, does it?"

"No, but..." Should I tell him? How much should I disclose? Stan might go off the deep end or off the grid.

"But?" Stan's gaze narrowed.

"Was Loretta doing any research?"

"For the company? Not that I know of."

"She might've been doing it on the side. Maybe she didn't want you to know. Like the storage compartment. Was she on the computer a lot? Acting secretive at all?"

Stan stilled. "She'd been spending a lot of time on the computer, lately."

I waited.

Stan cursed. "I thought she was online shopping again."

I nodded.

Stan reached out and gripped my upper arm. "You think she was researching King's Krank?"

The man had a grip. I tried to shrug out of his hold, but he tightened his grasp and pulled. I had a choice of fighting Stan or turning to face him. I turned. "Yes."

"Why?"

"I think her employer may have a connection to KK.

Your wife worked for a pharmaceutical company that spent a majority of its profits on drug research, and your wife's death is connected somehow to King's Krank, a new drug that has some super freaky-deeky side effects. Yeah, I think there's a connection."

Stan released my arm as if I'd burned him. His face contorted as his lips twisted, and his jaw clenched. "Any proof?" he whispered.

"Not yet."

Stan's body stiffened and he turned half-away before spinning back. He leaned in, close, so close the mouthwash he'd used earlier to rinse away the sherry wafted against my face. "We need to find proof."

"I know."

His skin glistened, and he licked his lips. "We need to be sure."

"I know."

26

Later that day, after a short morning cat-nap, I found myself sitting at "our coffee shop" with Mel. She'd shown up twenty minutes late, so I held my second cup of coffee, and the caffeine rushing through my veins left me jittery. As much as I tried to blink away the images, I couldn't get the memory of the dead couple from this morning out of my mind. At least the ache from my bullet wound had abated to a dull, somewhat annoying, throb.

Mel's knowing blue gaze, surrounded by a halo of big blonde hair, studied me from across the wrought iron table. I'd wanted to talk over the phone, but my old friend knew me better than that. My ability to dodge the truth decreased, and her perceptiveness increased drastically face to face.

With a perfectly French-manicured hand, she reached forward and plucked her latte off the table. After a long silent sip, she placed it gently back on the table. "How are things?"

"Well, I work for the VPD now, and I'm helping my cop friend find his wife's murderer. You may have seen some coverage on the news."

No point telling her about my little date with Sid tonight. Since I couldn't change the inevitable, she'd worry for no reason. After thinking on the whole Sid thing, the fear I'd experienced dissipated. He wouldn't harm his anchor. He didn't feed off pain or fear, and he'd manipulated and schemed too hard to get me just to throw me away.

"Is that why you're nursing one butt cheek and smell of dried blood?" Mel asked, gaze narrowed.

Dang it. I tried to hide that. "Yeah, sort of."

Her face scrunched up, obviously unimpressed with my answer, but after a moment, she relaxed back into her chair. "How's the investigation going?"

Technically, I couldn't divulge any information to a civilian on an ongoing investigation with the VPD, but this was Mel. We went way back. We'd seen each other at our weakest and knew what we'd both survived. Her mind was a vault when it came to any secrets I shared with her.

"It's going okay," I said. "A couple dead ends. No pun intended. But, I think I know who did it, and why. I just need proof." I quickly relayed what I knew about Loretta's death and the King's Krank investigation. "I can't help but feel it's all connected. The weird overdoses, the KK drug dealer, and Loretta's murder. I'm just missing the connecting dot."

Mel nodded. "Seems too coincidental for it not to be connected. I'm sure you'll figure it out. You always do."

"Why did you demand to see me?" I asked. Mel's tactics hadn't changed over the years, she buttered me up for something. Something she didn't want to tell me, but thought she had to. Since Mel belonged to Wick's pack, my brilliant mind narrowed down the topic possibilities. None of them good.

Mel shook her head and tsked at me. "Is it demanding to ask to see a friend?"

I speared her with my best better-start-talking-now-or-I-walk face.

Mel's shoulders sagged, and she bit her lip. "Okay fine. We need to talk."

Obviously. "About what?"

"Wick."

My spine straightened at the same time my stomach churned. Just as I feared. She wanted to talk about *him*. Was he okay? Had something happened? I swallowed stomach acid. Had he mated with Christine? Were they having skinny little love babies? "What about him?"

"Your decision hurt him."

I gulped back some more acid reflux before opening my mouth to defend my choice. Mel held her hand up to stop me and shook her head again. Her soft blonde hair brushed her slightly-flushed cheeks.

"I know you didn't make your choice lightly," she said. "But I thought you should know the ramifications."

My muscles weakened, and I slouched in my seat. At the same time, a burning sensation spread across my chest. "I saw him two days ago, he didn't seem to suffer any *ramifications*. He's already replaced me."

Mel glared.

I bit my lip. Okay, so he hadn't seemed fine, but he also didn't appear to be wallowing in self-pity, either.

"Christine is a part of the problem," Mel said.

With a long sigh, I picked up my cappuccino and took a long drink. My shoulders insisted on trying to touch my ears, and no amount of wondrous caffeine seemed to settle the unease circling in my gut.

"Okay," I conceded. "Hit me with it."

Mel set her coffee down again and nodded. She squared her shoulders, and her blue gaze softened.

Well, crap. This couldn't be good.

"Wick's wolf has seen yours," she started. "Wick *and* his wolf chose you."

"I know that. I dispelled my wolf."

Mel nodded. "But apparently that makes no difference to Wick or his wolf."

My brain cells stopped firing. My skin prickled with unease. "What do you mean?"

"They both know the wolf isn't truly gone, just banished to a different reality to make things easier for you."

I pursed my lips.

"No judgement," Mel quickly added. "I don't think anyone blames you for wanting to separate yourself from that pain. They just wanted you to separate from a different animal."

"Well shit, Mel. What more can I do? I hoped sending my wolf away would make things easier for Wick, not just myself. I can't and won't mate to more than one man."

Images from Sid's devious dreams streamed through my head. I shook them away. Not. Happening.

"I know," Mel said. She stared down at her cup. She had more to say. The deep furrow in the bridge between her perfectly plucked eyebrows told me so.

"Have you mated with Tristan, yet?" she asked.

"No. We're taking our time." I folded my arms across my chest, not caring how defensive it looked. Tristan knew how hard trust came to me—how much my past mistakes cast a shadow on the present and threatened my future decisions.

Mel smiled as if she caught all my thoughts. "That's good. I'm glad he's patient. But maybe when you're mated to Tristan, it will make things easier. Maybe then..."

"Honest to Feradea, Mel, if you don't spit out the rest of whatever it is you have to say, I'll find your entire shoe collection and burn it."

Mel sighed. "Wick's wolf won't accept Christine, nor anyone else, not when he knows yours isn't truly gone."

My stomach dropped as my skin prickled. "So Wick is rendered mate-less until...until what? Forever?"

"Until your death." Mel hesitated. "It's not like you've neutered him. He can still have relationships, still fall in love, but his wolf definitely won't. Wick will never have a true mate. At least not right now, and if what I sense through the pack bond is accurate, not ever."

My stomach dropped as if an invisible weight sank to the bottom. I hadn't expected this result. I knew I'd hurt him, but prevent him from mating in the future? My throat dried out and started to ache. Wick didn't deserve this fate.

If my decision had gone the other way, I would've left Tristan to the same fate.

Damned if I do...

The aching subsided and gave way to a racing heart. Mel's words replayed in my head. What she sensed... I straightened in my seat. "You can sense it through your pack bond?"

Mel nodded.

The wheels in my head clanked into place and started turning. "If you can sense it..."

"So can Christine," Mel finished for me. "And she's pissed."

Pain lanced across my face as I clenched my jaw. "Well, I'm certainly not happy about Wick's wolf, more than not happy, but causing that harlot grief is the least of my concerns."

"That may change," Mel said.

"What do you mean?"

"The only thing standing between Christine and her perceived happiness—"

Understanding hit me like a professional hockey defenceman. I stood in Christine's way. She wanted Wick and believed if I ceased to exist, the Alpha would be hers. She conveniently forgot I'd only recently entered Wick's life, while she had been around much longer. Had he wanted to take her as his mate, he could've done so well before I ever walked, or flew, onto the scene. Unfortunately, morons rarely thought logically. "I'm the only thing she sees in her way."

Mel nodded along with my changing emotions, expertly plucking the scents from the air. "That's why I needed to see you," she said. "I wanted to warn you and I didn't think you'd take me seriously if I sent this in a text."

My lips flattened. Had Christine been behind the mercenary attack? Had she literally become a pain in my ass? My butt cheek throbbed in answer. Or had the attack come from another direction? Lucien-lovers retaliating? The KK drug dealers trying to take out another of Stan's support pillars?

I sighed. I had too many enemies to definitively say who was behind the attack, but I'd find out.

My beast roared approval.

"Watch your back," Mel said. Her voice interrupted my mental plans to visit the hospital, then Christine.

I could always corner Christine for a little one-on-one girl chat.

With some even breaths, I managed to calm my racing heart and heated blood racing through my veins. The beast roared at me to "shank the bitch," and sent images of stabbing stick insects, but I ignored her. In the short time she'd become more vocal, she'd easily surpassed my other feras for saying ridiculous things.

If I took out Christine, it would be with my teeth and claws, not some handmade budget weapon. Sheesh. Beast needed to get with the Team Andy Program.

"You could've told me this on the phone," I muttered into my coffee lid.

"True, but then I wouldn't get to see my friend."

"And nag me about my skin care regimen?"

"Please, I gave you up as a hopeless cause long ago." She reached out and grabbed my hand. "No, I wanted to see my friend, talk to my friend, and let my friend know I'm here for her. No text can say that."

Part of me wanted to correct her. Technically, a text could say all that, but the swelling in my chest blocked the air flow to my voice box and prevented speech. I squeezed Mel's hand back instead.

27

L eft alone to my thoughts made the world spin and enhanced my need to scream. I hadn't heard from Tristan and after multiple checks of my phone, I'd come to the sad realization nothing was wrong with it. Battery at fifty percent and full signal. Tristan was avoiding me.

I'd been shot in the ass, again. If anything warranted a call, or a pity-text, bloodshed would be it. I could only play the cool and relaxed girlfriend so long.

My beast growled with approval.

Taking a detour on my way home from my coffee date with Mel found me pulling the car into the driveway of Tristan's upscale Port Moody home.

Time to boil some bunnies and demand answers. Getting out of the car sent bolts of pain down my leg and fed my anger.

Well, try to keep calm, I told myself. *There might be a reasonable explanation for this.*

All sense of being reasonable and calm flew out my mind when the front door opened to reveal Angie scantily clad in only a short, pink satin robe. She held it loosely closed around her moist skin, and made no effort to hide her ample cleavage or smug expression.

Red stained my vision. My gums ached as canines threatened to elongate.

Bite her face, my mountain lion hissed. The beast rumbled.

My falcon screeched, *Peck, peck, peck*, over and over again.

I surged forward, beast strong, clutched her neck and slammed her back into the wall. Her eyes widened, but she didn't struggle. My face contorted, stinging in a pre-shift phase as I fought to prevent a shift. If my gaze was capable of shooting laser beams, Angie's face would've melted off. Instead, she dropped her gaze. My pumping heart slowed a little. Angie finally conceded my dominance to hers in the prowl hierarchy.

Destroy, my beast whispered.

I took in a deep breath. The one long drag of air sent soothing waves down my limbs. She didn't smell like Tristan. She smelled of moisturizing body wash and burnt sugar from unrequited longing. Despite how it looked, she hadn't been in contact with Tristan. Not in *that* way.

Another deep breath.

Tristan hadn't been home in a while. His delicious scent ran stale and faint. My heart picked up. What if something had happened to him? And all this time instead of helping him, I'd been cursing his name and calling him a rat-bag?

"Where's Tristan?" I demanded, releasing Angie's neck.

"Not here." Angie didn't miss a beat. She straightened her robe and brushed back stray wisps of hair.

"Is he in trouble?"

"Hardly. He's away on...business. Phoned about half an hour ago to say he'd be home in a couple of days."

I sputtered. He phoned *her*? Not me? Rat-bag.

Angie's lip curled up. "Something wrong?"

I growled, and her mouth slackened.

"He's not returning my calls," I said. "Do you know why?"

"I told you he would hurt you in the end."

Truth, but it didn't stop me from wanting to rip out her eyes with my claws. "He's not cheating on me."

Angie tsked. "I said he'd hurt you. I never said how."

"Do I need to punch the truth out of your mouth?"

She frowned. "He'll be back soon enough to tell you himself. Don't expect him today. He'll be running the new moon by himself. He called to tell me to take lead with the prowl tonight."

Well, damn. He had wanted to talk to me the other day, but I'd jumped him instead. Hard to have a conversation when you're busy having multiple orgasms, and I don't think either of us were capable of speech after. I should've let him talk. Heck, he should've insisted I let him talk.

Be fair, Andy. You can't put that on Tristan.

Images from that night flashed through my memory. Ones of us naked, with sweaty limbs entangled, breathing in unison as we moved together.

My heart started to beat faster, and my body flushed with warmth.

Angie cleared her throat.

"I'll wait to talk to him," I mumbled.

"Good idea."

At home and miserable, I sat on the couch with an icepack under my ass and flicked through the television channels. I missed Tristan. Yeah, I was super pissed at him, but I wanted to know what was going on. I wanted his citrus and sunshine scent stuck to my skin and his warm body curled up next to mine.

Instead, I had the equivalent of radio silence.

B&B sessions with Stan were out, and there'd be no karaoke therapy to make me feel better either. The Witches were still not back, and I could've used a Ben pep talk right now. Nothing like belting out lyrics to 80s classics to work out my angst.

My pocket vibrated as the small phone shook with vigour. Tristan? Ben? I turned off the television and slouched in the sofa to slide the device out of my pocket. The screen flashed Stan's name. My heart sank a little, quickly followed with a pang of guilt. My life woes had nothing on Stan's.

I tapped the phone to pick up the call. "Yell-oh."

A pause. "Yellow?" Stan's voice crackled.

"Uh, sure."

"That's no way to answer a phone," he said.

"Whatever." I sat up. Stan's voice carried something different in its tone, something I hadn't heard since Loretta's death. "What's up?"

"The techies broke into Lo...into the phone."

"We got something?"

"We got something. I think we found the killer. There's a voicemail."

I fist pumped the air. "And?"

"Listen for yourself." Something shuffled in the background and a static voice carried over the line, presumably from the recording.

"I'd like to discuss your research some more. I think you're onto something. Let's meet at the warehouse near Main and Powell. Tomorrow. Noon." The oddly familiar voice clicked off, followed shortly by an automated woman saying the date and time—the message had been left a few days before Loretta's death.

"Bingo!" I said. My heart raced. The recorded voice sounded familiar. Not familiar enough to be someone close to me, but definitely someone I'd met. Something about the cadence and slight lilt of the words. And the meeting place. The street intersection bounced around on the inside of my skull. I knew that warehouse. I used it as a remote location to meet my handler back in my

SRD assassin days. Crap! Was there a connection somehow?

Stan cleared his throat.

"Can they trace the call?" I asked.

"Yes. Burner phone. Dead end."

"Well, that sucks."

"We have a location of the killer and your nose. The location is an abandoned building in Gastown. There shouldn't be anything else there."

"Except the homeless and a lot of waste from bodily functions. I know that building. I met my handler there, back in the day."

Another pause. "Think there's a connection?"

"Doubt it. We weren't the only ones to use the building, and it's been more than half a year since I used it for that purpose." Had it been only half a year? So much had happened since my botched assassination on Clint. Too much.

"When can you meet us?"

That's right. I'd told Stan I couldn't meet tonight for work because of "New Moon Supernatural Stuff." I was so full of it. He'd grumbled, but he seemed to buy it at the time, or at least not care enough to push it. But that was earlier today when we didn't have any leads. My chest tightened and pain sprang up at the back of my throat. If I didn't have this personal Demon shit to attend to, I could help Stan sooner than later. Bring him closure sooner than later. If I hadn't been compromised by a lecherous Seducer Demon and a now-deceased douchebag Vampire. Goddammit!

"Andy?" Stan asked, some of his excitement draining from his voice.

"Tomorrow. Two hours after sunrise," I said. May as well forgo sleep.

"Perfect. Meet there?"

"You bet."

Stan didn't bother with an elaborate goodbye. He grunted and hung up on me, leaving me to twist in my own self-loathing.

28

The sun set with a beautiful cascade of red and orange light. A cornucopia of scents drifted through the open window, and flooded my senses—mint, oregano, ginger, and pumpkin spice—as if each household delved into creating comfort food.

I certainly had. Two banana nut loaves and a bunch of cupcakes cooled on my stove top. If I survived this night, I wanted to gorge on food I loved. Napping had alluded me. If I survived this night, I'd have to meet Stan without a wink of sleep.

Was I really worried Sid would harm me? Not really. He seemed attached to the idea of having an anchor on a permanent basis. No. If harm came to me tonight it would come from stopping Sid doing something stupid.

Just enjoy the moment. I watched the horizon. If only the sun wasn't setting on my freedom as I knew it. If only it didn't signal the beginning of my own personal hell.

I sat on the sofa, curled up in a fuzzy gray-blue

blanket and watched the dying light of day fade into the peaceful abyss of night. If Tristan's strong arms held me, maybe this desolation wouldn't hit me so hard.

I sighed.

Who was I kidding?

Even if he'd returned my calls, or tonight wasn't a new moon where Tristan ran around as a leopard, no way would I allow Tristan here tonight. His Alpha nature and dominant leopard wouldn't tolerate Sid's use of me, and after our failed attempt to take down Bola, I doubted Tristan and all his awesomeness could match Satan's Assistant.

When the last rays of day disappeared, my core clenched. As if someone lassoed my uterus and started yanking, intense abdominal pain radiated from my trunk outward, down my limbs to the tips of my fingers and toes. Like menstrual cramps, but a bajillion times worse.

What the fuck?

My nails elongated and sank into the couch cushions. I ground my teeth together and snarled. If I had to birth Sid into this world, I'd gut him right away. To hell with the repercussions. No one played with my lady bits without permission.

The tugging continued, hard and relentless; pain shot through my body. My limbs curled and coiled under the onslaught, and I slid from the couch and crumpled to the floor. Not even the fetal position provided a reprieve.

My mind floated up and out of my consciousness. I looked down at my writhing body as my essence distanced itself from the pain. I'd done this before. Many times during the Dylan abuse years, and once when Lucien almost took my life to blood bond me.

This time it wasn't so bad. My feras still paced in my head, waiting, wanting out. The beast remained tethered. My heartbeat pounded heavy in my chest, echoing in the living room. My body snapped back, like a victim of tetanus. With a gaping wide mouth, an unearthly scream ripped from my throat, spewing a milky white cloud. It spiralled with force out of my body like a mushroom plume from a volcano. When it cleared, a naked Sid stood over my prone body, hands on hips, lips twisted up in a smug smile.

Sid slowly surveyed the room until his gaze fixated on where my essence hovered. "Nice trick, Carus. I'm glad you can dissociate. Though it shouldn't hurt as much, I suggest not waiting so long next time."

Fuck that. There'd never be a next time.

"You can come back now. We have much to discuss." Sid stepped away from my prone body.

I drifted in the space above my body and focused on it. My awareness gathered like pooling heat above a bathtub before it dove back into my crumpled body in circling tidal-pools.

My eyelids popped open. Pain emanated from behind my eyes, my limbs lay limp and heavy, the floor uncomfortable against my bruised flesh. Surprisingly, the ache from the bullet wound had disappeared.

"Get up, sunshine." Sid shuffled his bare feet from where he stood beside me, only a couple feet away.

All seven feet of naked flesh.

I squeezed my eyes shut. Not a view I wanted. At all. "There's spare extra-large jogging pants in my closet. Go put something on."

"You sure?"

"Absolutely. No one should have to see that."

"A lot of ladies love it."

"A lot of ladies also love Cool James, but you don't see him prancing around naked."

"Who?"

"Never mind. Just go put something on."

When I heard his bare feet pad along the wood flooring and hit the cushioned carpet in the bedroom, I opened my eyes up again and got up.

Or at least tried.

My limbs flopped around, heavy and boneless.

Well, this sucks.

I smacked at my sofa and hauled my useless body onto the soft cushions. The muscles of my arms shook with fatigue.

Sid sauntered back into my living room, wearing jogging pants that made it to his mid-calf. No shirt. His chiseled eight-pack gleamed across the room at me.

"See anything you like?" Sid raised a dark eyebrow and brushed his hand along his olive-toned abs.

"There is nothing to like about this situation." I glared at him. I would've waved at my useless body, but my arms defied the message and lay limp and useless beside me.

"Oh. That." Sid frowned.

"Yeah. That. Why the heck am I so useless?"

"Being a portal to a Demon requires intense energy consumption. Most norms would die from the transfer. Supes, too. Your semi-divinity allows this to work."

"It sucks."

"It will get better."

That's what that loser, Caden, had said after he took my virginity, too. Liar. A wave of nausea wracked my body as my toes regained feeling. Well, Caden hadn't lied completely. It did get better, just not with him. "How long will it take to regain my faculties?"

"Not long. Your bond with me will help accelerate the process."

"Hoooo-ray."

Sid tilted his head. "I sense sarcasm."

"You sense correctly."

Sid pursed his lips and glanced around my room again. His body twitched and a loud rumble erupted from his perfect washboard stomach. He clutched his stomach and turned back to me. "Have anything to eat?"

"What the hell does a Demon eat?" Didn't these guys leech emotions? Never thought to see one chow down a cheeseburger.

Sid shrugged. "I don't know. I feed off sexual energy." He paused and looked at me again. "Not going to get that from you, am I?"

"You sense correctly, again."

"But that's in hell or when summoned in a circle, which is different. I'm not sure what I can or cannot eat." He eyed my kitchen.

"Don't even think about it."

He cast me a wicked grin over his shoulder as he strutted toward the cupcake riddled kitchen; his lips twisted up. "Try and stop me."

MOTHERFUCKER ATE ALL MY CUPCAKES. IF I'D been capable of moving, I would've done some damage. Serious damage. Punching him in the junk multiple times would've been appropriate. Everyone knew not to eat a woman's chocolate with vanilla icing comfort cupcakes. Did they teach these Demons nothing in hell? I lay on my couch, as useful as a glass hammer, and watched the Seducer Demon hoover my food.

When he finished the last of my cupcakes, he moved to the banana nut bread. My limbs tingled, and I wiggled my toes. They moved. I tested my arms next, swinging them off the couch as if I could fly away.

Sid glanced at me before popping half a loaf into his mouth. Crumbs fell down his face, bounced off his chest and clung to his sweats; some pooled at his feet with bits of chocolatey goodness and vanilla icing.

With a breath sucked in, I wrenched my knee up. It worked. It drove up into the cushion and sent my body flying off the edge of the couch. My body smacked against the hard floor and sucker punched the breath out of my chest.

Sid barked laughter from the kitchen. Before I could

tell him where to shove his nether bits, his laughter broke off in a strangled gasp.

I pushed off the floor and used the couch to pull myself up into a semi-respectable position. What the hell was that noise? Like a cow trying to crow.

Sid thrashed around frantically in the kitchen. Face red, arms flailing around. He turned to me with bulging eyes and panicked eyebrows.

The big bad Seducer Demon was choking on my banana nut loaf.

Sid clutched his throat and pointed at his gaping mouth.

"What do you want me to do about it? Throw yourself against a chair."

Sid stopped his frantic motions and glared at me. "I'm serious! I can't give you the Heimlich maneuver in my current condition, and you can hardly do it by yourself. You need to dislodge the food with abdominal thrusts."

Sid's glare darkened, and his mouth flattened into a hard line. His face had passed red and went to purple.

I sighed and relaxed into the side of the couch. If he died on the mortal plane, he'd just go back to the Demonic realm and I'd be rid of him. Rid of him until he decided to torment me in my dreams. Even if this debacle wasn't my fault, Sid seemed like the angsty type to take it out on me anyway.

"Okay, listen up, Demon," I said. "Make a fist." Sid clenched his fist and waved it at me.

"Place your fist slightly above your navel." I paused

until Sid complied. "Good. Grab your fist with your other hand. Good. Now bend yourself over the back of my dining table chair."

Sid shot me another death glare.

"Do it! We're running out of time, idiot!"

He bent over the chair. If only I had my phone. It sat useless on my bed, ensuring no photographic evidence of this moment.

Sid made another strangled sound. "Shove your fist inward and upward." He did, barely.

"Again! Harder!"

Sid cast me one last death stare before ramping his body down on the chair while thrusting his fist upward.

My stomach cringed.

Banana loaf spewed out of Sid's mouth. The hard almond pieces, slathered with saliva, splattered against the table's surface as Sid sucked back air. He doubled over the chair and gagged on more loaf, leaving a pool of chunky drool on the seat's cushion.

"You're cleaning that."

Sid stiffened and straightened. His arm flung out, and he jutted a stiff forefinger in my direction.

I raised an eyebrow.

"You will never speak of this," he whispered.

"Please, like I want to acknowledge any involvement with you." My words were true, but I eyed my bedroom door again, which blocked the view of my phone, out of reach and out of assistance. Drat! A video of what I had just witnessed would've gone viral on social media. If possible, I might've used it as blackmail.

Sid studied me for a few tense minutes before he nodded, more to himself than to me, as if he'd come to a decision.

"So?" I asked.

"So, what?" Sid tilted his head.

"What do you plan to do?"

"Does it matter?"

"Yes." With the couch's help, I pulled my body up until I could get my shaky legs under me enough to stand.

His lip quirked in a condescending smirk.

I wanted to punch it off his face.

"Why bother asking when you can't stop me from doing whatever I want?" Stan asked.

"I'm not useless." The beast stirred as she sensed my intent.

"True, but do you realize, little Carus, I could snap you in two before you even thought to shift into the Ualida?"

"Well, fuck you, Sid. I don't want you marauding the Lower Mainland pulling a Bola."

Sid snorted. "Please. I don't feed off blood and mayhem. I'm more likely to cause a mass orgy than slaughter."

He had a point. But still. The idea of him running loose in the city made my skin crawl.

Before I could voice any further objections, Sid spoke again. "Despite what you may think. I do not wish you harm. I want you to be...content...with this bond. I wish to have a permanent anchor to the mortal realm."

"Well, that's not going to happen. I felt like a knife had been shoved into my uterus and twisted around."

Sid jerked back. His face contorted into something between horrified and disgusted.

"Tell me your plans, or I'll reciprocate the pain." I ground my teeth. Consequences be damned.

Sid cringed. After a deep breath, his shoulders sagged. "I didn't plan much. I wasn't sure it would even work. I didn't anticipate it would cause such pain either."

I crossed my arms and tapped my foot. Dang it, if he didn't sound remorseful.

"Can we watch television?"

"What?" I sputtered. My arms fell limp to my side.

"I wish to spend time with my anchor." He held his hand out, palm forward, to stop my opposition to the idea before I had the chance to voice it. "And I wish to use this opportunity to acclimatize better to this day and age. I haven't had much time out of the summoning circle or bedroom on the mortal plane, and information is expensive in hell."

"Television?" If information was expensive, Sid looked to gain a pricy commodity.

He nodded. "Television."

29

T rue to his word, the Seducer Demon spent the night watching television, keeping his hands to himself and browsing the internet on my laptop during commercials. The rise of the sun ended the anticlimactic night in a similar fashion. Sid mumbled, "See you soon" before vanishing into the Demonic Realm.

Good riddance.

The domesticity of the night creeped me out almost as much as his regular Seducer Demon role. I'd dozed off a couple of times, only to startle awake and find Sid exactly where I left him.

I had little time to deliberate the inner mechanisms of the Demon's psyche, though. Today, I needed to help Stan, and with little sleep, and still no contact from Tristan, I'd have to strive to be on my best behaviour.

The early morning shone as I stood on the downtown east-side street, littered with garbage and the homeless. The wound on my butt cheek had healed, the skin shiny and red. The injury still sent pricks of pain with sudden movement, and my clothes chafed against the sensitive skin, but my bond with Sid definitely sped up the healing process.

The building across the street hadn't changed since I'd been here last. The windows remained broken and boarded up. The last owner had given up long ago and abandoned it. Now, multi-coloured graffiti decorated the outer walls. Colourful tags brightened the otherwise drab hue of the old, neglected bricks. The stonework reeked of urine, human excrement, and unwashed bodies.

This abandoned warehouse had been the perfect location for meeting my now-deceased handler.

I ducked under the new police caution tape and walked past the metal entrance doors. They hung off their hinges as a distant memory of their former glory.

Inside, the fetid body odour grew stronger. The homeless used these abandoned and condemned buildings as shelter, and I didn't blame them one bit. When I'd run off to live in the forest as a mountain lion, there were no showers and the elements were harsh. No way would I have chosen nature if I was a norm and could squat in a place like this.

As each step brought me farther into the building, though, another smell carried through the stench.

Death.

A couple weeks old. Not good.

A gaggle of officers glanced up from their post outside a room and nodded at me as I approached the end of the hallway. They must've been sent to secure the location. My nose twitched. Decaying flesh, something feline, like bobcat and sour, burnt plastic.

The officers stare at their feet and wouldn't meet my gaze.

What the hell was going on?

"Is it true?" Stan bellowed behind me.

Spinning around, I found Stan stomping toward us.

I leapt out of the way as Stan barrelled past me. Not even a pause or indication of recognition. His gaze focused straight ahead, intent on his target. "He's dead?"

"Yeah, Stan. Sorry," one of the officers mumbled.

He might've spoken low and garbled, but I made out his words just fine.

So did Stan. He pulled up short as his body lashed back straight and tense. His heavy breathing made his chest heave up and down, but otherwise, he stood frozen, legs shoulder-width apart, arms by his side, fists clenched.

"FUCK!" Stan spun suddenly and drove his right fist into the wall. The old wood splintered on contact, and bits of decaying plaster, plywood, and paint flew through the air. Stan snapped his hand back and blood pooled between his knuckles.

The scent of his injury flooded my senses along with the canned ham of his despair. My stomach dropped.

I waited with his comrades in complete silence. My skin itched to do something. My brain drew a blank. What could I do to take Stan's pain away?

Stan cradled his bloody fist and stared at the wall. Time ticked by. Finally, the tension of his shoulders eased and he let out a long, pained sigh. "Another fucking dead end." He turned to me.

"I'm so sorry, Stan. I should've been here last night." My throat grew thick as guilt clung to my limbs, and my stomach tried to invert inside my body.

Stan shook his head. "They told me it's not a recent crime scene. It wouldn't have made a difference."

His words took the edge off my guilt, but self-loathing still gnawed at my gut. "Can we go in?"

Stan grunted and opened his mouth to speak when one of the officers piped up."We're supposed to keep the scene clear until the medical examiner and forensics team get here."

Something close to a growl emitted from Stan's throat.

My mountain lion purred with approval. *Good friend*, she said.

Now my inner kitty was proud of a friend's growling. *What. The. Fuck*.

"But, um..." The cop glanced at his comrades. "We can, um, look this way," he pointed to the wall across from the door, "and if someone were to slip into the crime scene we'd be none the wiser."

Stan's growl cut off. He gave a jerky nod, grabbed my arm and hauled me into the room.

The smells packed a punch and nearly knocked me on my ass. Death and pain. Hot iron from a stone mason's forge coated the walls and dripped off, sending waves of the unpleasant scent across the room. I didn't want to see the mystery man's body. I didn't need to. He'd been tortured.

The familiarity of his scent pinged a lightbulb in my head.

"Agent Nagato," I murmured. That's why his voice had sounded familiar on the recording. And from the heavy stench of death, this was why he'd dropped off the radar.

"The missing SRD agent?" Stan asked.

I nodded.

Stan stalked to the limp body tied to a chair in the middle of the room. Flies buzzed around the cadaver.

Another smell hit me. A dead animal. My mountain lion's soulful yowl racked my heart, and my falcon screeched.

The snow and tree sap of Nagato's lynx fera reached me through the waves of death and decay. I'd once thought he might be a bobcat, but the tree sap smell was unmistakeable.

My gaze snagged on a furry mess in the corner of the room. I dropped to my knees. Nausea boiled in my stomach like a cauldron of acid. My mountain lion yowled again, the hollow and broken sound echoed through my mind and vibrated my bones.

The bond between a Shifter and their fera was sacred. *Sacred.*

They'd defiled it.

"Bastards," I spat. A sob lodged in my throat.

Stan spun around, and his brows furrowed. Instead

of demanding an answer, he followed my outstretched arm pointing to the corner of the room.

"His fera? Stan asked.

I nodded. "They tortured his fera along with him. From the smell of Nagato's despair, they killed his fera first, so Nagato would die the most painful death. One of loss and heartbreak. Beyond cruel."

"And unnecessary. They got what they wanted from him. My gut tells me his TOD is before Loretta's. Once he gave them what Loretta knew, they killed him and went after my wife."

"We just need to know who," I said. My nose already confirmed Nagato's death occurred within days of Loretta's.

Stan grunted. "Got anything?"

I closed my eyes and opened my senses to the room, letting the rot and misery wash over me until I could pick out other scents—Nagato, his fera, unfamiliar norms, something old yet familiar...and Aahil. The drug dealer had been here.

My eyes narrowed. If Aahil had killed Loretta, he'd been smart enough to use a Witch charm to mask his scent, and prevent VPD backlash, yet neither he, nor anyone else on his diabolical team of douchebags, had found it necessary to mask their scents where they tortured and killed an SRD agent. If any crime scene would potentially crawl with scent-sensitive supes, it would be this one. Why the lack of effort? Did they not fear repercussions from the SRD? Did they know how inept the organization had become, or did they have another, more loathsome reason not to dread retaliation from the supernatural government branch?

Sergeant Lafleur's voice sounded in my head, his speech a distant memory. *"Let's get one thing straight, McNeilly. The SRD is corrupt."*

I glanced at the expectant look on Stan's face. The SRD's integrity would have to wait. Stan first. He'd chase after Aahil and gun him down before we solved the second part of this mystery. Loretta's research. She discovered something big enough to get her killed. It got Nagato killed...and probably Lucien, too. I wanted to know what it was. Tancher Pharmaceuticals' involvement, the side effects of KK, or something else, something more?

"Well?" Stan gruffed.

"Yeah." My shoulders dropping. "I got something."

"And?"

"And give me a minute." I pulled out my phone and punched in Donny's contact info.

"Andy," Stan growled.

I shushed him.

"Andy!" he repeated.

I smacked my palm against his mouth, and Donny's voicemail picked up. That's right. He said the SRD had tapped it. He wouldn't answer.

"Fuck." I hung up without leaving a message and turned to Stan. "I'll tell you, but you have to promise to remain calm and not act on the information right away."

Stan narrowed his eyes at me.

"I know I'm asking a lot. I promise on the goddess

Feradea and all my feras, you will have your vengeance, but there's something else going on here. Give me until tomorrow to get things straight, and we'll make a plan."

Stan ground his teeth together and clenched his fists. He stood tense and took long angry breaths as burnt cinnamon rolled of his body in waves. "Fine."

Truth. I didn't need a blood oath to know Stan stood by his word. "Aahil was here. But he wasn't alone. We need to figure out who and how this all connects together."

"Let's pick him up and torture the truth out of him."

"That might tip the others off."

"I've picked him up often enough it won't raise any suspicions."

I nodded. Thinking it through. "If we pick him up for this, it would have to be off the books."

"So?" Stan shifted his weight, ready to move, to take action.

"So, it means we'd have to handle the information we get from torturing him off the books, too."

Stan paused and stopped swaying. "You said you're pretty badass. You think we need help?"

I nodded again. "I think this is bigger than we can handle alone."

Stan jabbed his finger into my abdomen, just below the sternum, so hard I took a half-step back and winced.

"You have until tomorrow afternoon," he said.

30

When I walked into my apartment, a familiar smell greeted me. I'd been wanting this welcome for days, but now my stomach quivered and my hearing buzzed. Blood rushed to my head.

Citrus and sunshine, laced with honeysuckle from a warm summer's day. Tristan's scent usually made me think of mojitos and sex on the beach, still did, but today, it also put me on edge, because under the deliciousness of his fragrance, something else lurked, something dark and ugly.

A sour tang of canned ham, parmesan cheese, and musk oil collided with smoke and cobwebs in stiff air, laden with an invisible weight and blue cheese. The almost indiscernible mix of anxiety, despair, guilt, regret, sadness, and shame.

I paused at the entrance. If I turned around now, I could go back to la-la land and never face whatever horrific truth Tristan had to tell me. I could stick my head in the sand and pretend everything was okay and this divine Wereleopard Alpha who'd walked into my life and heart months ago remained perfection.

But that would be a lie.

I walked into the living room where Tristan waited. He sat on my couch, elbows rested on knees, with his hands cradling his bowed head. As I took the last few steps to reach the area in front of him, his head popped up, and he started to stand.

I held my hand out to stop him. He rocked back in the couch.

"Let's just skip the awkward hello and get right to it. We both know something's up and the anticipation is killing me." What awful truth could Tristan possess to cause such a reaction? One obviously eating him up inside.

Tristan nodded and bolted from the couch. I took a couple steps back. He didn't run away; he walked toward me, as if to kiss me and then hesitated. He spun and started pacing.

"You're freaking me out."

Tristan continued to pace.

"Please don't make me play twenty questions. I'll hate you more afterward. You've been avoiding me. Why?"

Tristan stopped. "I have to tell you something, and I don't know how."

"I find the best solution is to just spit it out."

"That might be the quickest way, but not the nicest. I'd prefer some tact."

"Why? So you look better? So whatever it is you did seems less awful than reality?"

He shook his head. "No. So I don't hurt or shock you more than necessary. I'm thinking of your feelings, not mine. Please hear me out."

Ice flowed through my veins. Hurt me? What could he possibly say that would hurt me? Donny's explanation of my snake fera and her meaning rang in my ears, *"...you will be hurt, Carus..."* My stomach lurched and grew heavy.

"Please believe me when I say I didn't know before. When my suspicions were confirmed, I tried to tell you, and, well..."

We'd done the horizontal mamba instead. My chest tightened, and my gut sank even lower in my abdomen.

"I should've tried harder to make you listen. I know that, but..."

When he broke into a heavy silence, I cleared my throat. "But what?"

"But I wanted you. This news might drive you away, and I selfishly wanted to be with you one last time."

"Well, shit. This is big, isn't it?" My throat dried out and began to ache. The room spun, yet time slowed.

He nodded.

"So you haven't decided you don't want a mate?"

Tristan growled, the sound so deep and feral it vibrated the room and travelled along my bones. "I've never wanted something, someone, more than I want you. I want you as my mate. I want to mark the soft skin of your neck and claim you as mine for all to see. No, I haven't decided against mating. My heart is yours."

I threw my hands up and ignored my fast beating heart. "Then, this is silly. Honestly! What could be so bad to come between us now?" Whatever he told me, we'd work through it. We had to.

"I killed your family."

31

A splattering of emotions smacked the inside of my skull as stiff silence descended on the room. My mind raced, trying to find answers, but instead of coming to any destination, my brain cells kept desperately sending signals around in circles. My chest constricted as my feet grew heavy as lead, sinking into the plush rug. Killed my family? What did he mean? How was that possible? "My dad died in a car accident and my mom of natural causes at a ripe old age."

"Your biological parents."

His statement replayed over and over again in my mind. I must've misheard him. He couldn't possible have killed my biological family. I didn't know who they were. Besides, he wouldn't have done that.

Would he?

Well, maybe... He'd been under Ethan's control. By Tristan's own admission, he'd done awful things at

Ethan's orders. His past held secrets, darkness, and shame.

The scrambled, hot mess in my brain gave way to a wave of hot anger. My knuckles popped and my canines elongated as my muscles quivered, demanding action. Heat flushed my veins as my pulse sped up.

Tristan killed my family, and he'd slept with me knowing the truth.

"Explain." My voice cracked.

He hesitated. "Norms weren't solely responsible for the Shifter Shankings. A lot of supes cashed in on the anger to take out threats, competition, and those with power or territory. The Shifters had a lot of influence, finding it easy to assimilate with norm society before the Purge."

He took a deep breath, probably to give me an opportunity to comment. I didn't.

He continued, "Ethan was among the supes to capitalize on the mass exterminations. He ordered me to systematically eradicate Shifter families that held prominent positions. I destroyed a lot of families. It's a past I cannot escape and one that haunts me to this day."

Digest information, breathe, repeat. Who the hell had my parents been that they made it on some douchebag's kill list? "Go on."

"Ethan specified I was to kill the targets and anyone else inside their home. I tried to end their lives as quickly and painlessly as possible, as Ethan hadn't dictated that detail, but your mother and father fought back valiantly. After it was over, I understood why." His mouth turned down, and the lines in his forehead creased.

The sour tang of his emotions wafted from his pores in a steady stream. The air in the living room compressed, as if our sadness bogged it down into a stuffy cesspool of emotions. Tristan ran a hand through his dark locks before continuing. "A baby. There was a baby in the house they protected with their lives. I'd avoided killing children on Ethan's orders previously by choosing a time they were out of the house. You weren't supposed to be there. The babysitter had stopped by to pick you up."

My chest tightened.

"The compulsion rode me hard, but I couldn't bring myself to kill an innocent baby, one that didn't smell of the forest, but more like a Christmas tree lot, filled with saplings and young spruce, cedar and fir. One that smelled of potential." His soft sapphire gaze flicked up to meet mine.

My body trembled.

"I fought Ethan's control long enough to carry you out of the house. The compulsion lifted. Ethan had ordered me to kill your parents and those inside their home. I could've saved a lot of lives, had I figured out the loophole sooner, had I not been in such a servant daze. My stupidity and weakness will forever be one of my greatest shames." His voice shook with his last words. He clenched his jaw and balled his fists.

"Have you always known?" He already implied he hadn't, but I needed to ask.

He shook his head. "Your scent has changed a lot since then. When we met at Lucien's, it struck me as familiar, as comfortable, as home, but I couldn't place it. I assumed it was a part of the mating call."

"What changed?"

"A moment. Almost two weeks ago when you came to my place. A movement of yours, a gesture, it triggered a memory of your mother. The flashback memory and knowing you were born during the Purge and adopted created this awful realization that our paths might've crossed before. As soon as that thought surfaced, I couldn't rest until I discovered the truth."

"Why wait to tell me now? Why not tell me your suspicions right away?"

"On a suspicion? Why drag up your painful past only to learn I had nothing to do with it? I wanted to be sure."

"And now? Now, you're sure?" I gulped, knowing his answer before he spoke, dreading it, yet hoping beyond reason he might answer differently.

His shoulders dropped, and he nodded. "I tracked down the adoption agency, and my team hacked their records. I'll never forget the day, much less the date, I dropped you off at that agency. Your file's information confirmed my worst nightmare."

"*Your* worst nightmare?"

He squeezed his eyes shut. "This happened in the past, before we knew each other, when my life wasn't my own to live. Ethan was responsible, and he's dead."

I'd chopped the fucker's head off myself.

"There's a silver lining."

My upper lip snarled on its own. "What good could possibly come of this?"

"You have a family, Andy. There were kid toys in another room. The babysitter must've picked up only him instead of both of you."

"Him?"

"You have an older brother. You have a family, Andy. And I know where to find them. That's where I've been. Unfortunately, there was no cell reception."

He still could've called when he got back to civilization, like he had with Angie. Or used a landline.

A family? I had a family?

A brother?

My heart spasmed in my chest again. No. No more. I couldn't take any more knowledge bombs today. An invisible weight settled on my shoulders. "I need some time to process this. I'd like you to leave."

"Andy—"

"Leave."

Tristan's sapphire gaze glittered. He squeezed his eyes shut, and his jaw twitched as he clenched his teeth, and balled his hands into fists. With a deep breath, he turned his gaze to me. He leaned forward and reached out with his hand. When I didn't move, he dropped his hand back to his side. His lips pursed. "I will give you time, Andy, but we're not done."

My chest became empty, numb. My muscles weak and tired. Coldness seeped into my veins, washing away the hot anger. Time appeared to slow again as I studied the conflicting expressions on Tristan's face through blurry vision.

Tristan continued to study my face silently until he slowly nodded, as if he answered his own internal question. After spearing me with a long soulful look, he walked out of the room.

I did nothing, said nothing, to stop him, yet the whole time, I couldn't shake this awful gut-wrenching feeling I'd failed him, not the other way around.

32

The conversation with Tristan left me raw and unsure. Yes, Tristan's actions were in the past, before he met me, before he had control of his life, but could I live with, bond with, have children with the murderer of my family? Knowingly?

He'd slept with me suspecting the truth. Maybe I should be thankful he didn't wait to reveal the truth until after the mating bond.

My heart convulsed in my chest as I crawled into bed. I still needed to connect the missing dots in the Loretta-KK case. I didn't have time for heartache and misery.

I wished Tristan had never told me.

If I'd never learned the truth, what pain or harm would it have caused? *Honesty is the best policy?* Not so sure on that one. Blissful ignorance looked real appealing right now.

Tristan admitted he had an ugly past. He struggled to live with it, as I did. We both had a pretty dirty rap-sheet.

Could he have lived with keeping this secret from me, too? Doubtful. He wanted no secrets. He wanted honesty. He wanted me. And despite knowing this truth would hurt both of us, he told me one of his deepest, darkest secrets.

I'd sent him away. Should I be the bigger person?

What did that even look like?

With a mangled cry, I shoved my face into my pillow and curled up, pulling the soft comforter around me. Tristan's stale scent still cocooned me, as if comforting me in his absence.

The last few attempts of sleep had been disastrous without him. My chest hollowed. I would've given my life for Tristan to live. Had that changed?

Another sob escaped my mouth. No.

I loved him.

Would that be enough? I'd loved Wick, too, but I'd broken things off with him for our mutual safety. In retrospect, he'd done far less to me than Tristan. But that was different, wasn't it? Neither man had a choice in their actions, but Tristan completed his sins before he knew me, Wick had hurt me while in a relationship with me. Sort of. He hadn't wanted to.

Tristan had fought the compulsion to get me to safety, before he knew I'd be his mate.

What was Tristan thinking right now? Did he hate me for sending him away? Had I failed him somehow? Not exactly the perfect picture of a supportive mate. Did Tristan lie awake in his Port Moody bed, staring at the ceiling, unable to sleep like me?

Sleep.

It should've been harder to come by, but I'd been running on empty for too long, that it shouldn't have come as a surprise when my thoughts began to drift into incoherent images.

I needed to forgive Tristan, make things right.

Visions of my lover's face grew fuzzy, distorted like objects in a deep fog. When the streams of light punctured the thick mist, Tristan's face was replaced with Sid's.

Sid!

I bolted upright, only to find myself on the mossy floor of a dense forest, not my bed. What the heck? I palmed the moist soil and held it out. It floated off my palm like fairy dust, carrying away its fresh earthy scent. Wind gently wove around the broad tree trunks, but instead of carrying the penetrating cold of Lower Mainland weather, it held the warmth of a summer's breeze on a beach.

Sid smiled and grabbed my hands. "Dance with me, beautiful anchor."

He twirled me around and around until the setting changed. Trees gave way to sand dunes, and green gave way to the deep blue of the Pacific Ocean.

"You look so much like Fera's daughter," he said before he ducked to kiss my cheek. Before I could punch him in the face, he skipped down the beach. Mermaids swam onto rocks offshore and called out to him.

"This is fucked," I breathed and followed after the Seducer Demon. Obviously, we were in some dream state, but this time things felt different. Before, Sid would invade my dreams and manipulate them with gleeful satisfaction and feed off any sexual energy he created.

This time the dream...my dream? I glanced around the unfamiliar landscape as it once again morphed into a different scene. This one looked like a stone room in a castle. Large slabs of concrete fit together like a jigsaw puzzle, and outlined the large space. Old tapestries hung from the walls and thread-bare rugs covered the floors, at least the parts I could see. The rest of the room was filled with naked humans, entwined together, writhing in ecstatic delight. Sid walked into the centre and flung his head back and his arms wide.

Seen that look before.

The energy in the room waned as Sid drew it into his essence to feed.

This was his dream.

Holy crap, I'd invaded Sid's dream somehow.

Did that mean I could control it? I closed my eyes and focused my energy on the graphic scene on the other side of my shut lids. What would ruin this for Sid? What took the sexy out of sexy time?

A leg cramp?

A man hollered in pain.

A stomach bug?

A woman moaned, and her feet slapped against bare stone as she ran from the room to vomit outside.

Explosive diarrhea?

"No!" A couple gasped. I opened my eyes and watched them spring up and run from the room covering their bums. Thankfully the sounds of their running disappeared around the corner so I didn't have to hear the result of that one.

The rest of the norm mass kept writhing and gasping with pleasure. I'd made a little dent in Sid's smorgasbord of sexual energy. He hadn't noticed anything...yet.

Challenge accepted.

With gritted teeth, I sent every person left in the room thoughts, actions and inactions—mood killers. Some lay prone doing their best starfish impersonations, some started barking like dogs, some talked incessantly about their days, while others just made weird slurping sounds.

More. Needed more. Garlic belches, eye-watering farts, bad clichéd dirty talk, kids crying in the background, and mother-in-laws talking in the next room. My favourite was the one man who bumped around awkwardly, apologized, and asked permission for each kiss, lick, or, well, otherwise, with a fake English accent.

Nice touch, McNeilly.

The energy in the room quickly dissipated, and not from the sex leech sucking it up. My job done, I beamed.

Sid's head snapped down, his eyes bugged open and he turned toward me. "ANDY."

I bowed. "At your service."

He glanced around, dark eyebrows furrowed in olive skin. "How are you here?"

"No idea. I'm not exactly an experienced anchor."

"Let me rephrase. What are you doing here?" He

swept his hand in front of him to indicate the room, now full of angry, insecure, and whimpering norms.

"Making your life as miserable as you've made mine?"

"I thought we worked things out."

"By watching television?"

He nodded.

"Do you still plan to use me next new moon?"

He nodded again.

"Then we worked nothing out."

Sid's lips snarled up. He flung his hand out, palm forward and an invisible force knocked into me. "Get out of my dream."

I sat up in my bed, still carrying Tristan's faint scent, and smiled.

33

With my phone tapped and Donny refusing to answer his phone—despite my best intentions to avoid saying anything incriminating—I decided to drop by unannounced at the SRD headquarters.

My heart sank when unfamiliar guards greeted me on entry. No Ben or Matt to brighten my day. The new guards at the front door accepted my old ID. Without any hassle or ATF run-ins, I found Donny in his dusty office, cluttered with ancient texts and smelling of coyote mischief.

"Carus, what a surprise." Donny smirked.

"Cut the crap." I had yet to surprise the old Shifter, and he knew it.

Ma'ii, his coyote fera, popped his head up from his dog bed nestled in the corner and barred his teeth at me. I stuck my tongue out in response.

Super professional.

"How can I help you?" Donny asked.

"Do you have any idea how difficult it is to find an expert on hieroglyphics in Vancouver?" I flopped down in the empty chair across the desk from Donny.

He frowned.

"Not the complaint you expected?"

He leaned back and laced his long wrinkly fingers together. "Honestly? You whine so much it's hard to know what to expect."

Well, Donny certainly didn't hold back on the truth. One of the things I liked about the old man. Sometimes, though, it would be nice if he kept his thoughts to himself. I didn't whine that much.

"Why do you need an expert?" Donny asked.

"A logo for a pharmaceutical company seems connected to a prominent KK drug dealer and quite possibly the murder of an officer's wife. I wanted to know if the hieroglyph has any significant meaning."

"But you can't find any?"

I shook my head. "Reverse image searches just lead me to the pharmaceutical company, and the ancient Egyptian expert from UBC overdosed suspiciously on KK a few weeks ago. We think loose ends are being tied up. There's a small Egyptian community in Surrey, but they're not exactly experts on ancient Egyptian hiero-glyphs." If Booth, the Egyptian goddess who'd posed as an SRD Agent to find her long lost love, still roamed the mortal realm, I'd ask her, but once I reunited her with Sobek, they'd taken off.

My brain stilled.

Booth was Egyptian...The hieroglyph was Egyptian. Was Booth connected to this in some way? My gut sank, but my brain kept processing. It didn't feel right. Not that Booth and I were besties and braided each other's hair, but this didn't seem like something she'd dip her goddess fingers into.

"Show me." Donny interrupted my internal musings.

"Excuse me?"

"Show me the hieroglyph."

"You're an expert?"

"I've been around for a long time."

My chest tightened as I pulled out the torn letterhead from my pocket, the one we retrieved from Loretta's storage locker. Without a word, I smoothed it on the edge of the desk before sliding it across the smooth surface toward Donny.

He grunted.

"What?"

"I'm glad you're not an investigator. Your handling of evidence is atrocious."

My fingers twitched, but I laced them together before I did something stupid, like flash Donny an inappropriate gesture. "One, there were tons of these retrieved at the scene, and two..."

"Two?"

Two, Stan and I didn't plan to go through the legal system for justice. I bit my lip and shrugged at Donny. He probably wouldn't rat on us, but he didn't deserve becoming an accessory.

Donny's mouth twitched as he reached forward and

snatched the crumpled paper from my hand. He flipped it over. And stilled.

His slight smile drooped into a flat line. Like a Vampire, Donny seemed to withdraw into the recesses of his mind, his body froze and his eyes trained on the paper before going blank and distant.

My scalp prickled.

Fly away, my falcon screeched.

Donny definitely recognized the symbol and from his reaction the information was bad, real bad. My sissy falcon kept flapping her wings in my head, wanting to get away before another knowledge bomb dropped.

Would Donny even share the truth with me? Or would he try to hide it? Donny played his own game, one that had never harmed me before, but first time for everything. As one of the oldest Shifters I'd met, Donny obviously played his game very well.

After three million ticks of the second hand, or thereabouts, Donny's stiff posture loosened; as if every muscle relaxed from his heart outward as he came back to reality.

He cleared his throat and slid the paper back to me.

"Please don't bullshit me," I said.

"You swear too much." Donny's voice had dropped an octave and gained some gravel. He cleared his throat again.

"They're sentence enhancers, not swear words."

Donny smirked, but the humour had drained from his face when he saw the logo.

"You recognize the symbol." Statement. Not a question.

"I do."

"Will you tell me what it means?"

He pushed back from his desk and clasped his hands. His gaze drifted off into never-never-land again for a minute. "I'm deciding whether it's better for your health to remain ignorant."

"Ignorance is rarely bliss."

"It might be in this case."

My blood pressure increased and an ache developed behind my eyes. "If you don't tell me, I'll find someone who will, even if I have to fly to Egypt."

"That's what I'm afraid of."

"I'm pretty badass, Donny."

"Not badass enough," he muttered.

"Excuse me? There're very few individuals who can best me in a one-on-one fight when I'm in beast form."

Except Demons, my beast hissed.

"At least, not on this plane of existence," I added. "You don't need to protect me, Donny. Besides, remaining ignorant might be more dangerous for me, since I don't plan on stopping my investigation."

Donny nodded slowly, his shaggy white hair fanning his face. "You're right, very few can best you. Very few still means some."

A slight chill travelled through my body. "This is one of the few?"

Donny nodded again.

"Then tell me who or what I'm dealing with. I'd rather go into this with full disclosure than get blindsided. I'm not going to stop just because the bad guy is scary." Inside, my gut twisted into a complicated knot.

"Are you sure about that? This may mean your death."

"They killed my friend's wife. Someone I care about. Yes, I'm sure." Truth.

Donny pursed his lips.

"Tell me. Which of the few ass-kickers am I up against?"

"The Pharaoh."

THE PLASTIC OF THE CHAIR CREAKED AS I shifted my weight. Goosebumps prickled along my spine and settled like cold icicles at the base of my skull.

Donny sat across the desk, observing me like a puzzle with a missing piece. His craggy skin bunched up between his two white shaggy eyebrows.

"The Pharaoh?" I asked. "The ridiculously old Vampire who makes the new ones all pee themselves when he's mentioned?"

Donny chuckled. "You've met him?"

"Briefly. At a NAVA convention when I served Lucien."

"What did you think?" He drummed his fingertips on his desk.

"Old. He smelled old, like frail, deteriorating parchment, yet powerful."

A pause. "You can't best him as you currently are."

"Time to hit the gym?"

"It will take more than a six-pack to best the Pharaoh."

My skin rankled. I grunted. "So what's the hieroglyph?"

"Few know it. It's from his past, from a time when he ruled as a pharaoh in ancient Egypt. The hieroglyph is a symbol of his name, from the time before he was turned."

"Is there anything else you know about him that would be helpful?"

"No. The Pharaoh is subtle though. If he wants Vancouver as a territory, he'll take it. If he wants King's Krank on the street, he'll do it."

"Why would he want KK on the street?"

"I've been thinking about that myself."

"And?"

"I got nothing. The pharmaceutical company must play a part somehow."

Tancher Pharmaceutical. The drug company specialized in research. The company, KK, Aahil, and now the Pharaoh were connected; Donny was right, if the Pharaoh wanted KK on the streets, he had enough power to make it happen. So why the charade of the drug company?

A thought hit my brain, so dark and twisted it made

my neurons recoil. My mouth grew sour and nausea heaved in my stomach.

Research. The Pharaoh had the drug company researching KK, which meant the introduction of King's Krank to the streets also served a purpose.

"Human trials," I gasped. "They released KK on the streets to test it on humans."

Ma'ii and Donny growled in unison.

"Motherfuckers," I said. My nails dug into the soft skin of my palms as I clenched my fists tight. My gums tingled, canines aching to elongate and sink into someone's flesh. The human trials must've been what Loretta stumbled upon. And it got her killed.

Hunt, my mountain lion hissed.

Destroy, my beast growled.

The falcon let out an eardrum-shattering screech and demanded we fly away to expunge the grime still coating my neurons. After a hurried goodbye to Donny and Ma'ii, and a thirty minute drive home, I gave her what she wanted.

34

S tan's hotel room reeked of old popcorn kernels, and a slew of alcohol. The air remained stiff and stagnant, invisibly weighed down by Stan's grief.

He hauled me into the main room when I knocked on the door and now he paced in front of me, back and forth, wearing down the already worn carpet, to the point of exposing the concrete underneath.

"Dish it, Andy. I waited," Stan said.

"I know. You sure you don't want to sit down? It's a doozy."

"Andy!"

I held my hands up. This involved his wife's murder. I got that, but I also had no idea how to share the information in a tactful way. Sensibility training wasn't exactly a mandatory requirement when the SRD trained me as an assassin.

Just spit it out. Factual. Concise. Without emotion. Like I handled all the other big reveals in my life. I might lack finesse, but at least I didn't spray poop with perfume and call it roses.

"Okay, Stan. Loretta stumbled upon Tancher Pharmaceuticals' real purpose in Vancouver. They're manufacturing KK and releasing it to the public as a form of human trials for their research. Aahil must be the main drug dealer spearheading the operation, but an ancient and extremely dangerous Vampire, simply known as the Pharaoh, is behind the whole thing. He's bad. Like super bad."

"Really? Super bad?"

"Donny, my old handler at the SRD, doesn't think I could take him in beast form."

Stan blanched. "Beast form?"

I winced. "Oh, right. Haven't told you about that. In summary, even my most dangerous form can't stand against this guy, and that's saying a lot."

Stan shook his head, mumbling "beast form," a couple of times. He finally straightened, and pinned me with a steely gaze. "Do you have a plan?"

"I want to make sure the Pharaoh is out of town and then take down the pharmaceutical company with the VPD. We stop their operation and raid their servers for more information. That way we can take down everyone involved. Later, after the dust settles, you get Aahil. After the fact, and off the books, so you can walk away from whatever you decide to do."

Stan blinked.

"We'll weaken the Pharaoh's hold on Vancouver. Not

sure how to defeat him in the long run, but at least we'll take care of the KK threat and Aahil."

Stan nodded. "I like it."

My mouth twitched. Stan wasn't exactly heavy with the compliments.

"We need surveillance," Stan said. "Information on the building plans, and their security system. I'll get the tech team on it, but they take time."

The word "security" sent a pang to my heart, followed swiftly with hollow longing. "I know someone for the security side of things."

Stan grunted. "Let's get this done."

ONCE AGAIN THE LARGE RED DOUBLE DOORS OF Tristan's Port Moody home stared back at me, daring me to run away or knock, mocking me, questioning whether I was good enough for the man on the other side. From the fierce bouquet of lemon with a pinch of pepper, Tristan already knew I stood here. I'd surprised him by coming to his place.

The citrus and sunshine scent of the pack permeated around the house, but a certain stiffness weighed it down.

Did they think I planned to break up with Tristan? That would make Angie happy.

Break up with Tristan?

My heart dropped in my chest. Could I live without him?

My stomach rolled. No. I couldn't.

Could I forgive him for killing my birth parents? Could I accept his history, and share mine with him? I had shameful things in my past as well. I'd used people and myself.

My breathing hitched, and the answer to my unspoken question remained hidden.

Hadn't I dumped Wick for less? My gut grew heavy and an invisible weight plunked down on my shoulders as the recurrent thought niggled at my brain.

Wick was probably laughing his ass off at the karma of the situation. Laughing with Christine.

Yeesh!

I slapped my palm against my forehead. Repeatedly. Wick's thoughts on this matter were irrelevant. And who he was with didn't change anything. I'd made my choice and whatever was going on right now was between me and Tristan. I had to wipe thoughts of Wick completely away. *Wick was then. Tristan is now.*

Andy, you're killing me. Tristan's voice filled my head. Usually deep and smooth he sounded rougher, more gravelly. *Are you coming in?*

"Yes." I spoke to the door. *Yes.*

The door swung open and a disheveled angel in baggy sweats stood before me. A plain white shirt emphasized his broad shoulders and fit body. My first instinct was to run my hands up his six-pack, tracing each defined muscle before resting on his strong pecs. His citrus and sunshine scent laced around me, the honeysuckles of his leopard teased my mountain lion and beckoned for her to come play. My pulse picked up and warmth flushed my body. Uncharacteristic stubble darkened Tristan's face and accentuated his piercing blue eyes. I wanted to drown in their pools of sadness.

"I've missed you." His jaw clenched and yellow flashed in his eyes. His Alpha power rode him hard not to play docile or patient with me. His fists clenched, yet he remained immobile, waiting for me to say something, do something.

His strength over his animal still impressed me.

"I need your help," I said.

He rocked back on his heels, and his lips flattened. "Andy—"

I held my hand out to stop his protest. "I know it's a dick move to ask something of you when I asked for time, but I really do need your help. It's not for me."

"Stan?"

"Yeah."

Tristan sighed and then stepped aside. "Of course, I'll help you. Come in."

In the living room, I quickly outlined the story and what I needed. Tristan simply nodded and led me to his bedroom.

"Um..." I looked around. For the first time, Tristan's house was completely void of prowl members and various items lay strewn across the place giving the whole home a messy appearance. Not that I cared. I was in no position to judge housekeeping skills. The only time my place looked spotless was when I procrastinated from getting other things done. Or I expected guests.

"I sent them all away," Tristan muttered as he dug around in his drawers and pulled out clothes. "They're taking vacations, visiting family, or staying somewhere else. A lot of the prowl kept their places from the Ethan days. Sometimes even felines need a break from their prowls. We're a small group. The ones who work for me are staying in the rooms at the office."

I nodded, not that he could see me. The majority of the prowl lived at Tristan's since Ethan's death. The silence and emptiness of the place bore down on me like a lead blanket.

When Tristan threw the blue shirt I loved so much on the bed, he spun to face me. "I will find a way for you to forgive me." His gaze drilled into mine.

I looked at my feet.

Coward, my mountain lion hissed. *Not submissive.*

No, but not nearly as dominant as Tristan.

"I want to," I muttered.

"What?"

"I want to forgive you. I want to get past this, but..." Feradea help me! I sounded like a broken record. How many times would I push a good man away?

"You need time to process?" Tristan's tone was soft, but it carried an edge. As if he understood why, but didn't like it. "I'll give you whatever you need, Andy, but don't push me away. Let me help you."

"You are helping me."

"Not just with Stan's stuff. With everything. Let me be here for you." He reached out and gently squeezed my shoulder, letting his hand slide down my arm until he held my hand.

"Where are we going?" I asked.

Tristan raised his dark brow.

"You're pulling clothes out of your dresser. You're not the type to make up an excuse just to change in front of me."

Tristan's lips twitched into a smile for the first time since I arrived. His white teeth flashed as he released my hand. *Whoosh!* He shucked his sweatpants off, and his shirt followed to provide a world-class view. With a solid defined six-pack, my gaze naturally followed the indented V down to...

Perfection. A view that was all mine, if I claimed it, if I marked the soft skin of his neck during the throes of passion.

Mine, the mountain lion hissed.

The falcon squawked.

"We're going to my office," Tristan said as he pulled the blue shirt on and stepped into dark denim jeans.

Going commando. *Feradea, help me.*

Tristan had never taken me to the office, saying he didn't like to mix business with pleasure. I understood. The SRD and VPD headquarters hardly made for good date destinations, but curiosity nipped away at my mountain lion and my mind, and I would've found some excuse sooner or later to visit Tristan at work and have a looksee.

Now, it seemed, an excuse wasn't necessary. It was show and tell day at the office.

35

The simple-styled business building with reflective windows and four stories loomed over me as we approached. Kayne Security Solutions owned its name and offered a bevy of personal and business solutions for safety and security of people, information, possessions, and property. Electronic security systems, personal security detail, temporary guards—it provided everything for a pretty price. I searched it on the internet months ago.

No wonder Tristan drove the latest hybrid sports car, and ripped out of designer clothes with little thought. He did very well for himself.

The drive over had been quiet, but tense. Even with the windows cracked, Tristan's delicious scent bottled up in the confined space. Part of me wanted to launch my body across the centre console and lick him all over like a lollipop, and the other part of me drowned in self-loathing that I'd even consider jumping the man when I hadn't figured out how I felt about our situation. If Tristan's leather seats could've swallowed me whole, I would've gladly welcomed it.

Now, as we walked to the main doors, the man beside me vibrated with warmth and love. I wanted to reach out and touch him. But I didn't. Why? Why did I hold back? For something he did in his past before he knew me? For having to serve a sadistic Master Vampire that made Lucien look like Bambi? For having the strength to be honest with me instead of trying to hide his shame? For some convoluted belief I should be angry and upset at him when all I wanted was...

"Penny for your thoughts." Tristan held the glass doors of his company open for me.

"I'd really like to understand my brain someday."

Tristan chuckled and followed me in. He reached down and clasped my hand. The contact of his skin sent tingles up my arm. I didn't let go. I squeezed his hand back as we walked through the sparse lobby.

A long receptionist desk with an elevator to the right and a door, presumably the stairs, to the left sat on the opposite side of the lobby. Cameras tracked our progress along the dark slab tiles. The little motors purred as the machines moved along with us.

"Hello, Mr. Kayne," a middle-aged receptionist with graying brown hair and kind eyes greeted us. Her gaze flicked to me briefly, before dropping to our joined hands. Her smile broadened.

"Hello, Suzy." Tristan smiled back. "This is Andy."

Suzy nodded and stood. Reaching over her desk, she

offered her hand and I shook it. Chamomile tea swirled around in her nutty scent. Shifter, not Were. Feline, but not leopard, mountain lion, or bobcat. I couldn't put my nose on it, but asking, "what are you?" would be rude.

"Ocelot," she whispered with a wink.

I grinned and nodded, but my internal badass recoiled. I kept my happy-to-meet-you face plastered on, while my mind raced. How had she read me so easily? I'd kept my expression pleasantly neutral. Only Tristan still gauged my internal musings with ease. Since the tattoo shop receptionist, I'd made more effort to shutter my emotions from my expression. Had my face become an open book for others to read despite my best efforts? My feras bristled.

I searched the receptionist's face, but she wore an open smile, and her kind eyes held no calculations.

No. She hadn't read me at all. My own insecurities were bubbling up. Suzy probably got asked the "what are you" question all the time, and knowing I could tell she was something, decided to throw the truth out there. Tristan pulled me toward the right. When we stepped into the freshly-scented elevator, Tristan called out to Suzy, "Hold any calls. I'm here on personal business."

"Got it," she replied. If she said anything else, the closing doors cut her off.

"Seems nice," I said. A lot nicer than Angie. But why would Tristan choose an older, kinder receptionist over sexpot Angie with the good looks and killer body? "Clients come here to feel safe. Suzy is open and honest.

She puts everyone at ease. Angie has a lot of qualities, but that's not one of them."

I snorted. "I didn't realize being a bitch was a quality."

"Angie...she's had it rough. When we were under Ethan's control..." His mouth flattened into a straight line, and his muscles tensed. "I tried to protect her, and everyone else in my prowl as much as possible, but she's an attractive woman. Bad men took notice..."

I held my hand up. "I get it." And I did. It made my heart soften a little toward Angie, and a lot toward Tristan. His sad gaze told me who he blamed for Angie's suffering. I needed to lighten the mood.

"If she keeps pushing me, though, Tristan, you're going to end up with a cat fight."

Tristan's lips twitched, and his gaze flicked to me before he leaned forward and pressed the button for the third floor.

The elevator jerked into motion. "This place is bigger than I expected."

"There's a room behind the receptionist desk for training. The basement has parking, supplies, and artillery. Second floor is offices, meeting rooms, storage, et cetera. Third floor is where most of the grunt work is done. It houses the IT department, our security programs, and all our surveillance footage. Fourth floor is housing, where a number of us stay after long missions or during intense projects. It's like a floor in a mini-apartment building."

I nodded to acknowledge I heard him, but my mind

had travelled someplace else. The small elevator offered little in the way of air circulation. If the car had been bad, this was worse. Tristan's scent accumulated into an overwhelming concentration. So potent, my head spun. Speaking was impossible. The citrus and sunshine melded with honeysuckles on a hot summer's day. I wanted to wrap his scent around me like a blanket and roll around. I wanted to sip raspberry mojitos, and have sex on the beach. Have him plow—

"Andy?" Tristan turned toward me, his eyebrows pinched. He took a long drag of air and shuddered. His eyelids half-closed and a purr erupted from his chest.

Well, damn. Guess he knew where my mind went.

He leaned toward me. "I've thought about taking you in this elevator every day at work. Pinning you against the wall, with your long legs wrapped around me..."

I melted. Something clenched. Heat pooled. I shut my eyes and swallowed. Deep breaths pulled in more of his intoxicating scent. My head swam with possibilities.

"Only one problem..." His smooth voice drifted off.

My eyes snapped open. "What?"

The elevator dinged, and the doors opened.

"The ride's too short for what I have in mind," he finished, before hauling me out of the small compartment. If the elevator ding hadn't announced our presence, the air rushing out with our scents and the smell of our arousal certainly did.

Multiple men and women—some Wereleopards, some Shifters, some norms—all glanced up from their computers. The supes in the room shared smug glances and knowing looks. With a flash of a few red dollar bills, I was pretty sure money exchanged hands. Our little elevator interlude didn't go unnoticed.

The floor held multiple cubicles and large screens adorned the walls, some showing images from this office, some displaying unfamiliar rooms and people.

"Olly?" Tristan turned toward a beefcake with no neck. Wereleopard, and one of the prowl members. Tristan had mentioned his second-in-command a few times.

"Yeah, boss?" His gaze darted to me, quick and calculating, probably assessing whether I'd hurt his Alpha again.

I kept my posture relaxed and my face open. If Tristan and I made this work, I'd become a part of the prowl.

Olly's gaze dropped to our clasped hands, and a small smile broke his stern expression.

"I texted you about Tancher Pharmaceuticals," Tristan said to Olly. "We got anything on them?"

Olly's grin widened. "We installed their entire security system."

Tristan nodded. "I'd like everything we have on them, on and off the books, sent to the IT conference room."

Olly mock-saluted and winked at me. Tristan didn't seem insulted or shocked. He simply nodded again and pulled me to the room at the back of the floor.

Tristan motioned for me to precede him, and I stepped into the small conference room with no windows, three monitors on the wall, and a large rectangular table surrounded with ten large office chairs.

"Have a seat. Olly will get us the information soon. I'm sure he started compiling it as soon as he got my text. Very efficient."

I quirked a brow. Tristan seemed tense.

"You smell so good," he said. "If you don't sit down and distance yourself, Olly might walk in on more than his pay grade allows."

At least I wasn't the only one hypersensitive and aware. I pulled out one of the chairs while Tristan grabbed a laptop from the cupboard, plugged in, and booted up.

"We should talk," he said without glancing up.

"Thought we were talking."

Tristan grunted and tapped away on his keyboard. "About your family. Whether you'll let me help you find them. I have the connections. About whether you can forgive me."

I sighed and leaned back. The office chair was real leather and super cushy. I rocked it back and forth a little before spinning it around once. To test it, of course.

Tristan cleared his throat and finally looked up, pegging me with his gem-cutting gaze.

"I'm not sure it's even forgiveness I'm searching for. I feel like I should be angry at you. Like I shouldn't be with the person responsible for the murder of my biological parents, but..."

"But?" He pounced on the word, his tone gruff and low.

"But, I'm not angry. I don't hold you responsible for my parents' deaths. That doesn't sit right with me. It was Ethan. I know that. There must be something wrong with me, because after the initial wave of confusion and anger, I just feel...weird."

Tristan tilted his head and studied me. "So, you've been upset with me because you think you should be upset with me?"

Well, when he said it like that... "Pretty much."

"Huh."

"Now I just feel stupid. I also feel like I failed you."

"Failed me?"

"The first time you divulge some of your painful past, which couldn't have been easy, I not only threw it in your face, but pushed you away. I wasn't a good mate to you." I looked down at my twisted hands. "Can you understand?"

Tristan reached over and placed his hand on top of mine. "Yeah, I can understand. You have the right to be upset. To be angry and confused. I suspected you would need time to process. Now that you've had a bit though..." He paused. His gaze flashed leopard-yellow. His jaw clenched. "Can you forgive me?"

The indescribable tenderness—the one I'd experienced during our first true night together, the one so fragile yet strong and potent at the same time—built in in my chest, expanding again to the brink of pain. Watching Tristan struggle to maintain control of his animal while asking forgiveness and trying to hide how much my answer meant to him, sent comforting warmth through my body.

Could I forgive him? "I think so. But why do I feel so awkward? Like I've emotionally shut down?"

Tristan's mouth widened, and his white teeth flashed. Musky coconut infused in his scent as he leaned forward. "I know the perfect cure for that." His muscles tensed as if he prepared to haul me out of the seat and throw me on the board table.

My heart raced. "What about—"

"Got everything!" Olly exclaimed as he knocked and opened the door in a single motion. "Oh! Um...sorry."

"Thank you, Olly." Tristan straightened and snatched the thick folder and a large document tube from Olly.

Olly rubbed his shaved head and shifted his weight back and forth. "I sent the rest to the laptop." His cheeks flamed red. He nodded at both of us before hastily backing out of the room, and shutting the door.

"Might have to increase that paycheque," I said.

Tristan nodded and pulled what looked like floor plans from the document tube. "Let's pick apart Tancher Pharmaceuticals first."

36

Sleep came quickly as I lay in bed and ran my fingers along my lips, the same lips that had pressed against Tristan's before he said goodbye, and reconfirmed our date for after the Tancher takedown.

Soft, full, and pliable. His lips had covered mine while his tongue delved into my mouth and stirred passion strong enough to vibrate my bones.

My heart swelled with the knowledge we'd work things out, that my emotional block would go away, and we'd get back to where we were, only better and stronger.

My mind drifted in a deep sleep, roaming through memories, more good than bad.

The flickering film reel of images slowed, then cleared, and suddenly my feet sank into the mossy bank of a river. Mist caressed the shoals and trickling water, while large rocks protruded from the flowing mass with a glossy sheen.

Movement across the water caught my attention. A dark form took shape. Tristan?

I straightened and smoothed down my gossamer nightgown.

Nightgown?

My gaze narrowed, and the mist parted to reveal a seven foot Seducer Demon.

"Sid," I spat.

He held his hands up, palms out. "Truce, Carus. I came to talk."

I grumbled, but my slurs didn't faze him. When he continued to study me, I caved. "What do you want?"

"A truce."

"A truce?"

He nodded.

"Because you've realized I can jump in and manipulate your dreams to make your sleepy-time as miserable as you've made mine?"

He scowled.

"Isn't nice, is it?"

"No."

"Well, remove your mark. Find a more willing anchor." My heart beat quickly in my chest. Maybe this would get me out of the bond.

Sid folded his arms across his chest. His pectoral muscles bubbled up. "I want to come to an agreement."

I waited.

"I will continue to use you as my anchor. That's not something I'm giving up. However, I'm a reasonable

Demon. I'm open to negotiation, I can give you things, many things."

My body tensed. "I don't need assistance in the multiple orgasm department, Demon."

Sid smirked. "I know."

My brain scrambled. He would continue to use the bond regardless of tonight's outcome. My shoulders sagged. Maybe... Maybe I should negotiate with the Demon, set some boundaries, and make the situation more tolerable until I found a way out of it altogether.

"Okay," I agreed. "Let's make a deal."

He nodded. "Name your terms, little Carus."

"Find a way to make the transition to the mortal realm less uncomfortable. That shit hurt." I flicked up a finger for each point. "Stop manipulating my dreams, and I'll promise the same. Stop feeding off my sexual energy, and I'll promise to feed you real food on new moon nights. You can use me as an anchor once a month, but you have to promise to do no harm while you're here."

"No nuts."

"Excuse me?" Coming from a Seducer Demon, it was a reasonable request for clarification.

"No nuts in whatever you feed me, and a proviso on the no harm term and we have a deal. Your parameters are quite reasonable."

"What kind of proviso?"

"I will not harm you or anyone under your protection. I reserve the right to harm those who attack either me or you, and I reserve the right to harm others on an individual basis. These would be people who've wronged me in the past or present, not random, group slaughters, like Bola. I don't feed on pain, fear, or bloodshed, and typically avoid it. You know this."

I nodded. Crap. Should I have asked for more? He agreed so easily. "No nuts. I agree to the no harm revision, but I also reserve the right to renegotiate, should other situations arise."

Sid narrowed his gaze.

I shrugged. I could turn his slumber into a nightmare. No more wet dreams for him. "Take it or leave it."

"Deal," he said.

"Do we shake on it?" I eyed the river.

"Silly mortal." He grew a talon and sliced open his palm.

Demons and their fascination with blood. I mirrored his actions and recited my agreement to the terms.

I'd just made a deal with the Devil.

Well, his assistant, anyway.

37

The cool fall wind rustled the soft feathers on the underside of my wings as I glided through the night toward Anacis Island—home of Tancher Pharmaceuticals.

With the plan firmly in place, now was not the time to take a joy ride, no matter how perfect the flying conditions.

The aerial view showed the VPD task force moving into position. With radio silence, they counted on me to get the job done. I couldn't let them down.

I wouldn't let Stan down.

After confirming the Pharaoh's presence in Denver at a Vampire convention, we chose a night raid to obtain the files and servers and to seize any King's Krank on site to avoid the daytime office workers. We didn't want to unnecessarily risk lives or risk the staff holing up in their offices to destroy evidence before we reached them.

The wind pushed and pulled as it swirled around the

trees and multilevel buildings on the island. Tucking my wings in, I flew to the top of Tancher Pharmaceuticals. With both feet perched on the ledge of the roof, my falcon eyesight spotted the north tactical team moving to the ditch across the street. One of them, Stan, took out a mirror and caught the light from the overhanging street-lamp to flash me the message.

Go time.

With a few hops and flaps of my wings, I made it to the central air duct on the rooftop. A quick shift to human form allowed me the use of fingers. The small grate and six screws provided little resistance to my supe strength. Metal scraped against metal for a brief second before I flung the grate off the vent. I paused. My heart stuck in my throat. No alarm sounded. I relaxed.

This was the hard part. I couldn't slither up metal, nor could I fly down the narrow duct. So I'd have to prop myself up on the vent and then shift into the snake. The building plans Tristan provided showed a drop until the duct branched into multiple directions. The trick would be to not die from the three meter drop. When my tiny, vulnerable, non-badass snake-self hit the branching part, I needed to pick the right direction, too.

Here goes nothing.

The shift back to a falcon, left my head dizzy and ears ringing. Never good to shift in quick succession. I could handle it though. I had to.

Using the air flows, I flew to the open grate and braced my small body with my talons gripping the thick metal on each side of the hole. The wind pushed against my sides. I wobbled. Teetering to maintain balance, my little bird heart hammered in my chest.

Deep breath.

I focused inward and called Kaa. As soon as her cold energy appeared, I pulled her essence into me and shifted. The shape came swiftly. My blood cooled as the scales crawled up my skin and replaced feathers. My beak receded and my tongue elongated, becoming forked. Flesh compacted. After sharp pain raked my body, my shift completed.

And I dropped.

I bounced off the sides of the duct as I tried to wrangle my small body into some sort of orientation. My brain spun as the air rushed by me.

Splat.

I hit the junction. The hard metal stung every cell of my body. My head whipped against the air duct. My ribcage narrowed, and my breath whooshed out. Stunned.

That fucking hurt.

Slowly, feeling returned to my body. With no diaphragm in snake form, my ribcage ached as it widened to suck in more air. Apnea set in after each exhale. Stillness flowed over my skin. Was this normal? Did snakes stop breathing? It seemed...wrong.

Normal, Kaa hissed. *Get a wiggle on.*

The light travelling down the duct from the roof illuminated four directions, not three, like the building plan stated. Which way was the correct one?

My tongue flicked out, tasting the air. Tiny nodes

gathered odour particles and transferred them to fluid filled sacs at the roof of my mouth. Not quite tasting, not quite smelling, either. At least, not in a familiar way. The sensory details flooded my mouth and gathered behind my eyes, as if my pea-sized snake brain translated the air information into a thought or scent memory.

Paper and pencils floated up the duct directly ahead of me. That way must lead to the offices. I twisted around and repeated the action. KK and something else, something "other." I couldn't describe it, but probably not the right way, either. I turned to the next option. Cardboard and steel. Probably the warehouse. The last direction delivered gunpowder, steel, and stagnant air to my tongue.

The security room.

Slowly, I started to move. Or tried to. The use of muscles didn't come naturally. The sideways undulation I'd used before didn't seem to work. I slipped down to the centre of the duct over and over again. I should've practiced more before the operation, but my thoughts had been focused on Tristan.

My breathing quickened as my pulse beat heavy in my tiny snake form.

I shook my little snake head and focused. Thinking of Tristan would have to wait. Moving the correct way through the air ducts mattered more at this moment. If I didn't find a way out, I'd never see Tristan again, anyway.

Never see Tristan again? My heart ached, as if it would rip in two.

With a snake hiss, I stopped and turned my attention

inward. Pulling harder on the snake fera. *Come on, Kaa. Do your thing.*

Relax, she hissed. *I got this.*

Her presence filled my mind as she took over my body, but not completely, more like she guided my motion while still allowing me to control it. With the soft scaly underside of my body I anchored to the metallic air duct by flexing in a series of alternating bends. This allowed me to press against the sides of the duct. Properly anchored, I straightened one of the bends in my body to extend forward. I started to slip. Quickly, I flexed the part of my body right behind my head to form another anchor and pulled the latter half of my body forward.

Flex, bend, anchor, straighten, extend, flex, pull, repeat.

I can do this! Just need to straighten and reform bends. Easy peasy.

Good, Kaa said. She relinquished her minimal control and receded into my mind.

Picking up speed, I inched through the metal air duct and made my way to the security office. As my tongue flicked forward to taste the air, more sensory details accumulated in my mind. Three men. Guns. Computers.

I pushed forward.

Muffled sounds travelled through the pipes—grumbling voices, the creak of a chair, tapping on keyboards. The air waves hit the side of my snake body, vibrating the scaly skin, transferring to muscle and bone before reaching the ear bones beneath my skull. The noise, though light, rippled through every fibre of my body.

After I turned the corner, the light from the room reflected off the metal and flooded the air duct. Lateral slats across a vent at the end broke the lighting up into sheets of bright bands.

Fuck.

I halted.

We hadn't thought about the grate on this end of things. How the heck would I rip it off? None of my other fera bodies would fit in this duct. Well, my falcon might, but she'd be squashed flat and useless in removing the grate.

My heart picked up speed, pumping cold blood through my quivering body. I continued forward, each pulse of my muscles bringing me closer to the gate of my jail cell. When I finally made it, though, relief washed through me. My heart slowed down, and my muscles relaxed.

I could fit through the gaps in the grate with my snake form.

For the first time since I gained Kaa as a fera, I was thankful not to be a huge badass reptile.

With my head close enough to the edge of the grate to see, I surveyed the guard situation below me. Three guards. Less than a meter drop. My landing would be on the fax machine. It would make a sound, so I'd have to act fast. Three guards meant I'd have to go mountain lion and possibly kill some of them. Two, I could handle easily in human form and not have to worry about getting shot.

Did these guys deserve to die? Maybe. Stan would

probably say yes, but he thought anyone remotely connected with his wife's murder deserved painful annihilation.

"I'm going to squeeze the lemon," one of the guards said. His voice broke the silence in the room and surprised me. My head snapped up and thumped against the grate. My head spun and my vision blurred for a few seconds before clearing up.

Idiot!

Without waiting for a reply, the guard stood up, stretched his lean body, and sauntered out of the room.

"Fucking hate that douche," the guard on the right muttered after the door swung closed. He pushed away from his seat a bit and folded his tattooed arms across his chest.

"Tell me about it," the other guard replied with a slight French Canadian accent. He had dark olive skin and thick black hair. His face flushed a little as he spoke. "Fucking gets off on pushing our buttons."

"Almost as bad as our boss," Tattoo said.

Frenchie grunted in agreement, and they returned to watching the monitors.

Time to move. This was my chance.

I propelled forward, slithered through the grate, and fell onto the fax machine. My body smacked against the hard plastic. Pain shot through my body.

"What the fuck?" Frenchie spun around.

No time to feel sorry for my bruised and battered body. I reached inside and pulled my human form. Fast and swift, my regular skin wiped out that of the snake as I grew and fleshed out.

Sitting naked on the fax machine, I had time to register Frenchie's fist before it slammed into my face. My body jerked back, and my head whacked into the hard wall behind me. My vision blurred, and pain radiated through my body like electricity. The drywall cracked from the force of impact. Before he could do more, I kicked out and sent him flying against the computer. I hopped off the machine and dodged Tattoo's attack. With a flurry of blows, leg kicks, and defensive tactics, I had both the guards pinned and secured with their own handcuffs.

"Fucking hell," Tattoo grumbled into the smooth flooring.

Frenchie groaned.

"That's enough from both of you," I said. Using spare T-shirts I found in the supply room off to the side, I gagged Frenchie quickly before he regained full consciousness.

Tattoo seemed to have a brain and hadn't attempted to call out. When I moved to gag him, he swivelled his head to look at me. "Marry me?"

I barked out a laugh before stuffing the shirt into his mouth and securing it behind his head.

Almost time for phase two of the attack. First, I had to find and take down the third security guard. With a quick glance at the security screens to make sure the floor was empty, I slipped out of the room and used an operating manual to wedge it open.

My ears pounded as the sound of my breathing and heartbeat filled the silence. The bathroom was three doors down on the left, and I found the third guard pissing in a urinal. After he shook it off, stuffed it back in, and zipped his fly, he glanced up into the mirror. His body stiffened when he registered my reflection and started to turn.

Leaping across the final steps, I hammered him with a Superman punch. His head flexed back and cracked against the mirror. A few shots to the guts and an uppercut left him incapacitated and unconscious on the bathroom floor. I breathed out a long sigh and my shoulders relaxed. After relieving the guard of his sidearm, I snagged his cuffs, hauled him to one of the stalls, and secured him in place next to the toilet. The last piece of the T-shirt gagged him, and I found his spare handcuff key in his back pocket. Typical.

A quick naked jog brought me back to the security room. Tattoo had flipped over to prop his body up against the wall. His dark eyes followed my movement and musky coconut wafted off his skin. Heck, maybe I didn't need to use force against these guys. Could've just let my animal magnetism do the job for me.

"The Douche is handcuffed to a toilet," I told him. "Don't expect a rescue."

His eyes widened at first before he winked back.

I turned away from him and surveyed the security monitors again. Two guards by the loading dock of the warehouse, two more in the main entrance, one floating guard in the warehouse. No guards upstairs on the same floor as the security room. Well, there had been three, but I'd already taken them out.

That was it? The Big Bad Headquarters of King's Krank and its illegal drug operation was guarded by a grand total of eight guards?

Had the VPD and SRD's incompetence lulled them into a false sense of security or were they really that dumb?

Well, maybe not that stupid. All the guards in the warehouse below carried Steyr AUGs. Very popular Austrian assault rifles. They weren't messing around when it came to artillery. I might not know designer labels and brands, but I knew guns. The ones the guards toted would be quite the match for the Heckler & Koch MP5s the VPD used. Hopefully, it wouldn't come to a shootout.

We had the numbers, but the idea of losing any officers on this mission made my heart sink in my chest. They'd lost enough already.

The screen to the very right snagged my attention. What the fuck? Lab techs walked around in what looked like a lab room. That couldn't be right. The building plans Tristan provided hadn't specified any lab, and the website claimed all pharmaceutical production occurred in the States. The label above the security screen, read "Basement." The floor plans had also left out a secret basement lab. The fourth vent! The one that smelled of sour, burnt plastic. It must lead to the lab.

I watched the screen a little longer. Two more guards and three lab techs in the basement. Hopefully, they wouldn't hear any of the commotion upstairs. I turned to Tattoo, and his eyes widened. I picked up the Beretta PX4 Storm from the table—one of the guns I'd taken from the guards. No safety. Nice. I racked it and pointed the prohibited gun at Tattoo's face.

I tapped my nose with a finger from my free hand. "If you lie to me, I'll splatter your brains on your comrade there. Understand?"

He nodded.

"I count five guards in the warehouse, the three of you upstairs and two more guards in the basement with three techs. Is there more?"

He shook his head.

"Is the basement soundproofed?" He hesitated before nodding.

I put the gun down and turned back to the monitors. The heat in my blood cooled as my breathing evened out. Even if Tattoo lied and the guards in the basement detected the invasion, they'd be too late to help.

38

S tan picked up on the first ring. "Yeah?"

"I'm in. Three guards subdued," I said without a greeting. The security office's phone grew warm in my hand as I relayed the information on the other guards to Stan. He listened intently before he grumbled the information into his radio for the tactical leaders.

"Wait on my signal," I said. My gaze remained glued to the computer screen to watch the floating guard. The attack would work best if he was close to the others so he could be taken out with them.

When we planned the invasion, we didn't know what to expect. Surveillance came back with a wide range of numbers for night-time guards and activity, so the most precise estimate we had to work with was ten to twenty guards with zero to fifteen night deliveries, with no apparent pattern.

Not exactly helpful.

Stan hadn't appreciated my colourful comments and said I'd insulted the team. I brought two dozen donuts from Timmy's to the next meeting with an apology.

All was forgiven.

I watched the security camera screens intently, specifically the roaming guard in the warehouse. He'd pose the biggest threat. When the roaming guard meandered over to the two men by the loading dock, I spoke into the phone to Stan. "Go now."

I sent a silent "thank you" to Tristan for the security system briefing he gave me. Nothing was labelled. I might've had to play "pick the pretty button" without Tristan's help and that would've cost lives. As I issued the order to Stan, I cut the lights and remotely unlocked the doors to the loading dock and main entrance.

What unfolded next, I watched what I could on the security screen.

One member of each team wrenched the doors to the main entrance and loading dock at the same time. My nerves itched to shift and jump into action. The Tancher guards hollered. Before they could act, another team member threw in flash bangs.

I loved those things.

White light spread across the screen of the security monitors for the factory and main entrance.

When the flash bang went off, my gaze darted to the lab screen. The techs and guards continued to move around as if nothing had happened, completely oblivious to the attack happening above. Tattoo hadn't lied. The room was soundproofed. Good.

The screens cleared in time for me to watch two officers come through the doors and move between the lead officers standing to the side of each doorway.

The stunned security guards by each entrance were taken down quickly and succinctly, zap-strapped, and flattened on their stomachs. They remained prone in the hog-tied position while the two invasion teams tasered and took down the one remaining guard.

Done like dinner. I switched the lights back on.

That's it? For the second time this evening, the simplicity of the invasion and lack of defensive effort sent a wave of nauseating unease up my spine. Sure the basement lab was left, but this screamed "too easy."

The teams yelled out "clear," as they moved through the aisles and rooms on the main floor.

"We clear?" Stan's grizzly voice came through the phone. "What about the basement?"

"Upstairs and main, clear. Basement is sound-proofed. They don't know what happened. Two guards and about three lab technicians."

"I've had more difficulty raiding a grow-op."

"Yeah, I know the feeling. Hang on."

The assault teams moved into position to take the basement as Stan barked orders through his radio. My supe hearing picked up his garbled codes through the phone connection. At least he wasn't barking at me this time.

My wolf would've hated that.

A pang struck my heart, and I shook it off. With a deep breath, I picked up the Beretta and pointed it at

Tattoo's face again. His eyes widened. He started shouting mangled nonsense into his gag. With a few steps, I reached him and yanked the balled shirt out of his mouth.

"There's no point in screaming," I said. "No one is left to save you, and it will just piss me off."

He swallowed and nodded.

"Start talking."

"What do you want me to say?" His voice was a deep, sexy baritone, but it had little effect on me. If Tristan was steak, this guy, for all his sexy tattoos, muscles, and good looks, was expired ground beef.

"Where's the other guards?" I asked. "Why is security so light tonight? This take down was too easy."

"I don't know."

I growled. My eyes tingled as they partially shifted. Tattoo squirmed. "I honestly don't know. They've been dropping our shifts all week, even laying off staff and approving transfers."

All truth. This guy couldn't buy a clue. His spicy scent carried no hint of a lie. All week? We started planning this invasion only a week ago. Coincidence?

Unlikely.

My veins heated, and my vision stained red. I stalked back to the table and picked up the phone. The plastic of the receiver cracked under the pressure of my fingertips. "I think they were tipped off. Take the basement."

Stan sword. "Affirmative."

Who the heck tattled on us to the Pharaoh? It could

be anyone from the VPD team, or maybe the Pharaoh had discovered the truth by other means.

Stan barked more orders over the radio. The north team reformed their group away from the basement and moved to come upstairs. They cleared the offices one by one. The pilfering side of the operation would soon begin.

The south team got a silent three count. On three, the team opened the door to the basement and flowed down the stairs to take out the lab. The security feed showed the instant they opened the door at the base of the stairs.

The guards spun around to suck in two smoke grenades.

Good thing the smoke didn't react with KK or its ingredients. I'd made them test it out prior to the raid. No way did I want to get blown up because some unexpected KK was found at the scene.

The south team moved into the room and tasered the guards and technicians before handcuffing them.

Instead of relaxing, my body tensed as if forming one giant knot. In less than thirty minutes, the Tancher Pharmaceuticals Company had been successfully raided and taken over by the VPD task force.

How come this didn't feel like a win?

39

The raid on Tancher Pharmaceuticals proved less informative than we'd hoped. The hard drives had been wiped and the little information recovered didn't provide any new insight or information we weren't already aware of.

This left a lot of unanswered questions; a ton of maybes, what ifs and if onlys would have to sit on the back burner, including how the Pharaoh learned about the raid. I needed to take care of another loose end. One I'd been putting off because there'd been no need to act on it.

Until now.

I thumped my fist against Lucus Klug's solid wood door on his polished Richmond house. With Ben and his coven still with the Elders, I had no other Witch connections. Klug in German meant clever or smart. Sid had warned me of this fact a few months ago when he'd first given me the Witch's name.

"Coming!" a high-pitched male voice wailed.

Lucus had caught one of the Kappa victims and kept him in his love den for who-knew-how-long. The information Lucus had given me led to my discovery of the Kappa's identity. I kind of owed him, but he didn't know that.

The door swung open to reveal a forty-something bald-headed man with a slight beer belly. Around five and a half feet, he stood shorter than me, and the glare he cast over his large hooked nose indicated he wasn't pleased.

"Well, now. Just who are you?"

"My name is Andy McNeilly." I held my hand out, but soon dropped it when it became apparent Lucus had no interest in a handshake. "We spoke on the phone a while ago regarding the previously possessed man you held in your love den?"

Lucus narrowed his eyes.

I held both my hands up, palms out before he could whip a curse at me. "I'm not here about that. I need your help."

"Mmhmm. And just what do you think you can give me in return?" He cocked a hip and placed his hand on it.

"Well, I'm not sure. Doesn't the task kind of dictate the price?"

"Good point. Sugar, why don't you tell me what you want, so I can go back to my business?" He pronounced it "bidness."

"I need to locate a Kappa named Tamotsu. I don't have any possessions of his."

"A Kappa? He the same one that used my Billy?"

"Is Billy the man..." *Well, crap. How should I phrase this?*

"In my love den? Mmhmm. He still couldn't remember his name, so I gave him one." He leaned on his door frame.

"Is he still... Never mind. Not my bidne... business. Yes, it's the same Kappa."

"Who do you work for again? The SRD?"

"I used to work for them. We had a few differences. Now I'm with the VPD."

Lucus nodded his head, as if answering a silent question. He peered up at me one last time before stepping back and swinging the door open. "I'll do a locator spell for you. But, sugar? You need to look into the SRD for me. I think they have my sister."

My eyes widened. "Couldn't you do a locator spell for her?"

"Mmhmm. Blocked every time. Only a few Witches have that kind of power, and most work for the SRD. My sister, Veronika? Well, she be a bit special. And knowing the SRD..."

"They retrieved her for their lab." Lucus snarled.

"I'll look into it for you." I stepped into Lucus' home, and he closed the door behind me.

Lucus had been swift and proficient with his locator spell and promptly booted me out of the house after making me repeat my promise to him. I didn't get to see the love den. What the hell?

Without a personal object, Lucus used Tamotsu's psionic energy to track him. There was only one Kappa in the area, and I'd bet my entire stash of mini-marshmallows it was Tamotsu.

I'd asked why he hadn't searched for Tamotsu this way when the Kappa had been on a wild rampage a few months ago. If looks could harm, the saying "curiosity killed the cat," would've spontaneously come true.

After giving me the best death glare I'd ever received, which said a lot, Lucus not-so-patiently explained he had to know the culprit was a Kappa in addition to a psionic energy user. And at the time, of course, he hadn't known that. Now had he? Mmhmm.

This mutant turtle still managed to be a giant pain in my ass. When I'd captured Tamotsu months ago, I'd given him the order to flee if anything happened at Lucien's, and then find me. He followed directions for the first part well enough, but totally bombed the second. Why hadn't he sought me out?

If I controlled him, he should've found me by now.

I hadn't moved.

Was he even under my control?

If he wasn't, though, why'd he stay with Lucien where he was undoubtedly treated like a slave? And if I didn't control him, who did? This left a whole gaggle of questions needing answers.

One thing I did know: Tamotsu and I needed to chat.

With a racing heartbeat and raw nerves, I tramped through the Alaksen National Wildlife Area, south of Steveston. Lucus couldn't pinpoint Tamotsu's exact location, but he identified the general area, and technically, that's all my Shifter nose needed.

A wildlife area? Really? The ocean and the mouth of the Fraser River surrounded me and filled my nose with water scents, and other, less pleasant ones. As a part of the Fraser River delta, this area acted as a wintering location and important stop-over for a large assortment of birds, which meant lots of bird poop.

When I landed and shifted to human, the estuaries, wetlands, and riparian forest created a mosaic of lush greens with vibrant blues. Despite the surrounding urbanization, the area smelled mostly fresh and earthy, with the exception of the tangy bird poop.

Why would a Kappa hide here? Last I checked, Tamotsu fed off energy, not flying chickens.

The quiet marshland sent a slice of ice up my spine. Surrounded by nature, it shouldn't be this quiet. Squawks, chirping and other annoying bird calls usually filled the air at the bird sanctuary.

My falcon screeched in my head.

Yes, like that.

I rubbed the bridge of my nose. Tamotsu had to be here. Nature understood predators, even the supernatural kind. I needed to find him fast before he tra-la-la skipped out of here and disappeared in the big blue.

My head fell back as I opened my senses to the environment. Tamotsu's scent blended in with the ocean, but not enough I couldn't pluck it out. Ocean and seaweed, infused with his otherness, wound in the other smells in the wind. I shifted to the mountain lion and loped through the marshland. I followed my nose like some perverse cereal commercial.

There.

Submerged in a murky pond, tainted green with algae and other photosynthetic microorganisms, the turtle shell protruded from the surface to bask in the limited sunlight.

As if he sensed my presence, most likely from my supernatural energy, his shell shook and what could only be described as a humanoid turtle, straightened from his amateur hiding place. Tamotsu stood around six feet tall and nearly as wide. No fat, just a muscular, circular body shape. Slicked with a sheen of slime, the brown outline of his shell peeked around his body. With feet and hands more similar to those of turtles, only man-sized, he looked unnatural and uncomfortable when he walked upright.

"I expected you sooner," his raspy voice slithered to close the distance between us.

I shifted back to human before replying. "Why didn't you find me?"

His head tilted, but he remained silent. In that one action, he answered my unspoken question. He wasn't under my control. My muscles tensed. My fingers itched as claws threatened to push through the tender flesh. How'd that happen? Was Tamotsu ever under my compulsion? Had he been faking it this entire time? Why?

My muscles tensed as Tamotsu's body jerked, and he shuffle-walked toward me.

Did the whys matter?

This meeting wasn't exactly going to end in a hand-shake. I needed something more powerful than a cougar to fight the mutant turtle.

Tamotsu lunged for me as I reached for the beast. She ripped through my essence, barrelling past her cage to assume control. My bones cracked, and my skin ripped as the Kappa's body slammed into me. We flew through the air, and my shift completed. The impact of the marsh floor and the large supe's body landing on top of me barely registered. I flung him off, sending him sailing through the mist-filled air. He twisted and landed belly first in the brambles.

After I straightened and stretched the kinks out of my beast form, I turned to where Tamotsu's body fell.

He didn't move.

A roar ripped through my dry throat.

I trudged to the fallen Kappa, gripped his scaly shoulder and flung him to the side. A large stick, more the size of a young tree protruded from his chest. It didn't go all the way through—the Kappa's shell prevented that—but it didn't need to.

Ah fuck. There went my answers.

Tamotsu gurgled. His eyes opened and failed to focus on my beast face.

"How did you shake my control?" I demanded, my voice rumbled low.

"Never yours," he wheezed.

How was that possible? He bowed. I filled his *sara* with water. Legend said he was mine to control, and he confirmed it. Unless...unless, someone had already filled his *sara*. Then he'd belong to them and it wouldn't have mattered how many times I splashed water at this supe. "Who controls you?"

Tamotsu hacked and coughed.

Even if he wanted to answer that, he probably couldn't. "Why did you pretend I controlled you?"

"My job... Kill you or infi...infiltrate Lucien's horde."

His breathing stuttered and his body shook.

"Why didn't you just give yourself to Lucien, then? Why the charade?"

"Had to...had to look good."

Well, the Kappa got an A plus for theatrics. I still cringed when I thought how close he'd come to besting me.

"Who controls you?" I asked again.

"You'll see." His cackle cut off in a gurgle as blood filled his lungs. His body shook again, but this time, his body went limp. His eyes glazed over as I watched his life flee his body.

As much as I wanted Tamotsu to name his master, he didn't need to. Not if my suspicions were correct. Since the beginning of my involvement with the Vampires, something had been lurking in the shadows. First Ethan's play for the territory, then the Kappa's homicidal reign, then Bola's, now a new drug on the market with a supernatural connection. Too many events back to back, all making Lucien appear weak and vulnerable... Was there a connection to it all? Had one Master played us like marionettes to a screenplay only he knew? If so, it had to be the Pharaoh. And if so, the Pharaoh truly operated at all levels. Did he want more than Lucien's territory? Or did he have other, more sinister plans?

40

The loamy scent of moist forest earth rose to meet me as I landed near Stan's unmarked cruiser and the folded outfit he left out for me. He'd parked on the side of a rural road that wove through the mountains north of the city. The cold air sliced at my skin, and I quickly pulled on the lightweight shorts and tank-top.

Stan's call had been cryptic, but one drag of the air and the answers came spiralling in. Even if the remote, isolated location hadn't given it away, the scent did. Stan and Aahil were down the path. I picked up the bag carrying the unregistered gun Stan had requested and trekked through the forest to find him. The bag had been surprisingly easy to carry in falcon form. A normal peregrine might've struggled, but the Glock 42 was light—less than half a kilogram fully loaded—and I had supernatural strength on my side.

It had been a month since the Tancher Pharmaceuticals take-down. My paperwork had finally been approved by the upper brass and shift work with the VPD kept me busy. Though we continued to work together on drug related crimes, I'd expected this particular call of Stan's weeks ago. When he finally rang me, I dropped everything. Tristan had been disappointed at my quick exit in the middle of a heavy make-out session.

When I reached the clearing, the bright moonlight and wind bombarded my senses. My falcon-shifted gaze took in all the details. Under the light, early-morning sky, Stan stood tense in the centre near a bound, gagged, and kneeling Aahil. My friend pointed his service pistol at the man's head. Stan's gloved hands visibly trembled. But not from nerves.

Stan's anger carried hot, charred cinnamon to my nose, so strong it almost blocked out the sweat of Aahil's fear.

"Did you bring it?" Stan asked without turning to me.

"Yes." I glanced down at Stan's feet. He'd covered his shoes with plastic booties. I waved a hand at my bare feet. "I don't want to mess up your scene."

Stan grunted.

"Did you bring him here in your squad car? There'll be evidence."

Stan snorted. "It's not the first time he's been in my car. It already has justifiable traces of him."

I nodded. "Witnesses?"

"I tailed him for days. Picked him up in the empty parking lot when he stumbled out after hours. Fucker thought I was just picking him up for more questioning at the station like all the other times. Just hopped in. No fuss. No witnesses. Even bragged about killing Loretta when I confronted him with the truth. Wouldn't shut the fuck up about it until he realized we weren't going to the station."

No wonder Stan vibrated with anger. "Cell phone?"

"Dismantled and dumped over the bridge on the way here." Stan holstered his firearm, stalked over to me and held his gloved hand out.

"Are you sure?" I asked as I held the bag open for Stan.

He snatched the unregistered Glock from the bag, actioned the slide and aimed at the drug dealer. Stan's voice came out gruff, as if shredded with sandpaper. "What do you mean?"

I turned to him and ignored Aahil's muffled pleading. "I mean, it's one thing to shoot someone in the line of duty. It's another to kill one in cold blood. You'll have to live with—"

Bang! A loud gunshot exploded. I jumped. My ears rang so loudly, blood probably flowed out of them.

Aahil's body snapped back, brains and scalp sprayed out from behind his head. His lifeless body flopped to the ground, dead eyes staring at the night sky.

"Damn," I muttered.

Stan pulled out a rag and wiped down the Glock before ejecting the mag. Kind of pointless since he wore gloves, but I admired his thoroughness. In short successive steps, he dismantled the firearm and placed the parts in the garbage bag I numbly held out.

"Fuck, this gun is tiny."

"Lady's best friend for purse concealment."

Stan skewered me with a glare. Pretty decent cop stare. For a moment, I thought he'd ask me if I had a permit to carry concealed guns, but if the thought crossed his mind, it quickly vacated. As it should.

Friends didn't judge friends on permit carrying, or unsanctioned assassinations.

Without a word, Stan picked up the nearby shell and tossed it in the bag. He grabbed the flashlight tucked in his belt, flicked it on, and tramped to the remains of Aahil's skull. After a little searching, he plucked the warped 9mm bullet from the slew of brain bits and bone fragments.

Stan straightened and gazed down at the body in silence. The smell of pungent snake skin and parmesan cheese with musk oil moved stiffly in the cold air along with blood and death. Stan's shoulders slumped, and his mouth formed a grim line. When he turned to me and started walking back, his hard gaze softened and a brief glimpse of old-Stan flashed across his face.

He dropped the bloody bullet in the disposal bag, and headed down the path. We walked to the gravel road in silence, and Stan's bloody booties and gloves joined the evidence bag.

"Take care of this?" Stan gruffed at me.

I nodded and pulled the strings on the small garbage bag to close it. "The gun was light enough to carry here. I can take this in falcon form and distribute the gun parts and this other stuff to all the deep and fast flowing rivers within flying distance. No one will ever recover this weapon." I'd have to stuff the lightweight outfit I wore into the bag and dispose of it as well.

Stan grunted. He turned to walk toward his car before stopping abruptly.

"Andy?" he called to me over his shoulder.

"Yeah?"

"You're a true friend." He didn't wait for a response and clambered into his car.

He was right. I'd have to live with this execution-style murder on my conscience.

It was worth it.

EPILOGUE

S traddling Tristan on the couch, I wrapped my arms around him and rested my head on his shoulder. He slipped his warm hands over my tight muscles and started kneading. "Why are your shoulders so tight? It's over."

"But it's not."

"Loretta's killer has been dealt with, the pharmaceutical company has been exposed, and the King's Krank lab has been shut down."

"Yes, but I think we can both agree the Tancher drug company raid went a little too well. Someone tipped off the Pharaoh and I want to know who and why. All those loose ends tied up nicely, too nicely. The Pharaoh must have a backup plan for his world-domination fetish."

Tristan's hands stilled on my shoulders. "You have a point."

"And Ben hasn't returned from the Elder's with his coven. I don't have a good feeling about that."

Tristan sighed. "Me neither. I like Ben. But he said their restitution might take months. You shouldn't worry, yet."

I pursed my lips. Telling me not to worry about Ben was like telling me not to drink coffee, but I let his comment slide and continued listing my concerns.

"Something's going on with the SRD—whether they're complacent or incompetent remains unknown—but I need to find out if they're holding Lucus Klug's sister." I sucked in a breath and kept going before Tristan could try to calm me down. "I want to know more about my birth parents, and I have a brother who might've survived the Purge. Plus, there's a would-be-assassin with mountain lion wounds running around who knows where I live."

"That will be dealt with." Tristan's voice turned hard and dark.

"Tristan..." I started.

His hands slipped forward to fold around me in a hug as he leaned forward. His mouth pressed against my ear through my hair.

"I've already got my team working on it," he said. "And now that you've finally given me permission, my company will be here tomorrow installing a security system throughout your building. I know you don't want to move from this place, so instead of trying to fight you on it, my company will continue to monitor your home twenty-four-seven like they have for the last month. It's going to stay this way, too, until I can convince you to live with me."

"Tristan..."

"It's non-negotiable."

"Tristan!"

"What?" he growled, but in a playful way. He nipped my ear.

Tristan's phone chirped and interrupted whatever Tristan and his wicked mouth planned to do next. He sighed and pulled back. I slid from his lap to sit beside him while he checked the message.

"Work," he groaned. "I have to go in."

"Will you be long?"

"Hope not. I have plans for you." Tristan leaned over and planted a kiss on my lips before getting off the couch and swaggering to the bedroom.

My heart beat faster and my cheeks flushed with warmth. Words bubbled up my throat on their own accord. "Hey, Tristan?"

"Yeah?" He stopped and turned to me.

"I love you." The words flowed out of my mouth, as natural as the rain on a stormy day. Why'd I choose now to say it?

Because it was right. And true.

"I know." Sapphire blue eyes twinkled back at me. "I love you, too."

I remained on the couch while Tristan gathered his things. I'd already showered and changed into clean clothes earlier but I'd eventually have to peel myself from these cushions and make it to the bedroom or I'd end up with more knots in my neck.

After getting ready, Tristan returned to give me another kiss. "I'll see you later?"

"Of course."

He headed around the corner to leave when the door to my apartment slammed open. I jerked upright on the couch, my vision wavering from the sudden movement.

Tristan growled.

I bolted toward the hallway and Tristan.

Men shouted. The eerily familiar rat-a-tat-tat of machine gun fire echoed through my apartment. I rounded the corner to watch Tristan's body jerk as bullet after bullet struck his body.

Anger wrenched my body and my demon shape ripped through my essence as foreign scents wrapped around me. Wait. Not completely foreign. A misplaced scent. Something familiar pulled at my senses but I pushed the thought from my mind as I completed the change.

Let the beast reign. Destroy them all.

Tristan hit the floor and I launched over him. The men's gazes widened as I pounced on them, slashing with my sharp talons. I didn't give them an opportunity to surrender, no time to escape. Instead, I ripped them apart, spraying the walls with their blood. With cold efficiency, I dispatched every single one of them, but anger still raged inside me, hungry for more.

The last body slid to the floor and I spun around to find Tristan still on the ground, not moving.

No.

I rushed to his side and gathered him in my arms.

He'd healed from worse injuries than this. His chest rose, but his breathing was shallow, wheezy. I searched his body, finding only bullet holes, but they weren't healing right and his blood...

Something wasn't right. Something didn't smell right.

The bullets were poisoned with something. The bleeding continued and the smell of death rose in the hallway.

"Tristan?" My voice rumbled. "You have to be okay."

Tristan's eyes fluttered open and his piercing sapphire gaze found mine. A smile spread across his face for a brief moment.

"Stay with me. You're going to be okay." I pulled him onto my lap and held him close. What should I do? What could I do. There was so much blood. *Please Feradea, No.*

"Andy..."

A sob bubbled up my throat. I held Tristan in my beastly arms as he continued to bleed out and grow cold on my lap, his body racked with each laboured breath. "Shh...It's going to be okay."

It had to be.

My heart thundered as if trying to make up for the slowing of Tristan's. My skin prickled as a wave of ice spread over my body. Tristan's breathing grew shallower, his heartbeat continued to stutter and slow.

No.

"Andy. I love...you."

And just like that, the warmth of sunlight I had

grasped for only a brief moment slipped through my reach. Tristan's last breath shook through his body, his purr now gone, his warmth forever leached away. With the sweet air expelled from his mouth, his citrus and sunshine scent, the one laced with honeysuckles, the one that reminded me of sex on the beach, faded...faded and turned to something dark, something morbid and sad.

Death.

"No," I whispered.

The beast pushed.

"Noooooo!" My talons dug into Tristan.

Let the beast reign. Destroy. Destroy them all.

Pay. Make them pay. Destroy them...

The beast's control ripped through me, over me, everywhere, as fury slid to replace the overwhelming sadness. The beast took over.

My resistance gave way and I surrendered to her.

I stepped within myself, sealed the steely doors on my loss and let her reign.

Together, we roared.

They call me Carus...

Two months ago, I lost control and the beast reigned.
Seven weeks ago, the SRD caught up to me.
Nine days ago, they injected me with a vile new drug.
Today, I'll break free.
And tomorrow?
Tomorrow, I'll make them pay.

For I am everything they have ever called me—shifter,
beast, demonic, cursed. I am the Carus, and the world
will know my rage.

*Don't miss this fast-paced, addictive urban fantasy with
sugar and spice and everything not-nice by international
bestselling author, J. C. McKenzie.*

Previously published as *Beast of All* by the Wild Rose Press.

Acknowledgments

Cursed wouldn't have been possible without the support and expertise of my critique partners and beta readers—Charlotte Copper, Shelly Chalmers, Karilyn Bentley and Katie O'Sullivan.

I'd also like to thank Lara Parker, my amazing editor, and Olga Sauchenia, the talented artist who designed the cover.

A big thank you also goes out to my friends and family for their love and support.

And last but certainly not least, thank you to the reader. Your support and words of encouragement are everything to me.

I hope you enjoyed the story.

J. C.

ABOUT THE AUTHOR

J. C. McKenzie is a book loving, gumboot-wearing, unapologetic science geek. She predominantly writes urban fantasy and post-apocalyptic dystopian fantasy with strong romantic elements. When she's not spinning tales, she's in the classroom sharing her passion for science and mathematics while secretly warping the young, impressionable minds of our future to carry out her evil plans for world domination. She lives in the Pacific Northwest with her family.

Visit her at jcmckenzie.ca

facebook.com/j.c.mckenzie.author

instagram.com/j.c.mckenzie

tiktok.com/@jcmckenzie0

bookbub.com/authors/j-c-mckenzie

www.ingramcontent.com/pod-product-compliance
Lightning Source LLC
Chambersburg PA
CBHW030633020726
47493CB00006B/1686